DARK HENRY SMITH

A Novel By

Mike Johnson

Copyright © 2023 *Mike Johnson*.
michaeljohn@scratchline.com

All rights reserved. No part of this book may be reproduced, stored, or transmitted by any means—whether auditory, graphic, mechanical, or electronic—without written permission of both publisher and author, except in the case of brief excerpts used in critical articles and reviews. Unauthorized reproduction of any part of this work is illegal and is punishable by law.

ISBN: 979-8-88640-636-8 (sc)
ISBN: 979-8-88640-637-5 (hc)
ISBN: 979-8-88640-638-2 (e)

Because of the dynamic nature of the Internet, any web addresses or links contained in this book may have changed since publication and may no longer be valid. The views expressed in this work are solely those of the author and do not necessarily reflect the views of the publisher, and the publisher hereby disclaims any responsibility for them.

One Galleria Blvd., Suite 1900, Metairie, LA 70001
1-888-421-2397

*I wish to thank the following for
their meaningful contribution to this book:*

Judaism, with some Jews from the Tribe of Levi.

Islam, some Muslims, and the Prophet Muhammad.

Christianity, some Christians, and Jesus.

Catholicism, a few Catholics, and the Pope.

An early Victorian Cemetery in London.

Johnnie Walker *black label* whiskey.

*If the revered prophet is so fragile your
religion requires you to take up arms and avenge real or
imagined insults, please do not read this book.*

*"The most excellent Jihad is that
for the conquest of self."*

This Wisdom attributed to the Prophet Muhammad.

CHAPTER 1

Jack described Henry to me as an intelligent man, somewhat self-effacing, and always respectful of the needs of others. He was a lightning rod for trouble, though, and usually of his own making. The following few paragraphs describe a situation that escalated beyond reason and illustrate perfectly how many choices were available to change the outcome of a chance meeting that Henry involved himself with.

Dark Henry Smith bought a used car, a large Lincoln town car, born in 1969. Mechanically it was in excellent condition, with perfect black paintwork, tinted windows, and a roof rack. A Saint Christopher medallion hung from the mirror, which he would habitually flick with his finger. He smiled at the faint smell of leather and caressed the padded steering wheel.

The vehicle would be paid for in monthly installments using the wages from his evening job as a bartender at a small saloon some three miles from his home.

Behind *Ronnie's bar and grille* was a small paved yard where employees and patrons could park their automobiles. The vampire mobile was also parked in the yard when Henry was behind the bar.

Thursday evening, when he arrived late to work at around eight-thirty, he discovered that all available parking places were occupied. Muttering darkly, he backed into the street and parked a few yards from the bar. He had not yet shut the engine off when a sharp rap on the passenger's window drew his attention. He lowered the window, and a commanding voice, with a ring of self-importance, addressed him from the darkness.

"You can't park here, sir, too close to the intersection. Please move your vehicle."

Known for his pleasant and most accommodating attitude, Dark Henry Smith considered the request carefully before replying in a stern voice mimicking the enforcement officer.

"Away with you gurgling poltroon. Bother me no more, or I will make a pudding of your entrails."

This prompted a quick response from Andre, the noble parking enforcement officer.

"As a courtesy to you, I will pretend I didn't hear that comment. This is the last time I will tell you. Move your vehicle. If you do not, I will write a noncompliance ticket and call the police." Officer Andre did not know what a "gurgling poltroon" was, never having been called one before but realized instinctively that he had been insulted.

The frightened vampire, dreading a possible parking citation, replied softly,' "And I, as a courtesy to you, will not have your pointed head displayed in any Wall-Mart store or local coffee house."

The bemused captain of parking enforcement, believing he was speaking with a madman or deranged asylum escapee, foolishly leaned on the car door, putting his official city parking enforcement head through the open window.

"Excuse me," he said. "I didn't quite understand that."

The vampire Henry raised the window quickly as Andre spoke, trapping the officer's head inside his car.

Now guillotined by the window, gasping and coughing because of his suddenly restricted air supply, the officer was enraged beyond all reason. His peaked cap fell off as he flailed his arms and ineffectually beat on the window and door with his hands.

"I am so sorry," Henry said. "I am unable to understand you. Please speak clearly and slowly, or I will be forced to remove you, as this is a no-parking zone. Also, I have neither the time nor inclination to enter into a debate with an illiterate parking prostitute. If you are unable to converse in English, an interpreter may be found for you."

And here, the Inevitable disaster that could have so easily been avoided gives a glimpse into the character of Henry Smith. As you read, a complete account of the terrible incident will be found in chapter nine.

There is much more to tell about Henry and Jack, and as you will soon see, their stories come alive and are played out again as you read on.

I remember my good friend Jack, Jack Cordell. We had known each other for several years at the time he told me his story. He was quiet, somewhat studious, a little reserved perhaps, but altogether a decent fellow, usually with a ready smile. He worked primarily as a marine biologist at the prestigious *Aeron Glass* institute and proudly, with a recent doctorate to his credit. Describing his job at the institute as a researcher and scientist, sometimes as a window cleaner at the glass factory, he seemed a poor fit in a corporate environment, with long blond hair curling over his collar, well-worn blue jeans, and a ratty sweater. He must have excelled in his profession, for he was nearly four years at the institute when we met. We became friends soon after I moved into a small apartment next to his. I remember his birthday at thirty-nine years. We celebrated with a few drinks on my balcony. I was three years younger. I remember because I moved away soon after leaving California to take a job in London again. On one occasion, He introduced me to his girlfriend, Anneliese, soon to become his wife, he said. She was beautiful, slim, with almost waist-length black hair and a direct unnerving stare, with bright eyes that seemed to change from light blue to grey. Latina, I thought, but that opinion quickly changed when she spoke—a pronounced German or East European accent at odds with her looks. First impressions are important, I suppose, and my first impression of her was that I didn't like her and found her a little intimidating; there was just something about her that bothered me. She probably felt the same about me.

Anyway, Jack told me his story over a period of four days or so. And I will tell you everything he said to me. Believe me. It is a tale worth telling. Thinking back to that little apartment in Van Nuys, California, the memories come to me quickly like drops of rain on the window, with one running into the next. I think of my school days in London and, with some good reason, as you will see, remember well the old cemetery near my school.

In the days before Bob became Dylan, before the Beatles had learned more than three guitar chords, and gay was happy and bright without any queer connotations, the storied Highgate Cemetery existed as a foreboding walled reminder of early Victorian Gothic architecture.

For several minutes, I lost myself in the memories again and stared at a few grainy photographs of the cemetery my friend Maggi had given to me.

Early 1970, London's Highgate vampire story became a popular distraction in local and international news outlets. Whatever the creature was, it was seen many times by various witnesses and promptly declared a *terrible vampire* by two flatulent, over-inflated, self-appointed, and self-promoting *experts*.

Descriptions vary in detail, but most described a tall black shape with a white or pale skeletal face moving silently within and sometimes without the cemetery walls, quite unlike Dark Henry Smith. These sightings eventually encouraged several self-styled *vampire hunters* to converge upon the cemetery and perimeter lanes to rid the grounds of the beast. They did so noisily, without restraint, some brandishing large wooden stakes and mallets, most fueled with alcohol. Other paraphernalia was seen, much of it in accordance with doubtful information from recent movies and popular books. The only thing missing was a vampire.

My interest in this foolishness began many years ago. I was raised and sometimes razed as a child in the north London suburb of Hampstead. A short bus ride and brisk uphill walk would bring me within a few hundred yards of the Highgate cemetery entrance. A twelve-year-old schoolboy could, and often did, slip easily through broken ornamental iron gates or climb the crumbling perimeter walls to find himself in a vast overgrown garden of green mossy tombstones, marble statuary, and leaning pillars. Granite and Marble columns with arabesque and other intricately carved designs stood at the entrances of larger vaults. A maze of narrow grassy paths through arches of trees, hanging vines, and ivy-covered graves revealed the somber resting places of many notables.

No peasants lay here; this place was built to provide shelter and an everlasting sanctuary for the wealthy and many long-forgotten dignitaries. Old family wealth was once displayed tastefully here in the center of North London. An aura of desolation and watchfulness permeated the area now, quite apparent when first entering the place. There was something wrong here, a malevolent angry presence always at your heel. I would never go exploring there alone and would never enter the grounds after sunset.

At the center of this awful place was a circular pit, a carefully excavated depression below ground level, about half a mile in diameter and approximately twenty feet deep. A flight of worn stone steps gave access to the bottom of this place. Many rectangular vaults were cut into the grassy side walls of this pit, some perhaps fifteen feet into the earth, others much longer; all were about twelve feet high. Wrought iron or heavily carved wooden doors secured the entrances to these places and were locked and chained to prevent unwanted scrutiny or interference. Over the years, neglect and abandonment by the city revealed the contents of these grim mausoleums.

Ancient stone coffins, some with elaborately tooled inscriptions, some with brass or stone nameplates, were now made accessible to the curious and those intent on desecration. Later, I learned that this area was known as *The Circle of Lebanon* and was undoubtedly the hellish pit from which all the prevailing anger and evil originated.

Jack showed a great interest in my story and listened attentively when I told it. I re-told it several times when he asked. I understand his interest now after reading through his notes and having listened to the recorded information he left for me.

So, meandering through the cemetery, past overturned stone markers and neglected marble statues, one could find apparent signs of desecration and dark worship. Many other symbols were painted or scratched on the sculptures and plates—no resting place here for either the Godly or wicked. I remember well a lead-lined stone coffin with the lid removed and the mummified occupant clearly visible. Her long white hair was pulled behind her head and tied in place by faded red ribbons. I knew that in life, she was beautiful with long fair hair, laughing as she skipped barefoot across the short, damp grass of the front lawn. Rooms in her big house echoed the bright chatter and laughter, welcoming friends and visitors. She was angry now, though, and rightfully so, angry at the disturbance, her long sleep violated by this great sacrilege. Small black candles were carefully arranged around the rim of the casket, and dead flowers were placed as macabre decorations below the grinning parchment face of the deceased. For some time, I stared, fascinated with the sight before me, unable to turn my gaze. Suddenly, the wind snapped me from my reverie, blowing gently, touching my face, kissing my cheeks, and ruffling my hair. The same little breeze was now tugging at the dead flowers in the coffin and wandering through the empty eye sockets of the corpse. Then fancying something was moving and mumbling within the coffin, I ran. A breathless, headlong flight until I reached the safety of the narrow street beyond the cemetery walls. Still frightened, drawing painful ragged breath through a parched throat, I started for home.

As the area's sinister reputation grew, so my mother, horrified that such a place could exist without proper oversight or governance, forbade me from ever going there again.

The eyes cannot unsee, and although I never went exploring there again, my memories of that terrible place remain clearly. A recurring nightmare would find me wandering along the overgrown paths, all leading to a desolate field. I was lost and alone, then suddenly before me stood the mummified form of my darling lady with red ribbons still tied into her long white hair. She called with a sweet hollow voice for me to come to her.

Such was the clamor and mischief from Devil worshipers and occultists of every hue that local residents, now harassed by the ever-increasing attention from television, newspaper, and other media platforms, complained loudly and bitterly to the city. Subsequently, the ravaged acres were soon managed and supervised by a city-endorsed charity dedicated to preserving and maintaining select parks and buildings, reflecting London's early history. There was much worth preserving at the Highgate cemetery.

So, enough for my dusty old memories. Sadly, I never saw Jack or Anneliese again after I moved away. We drifted apart as people do, but his story remains with me and, with the telling, becomes clearer. And with the writing, clearer yet, as there is now a tangible record for my reference.

CHAPTER 2

JACK'S STORY

"I first met Henry Smith a few years ago, early in 2007, I believe, although reaching back through the years, it seems like a lifetime to me now. At the time of our introduction, I could not have imagined he would become the most important and influential person in my life. I found him to be at once infuriating and terrifying. Sometimes he was the object of my admiration and occasionally a hero to me. In times of need, he was always a good friend."

As I remember, the obligatory colleagues-from-work party was winding down. Music was still discernible as a vague cheerful noise over the background blend of conversations. Sudden laughter and the clink of glasses returned me to a slightly intoxicated awareness of my surroundings.

I struggled to my feet, leaving the comfortable sanctuary of a large armchair to shake the proffered hand of the slender black man standing before me. "I hope I'm not disturbing you, Jack. My name is Henry. I just wanted to introduce myself." His voice was soft, and the accent difficult to place—possibly Asian or Oriental, quite out of keeping, I thought, with his African features.

"You know my name, Henry. Have we met before?"

"No, we were never formally introduced. I overheard a conversation a while ago. Your friends were calling you Jack. I believe I have met everybody here except you, so this is my opportunity."

"Well, then, Henry, a pleasure to meet you. Perch over here while I get another drink. Something for you?"

He stared at me quizzically for several seconds. "Perch?"

"Sure, park, sit, perch, take the weight off…."

"Oh, okay. Sorry, I am not familiar with that expression. I thought you were referring to a fish."

It was my turn to stare. "You're not from around here, are you?"

"Recently, yes, about twenty minutes from here. Argyle Street—an unfortunately depressed neighborhood, but quiet enough for me."

He laughed suddenly. "Jack, I do know what you mean. I am from Spain, Barcelona. I have lived in America for about two months. Please help me here. I acquire the language, but sometimes slowly."

We chatted for half an hour or so, he extolling the beauty of Barcelona's architecture while I told of the drama and wonder of Southern California's coast road views. At length, he stood to take his leave.

"Thank you for your time, Jack. For me, there was much pleasure in our speaking. I know now we will meet at another time. I will look for you soon, perhaps."

Henry was likable, but a black man in his early fifties seemed strangely out of place in this gathering of students and young academic types from the institute. I wondered who had invited him.

Returning to my chair, I exchanged pleasantries for about another half-hour before leaving my friends and colleagues at the party. I slowly made my way home, happily anesthetized with celebratory alcohol.

As Henry might have said, I acquired a deep, dreamless sleep very quickly.

We met again a few days later. It was an unexpected encounter, but as I later realized, every action was carefully orchestrated. Every word he uttered was purposefully chosen. Every road he traveled was always by design.

I was sitting at a small sidewalk café, eating an overpriced European-style sandwich and sipping a glass of cheap red wine. The sandwich and two glasses of wine, rinsed away with a tiny cup of strong black coffee, would be my dinner tonight, with distant street noise providing the background music for my dining room.

I watched the late summer afternoon slowly embrace a purple evening sky that softly covered the city. A profusion of neon signs on Main Street gave an indirect glow sufficient to bring a measure of comfort to this quiet little side street. I had eaten at this cafe many times, always enjoying the simple food and attentive service.

Familiar green wrought iron chairs and glass-topped tables welcomed me again to the small restaurant as they always did. A comfortable, unhurried atmosphere invited me to drink a little more wine before eating. This small side street eating house has become a regular refuge for me.

The owner, Louie, a much loved, rotund, and respected father figure in the cafe, allowed me to commandeer a table of my choosing to work on my projects without interruption. There is a Louie dining room ambiance, a background blend of happy sound and smell, coupled with a nod of recognition from regular patrons and echoes of hidden subterranean activity somewhere below street level. In this mix, there is always the prevailing background of faint street sounds to reassure me. Also, there is the delightful lady serving customers, a family member or friend perhaps. Either way, I will ask her on a date if I can find sufficient courage to do so.

I can work efficiently in this place; for some reason, the atmosphere is far more productive than trying to write or study in my quiet little apartment or my austere glass-paneled company office.

"*Bonne soirée. Vous avez bien manger ce soir.*"

I started at the sound of the voice so close to my ear. Turning in my chair, I expected to see a waiter, perhaps the proprietor, at my side, but there was no one. Twisting around again, I nearly upset my chair at the sound of soft laughter. Henry stood before me, grinning hugely. I stood quickly, shook his hand, and motioned him to sit.

"My apologies for frightening you. I was only having a little fun. Beautiful evening, eh *mon ami*?"

"You speak French, obviously, and display a great talent for sneaking about and creeping up on people."

"I speak many languages, Jack. But the English I once knew is now very different from the language you speak. So, I am fast learning the English as you fuckin' Yanks speak. What do you think?"

I laughed, beginning to enjoy the unexpected encounter. "You speak the language well, Henry, but *fuckin'* is really not necessary. Anyway, good to see you again."

"And you," he replied. "How's the squid behavioral project?"

"You know about that? How? The research is not in the public domain yet."

He smiled and laughed softly. "The mortal mind is a many-layered book, pages upon pages. I turn the current pages at the appropriate layer and read as I wish. You are a new acquaintance; therefore, a little investigation seemed appropriate."

"Wow, so now you're a mind reader, then? Well, happy to know you. I'm just a Mongolian acrobat."

"No, Jack. You are neither Mongolian nor are you an acrobat. You are a researcher at the Aeron Glass Marine Institute with a penchant for infuriating the project manager. Also, my advice—if asked—would be to divert your affections from your assistant Angela and pursue the data coordinator, Maureen—ultimately a happier and more rewarding experience for you." He chuckled. "But then you didn't ask, did you."

The evening seemed suddenly darker, and I shivered in the warm-scented air. For several seconds I stared across the cluttered table at Henry, unable to form a reply.

Henry smiled, and again his quiet melodic laugh broke the silence. "I really must be going now, Jack. I saw you at the table as I was passing and just stopped in to say hello."

"Wait—wait a moment. Don't go yet. You've only just arrived, and this is beginning to get interesting. Since you have an advantage, knowing so much about me, how about telling your story? Do you work? I assume that you aren't married. What brought you to this country?"

"I have a curiously high regard for you, Jack Cordell, and will give a few explanations to satisfy your curiosity reasonably." He shifted his position sitting on the edge of his chair.

"First, I ain't some ghetto nigga; my features are borrowed for convenience. The downside to that, as I am beginning to discover, is that people in this neighborhood regard me with fear and suspicion, whether justified or not."

He shrugged and glanced at his hand, brushing something away from his sleeve.

"I am not opposed to working," he continued, "but I do have a great distaste for manual labor and therefore am unwilling to operate gardening implements or construction equipment. These are the tools of ignorance. However, rent must be paid; I need a car and wish to dress appropriately in various settings without attracting attention."

I ignored his "borrowed features" comment for the moment. "Surely you don't live without working? You're obviously educated, multilingual, and well-read. These qualities alone will get you accepted into any number of places."

"Certainly, you are correct, but at this time, I have a few temporary issues preventing me from integrating easily into the workplace."

I raised my eyebrows, waiting for him to continue. "Your issues?" I prompted.

He smiled slowly. "Very well, in no particular order of importance then, I need serious dental work. I am only able to function at a higher level after sunset. I am a spirit being you would choose to call a devil or vampire, although many call me an angel. And, as you can see, a black one, but only temporarily."

Although he seemed harmless enough, I laughed hesitantly at his joke, concerned that I was engaging in social exchange with an asylum escapee or madman. I watched carefully for abnormal behavior or sudden movements while continuing the conversation.

"So, you're a temporary black angelic vampire with bad teeth, then?"

"Yes, a dark angel, also a practicing Muslim and Christian, I play the accordion to relieve stress and anger. By the way, I think I will adopt the name Gaytooth—quite a ring to it, don't you think? Rolls off the tongue most pleasantly."

I decided to humor him and continue with his joke, waiting for the impending punch line. "Yes, it does," I replied. "But why Gaytooth for a name? Why not Ironfang or Razortooth? Don't you think Gaytooth is rather effeminate for a demonic vampire name?"

"Effeminate, yes, but tell me if this makes sense to you, Jack. My sexual preference is for young males rather than females. Preference, though. Not an absolute commitment. I enjoy the company of both; I am more inclined toward males. Girls, as they say, are okay, but you can't beat the real thing."

I shook my head, chuckling. "Well, Henry, whoever told you that is sadly mistaken. I will admit that women are wired differently than men, which is necessary to perpetuate the old hunters' and homemakers' differences, but that's where it ends. Personally, I can't imagine any other sexual preference."

He grinned, shaking his head. "Very well, Jack. You are obviously set in your ways. Let us say that perhaps this is a vampire thing."

His voice was soft and melodic, quite formal with no pause for dramatic effect, no attempt to convince me he spoke the truth, almost as if he were reciting from a grocery list.

I stared at him for several seconds, waiting for another revelation, but none came. Apparently, my look of confusion prompted a slight chuckle.

"Here is a quick demonstration for your amusement, as by the look on your face, you do not believe me. It is necessary that you do so, Jack, and that you trust me as we are soon to become friends. Look across the street and greet your new friend at the corner."

I glanced across the sidewalk to a small intersection. Around the corner came a figure walking hurriedly toward me.

"This is my friend?" I asked, turning again to Henry, but there was no Henry. The chair was empty. I jumped from my seat, spilling wine on the table, and stared in cold terror as Henry crossed the street and regained his place at the table again.

"Oh, come on now, Jack, that was only a trick. No need to be afraid. How about a little more wine?"

At that moment, the waitress appeared with a half-empty carafe.

"I brought more wine for you since you spilled your last drink; this one is on the house."

I smiled weakly, thanking her as she cleaned the table. I poured more wine into a clean glass with an unsteady hand, leaving the carafe between us.

"For you?" I asked, indicating the glass.

"Thank you, no, Jack. I really must be going. Again, the pleasure was mine. I am sure we will meet again—sooner rather than later." Standing, he inclined his head and walked quickly across the street to the corner from whence he had just come.

I sat lost in thought for several minutes, still shaken and confused, before deciding it was time for me to leave this unsettling dining place. The waitress took my credit card, grinning at the overly large tip as I signed the check.

"Many thanks," I said. "I'll be back soon. I don't think my friend ordered anything, did he?"

She stared at me, raising her eyebrows and clearly surprised by the question.

"Sorry, your friend? You were alone at the table, weren't you?"

CHAPTER 3

Nearly two weeks passed before I spoke with Henry again. Although I tried many times to reconcile the events at our previous meeting, it was impossible for me to do so. Vampires and spirit beings are the stuff of legends and mythology, existing only in books and movies. Henry was an illusionist, albeit a very good one. There was no magic. He was a personable, charming, sleight-of-hand stage artist.

Rather odd to develop a character as a gay vampire with bad teeth, though, and what about his ridiculous Muslim *and* Christian claim, this from a *vampire?* My logic did not comfort me. There was much more to Henry than appeared on the surface.

The local newspapers and TV news channels covered a story about a popular imam from the elegant "Light of Hope" Mosque on Main Street. Apparently, the imam had suddenly disappeared under the most mysterious circumstances. Scant information and no opinion or comment from the Muslim congregation did nothing to dispel rumors circulating about this strange situation.

The subsequent police investigation revealed that, in all probability, the imam had been abducted. No further information was available at that time.

Rumor and speculation hinted at the holy one's involvement with organized crime gangs and participation in bizarre sexual practices. Eventually, some details emerged, but the truth was never publicly revealed.

Apparently, demonstrations by gay vampires or others attempting sexual gratification are not encouraged in mosques. It is preferable to indulge in such activities far from public scrutiny.

Henry sat with the young cleric in the third prayer row. Call to *Maghrib*, the evening prayer had not sounded yet, and only a scattering of believers and visitors populated the mosque. Henry produced a small blanket, draping it over his young companion.

Having adjusted his clothing, the angel smiled serenely as the young cleric bent to engulf the dark angelic penis and produce a meaningful conclusion from his effort.

Unfortunately, the accompanying grunting sounds and rhythmic bobbing motion of the blanket attracted a worshiper's attention in the next row.

The outraged witness interrupted other worshipers by loudly decrying the immoral display and summoning the Imam.

The Imam Fahim Ibn-Abidin, a good and most holy man, a scholar above any at the Masjid, was quite beside himself with fury. He threatened to call the police, then ordered Henry and his friend to immediately cease their ungodly activity and leave the mosque, never to return.

The dark angel Gaytooth Smith, having not experienced meaningful results from the cleric's ministrations, railed loudly at the imam, promising to avenge the frustrating interruption and quickly bring down great punishment upon his scaly Mexican head.

CHAPTER 4

It transpired that the Imam Fahim Ibn-Abidin was a thief. However, In fairness, it should be noted that his propensity for and great skill in removing other people's property and converting it into cash was a product of his previous lifestyle. Some thirty years earlier, during the time before Fahim Ibn-Abidin was Pedro Morales, a child of the streets and sometimes a refugee of the Ciudad de Mexico. The pueblo Santa Cruz was home to young Pedro in those days.

His mother, Josephina, disappeared during a washing day by the river. A body was never recovered, but two empty clothes baskets were found in a small wooded area about a mile from the riverbank. Pedro continued to live with his father in the house he now knew as home for three more years.

A few weeks after his sixteenth birthday, his father died. The old priest was called upon to perform the perfunctory rituals before he and the doctor searched the small dwelling. They found enough money in a little-rusted cashbox to satisfy the church; in the trousers and jacket pockets lay sufficient coin to pay the doctor. The celebration and internment were traditions happily supported by the small pueblo community.

The many empty alcohol containers littering the stone casita's back porch were the only legacy from Pedro's father, Alfredo.

During the celebration of his death, Alfredo's corpse was removed and laid to rest in the mausoleum. Aunt Rosa decided Pedro would move to her house, being much larger than Alfredo's casita. Her home had two bedrooms, a kitchen, and a separate washroom. It was a reasonable arrangement for both and a fortunate one for Pedro.

Rosa, Josephina's elder sister, had no children. Her husband died from an unfortunate fall from scaffolding at a housing construction site where he worked. Now, six years after his passing, the deep aching loneliness was beginning to fade. She arranged to feed and house the boy in return for his help at the small general store she owned with her brother. He would further what little education he had by attending a Catholic school two miles from the house.

One memorable Sunday evening, when he and Tia Rosa returned from church service, they sat together in silence at a rough wood table by the back door. They listened to small animal sounds and the last rites of the evening performed by muted birdsong.

The warm breeze brought peace, a sense of belonging to Pedro, and a drowsy feeling of happiness to Rosa.

At length, Pedro broke the silence by asking Rosa about his mother, the truth about her death, and her life with Alfredo. A long silence passed before Rosa spoke of her sister.

"A body was never found to confirm her death, no signs of violence or a struggle. A short investigation by *la policia* found no clues, only a strong suspicion that she had started a new life with a secret lover—a companion from her past, perhaps."

She stared at Pedro for several seconds before continuing.

"I believe she left quietly, having thought about her life for some time. Living with your father was never easy, Pedro. This I know for a fact. He was not a bad man, but the God he worshiped was from a bottle and not to be found in any holy house."

She shook her head and sighed deeply.

"I do not judge her or condemn her actions. Our time in this world is given for us to do with as best we may. I think my sister chose her own path and is living in another place far from here. I have not heard from her and do not know where she may be, so these are my thoughts only."

Pedro listened intently, his large brown eyes wide with astonishment. Now for the first time, he considered the possibility that his mother might yet be alive. Such news brought no pleasure or comfort to him, though.

"If my mother lives, then she abandoned my father and me. Men and women do not always stay together. I understand this, but for a mother to leave her only child? How could she do such a thing? Was I such a bad child?"

Rosa could make no answer. Tears flooded her eyes as she shook her head. "No, Pedro, *mi Amor*. If Josephina abandoned you, she also abandoned me, her only sister. I am not able to tell you more, for this is all I know about the matter. I cannot say if this is the truth or not, but it is an answer to the questions you asked me."

Pedro sat quietly, thinking about the mother he thought was dead. He listened to the faint sounds of the evening, but no answers came to him.

Rosa watched the boy in silence, her chin resting on the palm of her hand, wondering if she should have shared her thoughts with him. There is no truth for us here; she whispered only my sister's actions, as I believe them to be. She stood, walking quickly to the kitchen.

A few minutes later, she returned with two glazed earthenware cups. Sitting next to Pedro again, she passed a cup to him. "Here, *Mi Amor*, a little mescal for two poor abandoned *niños*."

Pedro smiled for the first time that evening.

"*Salute*, Pedro," she said and touched his cup with hers. Raising her cup, Rosa drank a little.

Pedro drank with her, the liquor harsh in his mouth and hot in his throat. After a few seconds, the burning sensation lessened, replaced by the sudden warmth in his stomach, reaching back to his cheeks. He sat in silence again, thinking of his mother and father.

His sobs came quickly, shaking his thin body with the sound of his breath catching unevenly in his throat.

Tia Rosa watched him until she could bear his pain no longer. Suddenly unbuttoning her blouse, she pulled the thin material away to uncover both her breasts. She drew the boy's head into her dark-skinned nakedness and, with her free hand, moved a breast to his mouth. For her, an unthinking maternal reaction to the sound of a child in pain. At that moment, she would have fed all the children in Mexico from her breasts.

CHAPTER 5

Pedro found her nipple with his tongue, nibbled gently, then turned to the other breast. He sucked on the hard-brown nipple but found no milk to draw.

Rosa cradled his head in her hands. With eyes closed, she smiled softly as he felt her breasts with trembling fingers. Pedro found comfort at last as his choking gasps subsided.

She whispered soft crooning sounds in his ears as he continued to explore with nervous hands. Standing slowly, she pulled him with her, his hands and mouth still at her breasts.

"Do you like how they feel, little one?" she asked. "Would you like to feel more?"

Pedro nodded, not knowing how to answer her as a thousand new emotions entangled his tongue.

"Then I will give you more if it pleases you," she said. "First, we finish the mescal."

They both sat again as the gentle warm night drew them in. She pulled off her blouse, and Pedro gazed, hypnotized by her dark, naked beauty. Rosa tossed her long dark hair, letting the thick black braid fall across her shoulder and between her breasts. Both nipples stood in silhouette, defined and hard, caressed by the small mischievous breeze.

Pedro stared in disbelief. His small world was upended so quickly by a magical mature raven-haired beauty that stepped from the midst of an erotic dream. He had seen naked women many times, but always from the pages of books or periodicals. Never had he seen such perfection in the living flesh. Pedro never thought of his aunt as a desirable woman. To him, she was always the distant family icon, a modest, hardworking figurine to respect and admire.

They sat on the bench again, sipping the liquor until both cups were drained.

In the precious nervous silence they shared, neither wanted to contest their versions of this evening's reality. Rosa spoke haltingly, her hand on Pedro's shoulder.

"Come now. We go inside to sleep."

With the liquor clouding their thinking, they stood, moving uncertainly toward the door. Emboldened by the drink, Pedro slipped his arm around her waist as they made their way inside.

She lit two candles and two small oil lamps on either side of her bed.

"Go clean yourself, *Mi Amor*, and when you have finished, I will do the same."

Pedro washed in the cold water from a jug in the washroom. For the first time in his life, he had drunk the strong mescal liquor and looked upon the naked breasts of a woman. Both so occupied his senses that he never felt the cold water splashing over his body.

He returned to Rosa, still sitting on her bed, uncovered as before. She smiled brightly, with no hint of embarrassment, no attempt to clothe herself.

"I go now to wash. Please, light a good fire for us this evening."

She stood, walking to him, pausing for a few seconds while she ran her fingers lightly through his unruly black hair. Her body brushed him softly as she passed.

By the time his aunt returned, a smoky wood fire was warming the bedroom. He turned his head away quickly as she now stood totally without clothes.

She giggled playfully, dancing shadows from the fire moving across her damp, naked body. "Have you ever before looked at an unclothed woman?" she asked.

Pedro shook his head, eyes still averted.

"No girls? No young ones from the pueblo? No women by the river washing?"

"Never," he responded, shaking his head. "Except when you took away your blouse this evening."

"Then you can look at me now, so when asked that question again, you will answer yes."

He gazed at a seductive glistening statue that was once his aunt. She clasped both hands together, raising them high above her head. The thick black hair beneath her arms and between her legs held his gaze for many long silent seconds. With the passing of time, the vision remained, although the fragrance of her hair and the laughter in her voice faded.

Turning from him slowly, she lowered her arms and, holding her hips, bent slightly at the waist. Moving her legs further apart allowed him to see a small tuft of black hair against the dark olive skin between her thighs.

"Are you pleased with what you see?" she asked.

"You are the most beautiful thing I have ever seen," he answered quickly, hoping to please her.

She sat on the bed, her feet touching the floor. "Come." She beckoned him to her.

He knelt on the floor, resting his head on her lap. He felt her hands moving gently through his hair as she shifted her position slightly.

"Look again, Pedro. Touch and feel if you wish. Soon I will turn for you to see me from behind. You will know what gift I am giving you then."

Many seconds passed before she stood from the bed, turned slowly, and knelt, displaying her smooth rounded buttocks. "Look well. Spread me a little, then push your fingers gently into me. Let me guide your hand."

He did as she requested, following her fingers with his, then suddenly realizing how painfully hard he was, how restricted he felt with his trousers tied around his waist.

"Now, you have seen me. I will see you." He withdrew both fingers slowly, and she stood before him again. Wordlessly she untied his belt and pulled off his trousers. Her cool brown hand seemed very dark against his skin as she encircled him, stroking slowly. With every movement, he groaned and pushed unwittingly into her hand as she moved.

Within seconds she had brought him to a shuddering, gasping climax. His seed spilled thickly over her hand and onto his leg.

"Now, turn for me."

He knelt on the floor as she had done. He felt her hands spreading his cheeks and then a sudden shock as her finger pushed into him. Her other hand reached around his legs and held his member as it became hard again.

This time she squeezed instead of stroking, but the finger buried in him from behind moved purposefully, in and out, as she squeezed. He ejaculated again, quickly without control, unable to stifle a loud rasping cry.

They stayed kneeling for a time without speaking, their shoulders lightly touching.

Above the sound of their ragged breathing, he could hear the crackling hiss and spit of the fire. Fantastic moving shadow shapes danced on the walls around them as the flames flickered unevenly. The magic they were making in the little room hung heavily around them.

"Come into the bed with me, and I will hold you while you sleep. Later we will find many things to please us."

"Is this a bad thing we do, *Tia*? Will we displease God?" he asked, lying with his head upon her breast.

"How does it feel to you? Do you think our Lord is unhappy with us?"

"This feels like a perfect dream, a blessing, and so good that I think God will only be happy for us."

He closed his eyes for a few seconds watching shadowy mezcal visions dancing to distant music. They whispered softly and, with their sweet song, slowly pulled him into a deep sleep. Rosa smiled at his reply and held him gently, listening to the steady rhythm of his breathing before sleeping herself.

Rosa woke as the first gray light of morning slipped through the windows. The fire had burned low, leaving a chill in the room and a dull red glow beneath gray ash in the hearth.

Pedro felt her move and curled into her, pulling the blankets around them. They lay for a while, both luxuriating in the warmth of their bodies. Again, they drifted into sleep, with distant river sounds providing comforting music. He stroked her back and heard her little gasp when he felt her breasts as she turned to comfort him.

It was nine months or so before the young Pedro realized how bored and dissatisfied he had become with his new life.

He was paid a small wage for helping his aunt. The work was not difficult, food was plentiful, and for the first time, his sheets were clean and his bed warm. Something was missing, though. His life had no direction or purpose.

There was a distance now between him and Rosa. The scent of her hair was his mother's scent. Salt sweat licked from her stomach was his mother's sweat, and the smell of his mother was on her skin. When they lay together, he pushed hard inside her, and he knew it was his mother he was fucking.

He had heard on the radio about many opportunities waiting in the big world beyond the little stone house. He was also noticing other girls from the pueblo; these girls were very different from Rosa. They wore their hair freely flowing at the shoulder, without braids. They were lighter-skinned and much younger than Rosa's thirty-eight years, making her an old woman in his young eyes. These girls were his age, full of unnecessary laughter and chatter.

He saw them as bright flowers dancing for him in the sun. His statuesque, beautiful olive-skinned mother goddess was soon to become a commonplace boring old Indio woman.

Pedro decided to leave. This new year of 1990 was a year of promise and good fortune. He heard news bulletins on the radio and listened to stories of discontent in the south. There were murmurings of a possible rebellion. He was told exciting stories about how men and women his age would be welcomed quickly into the ranks of the noble dissidents.

Rosa noticed the change in him with sadness. No longer was he the polite, dependent, loving child. Instead, he was growing quickly into a greedy, ambitious man.

Like his selfish father, she thought, *but without the need for tequila to sustain him yet.*

Several months later, when Rosa left for the city center to attend her eldest brother's funeral, Pedro remained to run the store during the week she would be away. He saw a most convenient and unexpected opportunity to leave on his grand adventure. He could now go quietly without answering questions or listening to the inevitable advice from Rosa.

He decided to join the Zapatistas and fight like a soldier for their cause. The day after Rosa left, he entered the store, carrying a large backpack loaded with as many provisions as he would need on his journey south. Pedro searched the store thoroughly, took as much money as possible, and left by the back door after barring the front.

Sadly, the *rattero* to whom Rosa had given so much left like a thief, wearing the boots and clothes she had given him. Pedro never recognized that he had exchanged gold for a handful of sand through treachery and selfish ambition. He would never return and never again see the woman who loved him and gave so much

CHAPTER 6

Three days into his journey, Pedro reached the outskirts of Chiapas. He traveled as far as Tuxtla during his crossing through the Sierra Madres. About thirty kilometers before Centro, he met with a small group of mercenary fighters heading to San Cristobal.

He was very impressed with these jovial rough-talking men and later learned that four of the nine were Arabs from Yemen. Five times a day, almost simultaneously, they would join together, facing east and kneeling with arms outstretched, foreheads touching the ground.

"These brothers are Islamists," he was told by a soldier. "They come to support our cause and provide funding for the conflict. Our people are poor, betrayed by a corrupt government interested only in increasing its wealth and despoiling our land. We are poor, but many, and it is in our numbers this enemy will feel our strength."

Pedro listened, fascinated by the anger and determination he heard in the soldier's voice. He told himself, I will fight with these people now, more determined than ever to join such a good cause. Perhaps I will become a famous general and grow very rich.

At seventeen years of age, Pedro was the youngest of nine travelers. He bore the brunt of many jokes and good-natured insults from his new companions.

"We were nine; now, we are ten. We will soon be known as the terrible ten, feared and respected throughout all Mexico."

The "baby Zapatista" bore the name-calling good-naturedly, content to accept his position as the new revolutionary trainee.

The Arabs rented a large house in San Cristobal. Pedro was given a room there and received a small supplemental income for his work as a messenger. He was treated well and soon began his full-time occupation as a dedicated student of Islam.

He immersed himself in the Islam religion and the Arabic language during the next four years. Three of his four Arab compatriots spoke Spanish fluently, the other English and French. These newfound friends were studious and dedicated to their religious beliefs.

Since he was a baby, he was taught to believe the teachings of the Catholic Church without question. To be a good Catholic, one must be reverential to the Holy Mother Mary and obey the priest's instructions. This was as much as any man in the pueblo could aspire to.

For the most part, the Zapatistas condemned the established church and its teachings as a stage upon which they would parade their white Christian gods. Such was Spanish hypocrisy and a conquistador's legacy to enforce unwanted beliefs on a reluctant enslaved society.

Islamic doctrines and Muslim believers found wide-ranging acceptance in this fermenting cauldron of discontent. There was a logical system of belief—no blustering hierarchy to appoint and support, no contradictory teachings based upon a version of the scriptures issued from a remote Italian entity most people could never embrace or understand.

Muslims were straightforward and practical, preaching a core belief that resonated harmoniously with the exploited Indian population.

It pleased the Arabs greatly when Pedro decided to convert to Islam through shahadah's recitations and accept the Muslim way. They saw in him a serious and dedicated young student, fervent in his beliefs, respectful to the prophet's words, and humbly accepting Allah as the great and only provider.

Unhappily, his conversion to Islam was insincere, a mask of righteousness covering the face of deceit.

During the years until 1994, he pursued his studies relentlessly, learning the meanings behind the words recorded in the Holy Quran. He studied Sunnah with fervent dedication and delighted in discussing and comparing opinions from great Muslim writers and jurists.

On January 1, 1994, having declared war on the Mexican government, revolutionary forces mobilized and marched in several well-coordinated assaults. Police and governing officials were unprepared for the strike. Within two days, most of the southern state of Chiapas was under revolutionary control.

Their cause was right and just, and they rallied against the iniquitous trade agreement so beloved by the Mexican and American governments. The revolution was soon popularized and paraded on the world's news platforms with photographs and videos of brave young fighters raising clenched fists, holding E.Z.L.N. banners, and images of the iconic Emiliano Zapata.

Pedro was photographed in the front ranks, wearing a bandolier of 12-gauge shotgun cartridges, his face covered by a black woolen ski mask. Although he never fired a shot, the publicity and favorable propaganda were immense, generating international sympathy for the cause. His heroic image was seen in many foreign countries and broadcast throughout his Mexican homeland.

Within twelve days, government troops and paramilitary groups responded to the uprising, their actions ensuring many lost lives.

Later in the conflict at the pueblo of Acteal, 48 unarmed people, including women with babies and children, were slaughtered without reason.

The revolution quickly shifted focus to a more effective propaganda war, publicizing human rights issues and disgraceful treatment from the Mexican government. Their conflict continues to this day without resolution.

A few days after the successful 1994 southern uprising, Pedro continued his studies under the tutelage of the Arabs. Not his four friends, though. They were replaced one after another by others, friendly and knowledgeable. He could now speak many sentences in Arabic and some in English.

His earlier ambitions to represent the revolution on the battlefields were directed elsewhere. Pedro spent another three years of immersion in Islam and learning the ways and history of eastern cultures. Before long, his understanding of holy Islamic doctrine enabled him to recite the Quran almost without fault.

Although a quick learner and dedicated to his studies, he was never steadfast in his reverence for the prophet or belief in Allah's loving, merciful embrace. He gave as much lip service as necessary to satisfy his teachers, but the only god that ever pleased him was personal gratification.

The whores he paid reminded him of Rosa, but their artificial movements and superficial conversation gave neither the pleasure nor gentle love that she had unselfishly given to him. The liquor he drank temporarily erased memories of those simpler times that continually haunted him.

Apparently, Allah, the giver of peace and mercy, had decided to allow the young deceiver to continue in this fashion. For who are we, and who among us, even the most faithful, dare question the will of God?

No longer Pedro Morales, he was now Fahim Ibn-Abidin, holder of American and Yemeni passports provided by his Arabian friends. Soon he would live and work in the United States.

"Our business here is finished," he was told. "We joined hands happily with our brothers and sisters in the movement. We stood with

Sub-comandante Marcos and Compañero Galeano, as did you. The Zapatistas have prevailed over the oppressors and will continue to until the Mexican and American governments consider their political positions.

"If they order another serious military response, the Zapatistas will be forced into the jungles again. They will fight from these positions for a short time.

"The movement will always endure, though. The courage of the people will never falter. Although we now have a far greater cause to champion, we fight the same fight, an international program to purge corruption and disinfect satanic politics in the Western world.

"Join us today to remove the enemies of Islam and destroy the great hidden Satan. Your rewards will be many."

Within the year, he was living in the United States as a Los Angeles, California resident. A bank account established in his name provided well for all his needs. Funded by the Yemeni but ostensibly originating from Egypt, his primary purpose was to support other radical operatives destined for future arrival in the United States. Also, to facilitate the spread of the unsightly Islamic stain.

Three years later, he filled a position as an imam in the Light of Hope Mosque—an appointment he would hold for four more years.

CHAPTER 7

Later that evening, an erstwhile Mexican street brat, now Imam Fahim Ibn-Abidin, walked slowly to his car. No longer a skinny waif, his ample stomach reflected an abundant western lifestyle. With no surprise, the recent memory of the sexual acts brazenly performed and publicly enacted in the mosque was still clear in his mind.

He shook his head, remembering the audacity of the participants, particularly the belligerent attitude of the black man when told to remove himself.

Here was the personification of ignorance, loud and obnoxious, *the very reason* he thought why so many blacks were disliked in this local Muslim community. As a good Muslim, he knew he should harbor no prejudice, for, in the eyes of Allah, all men were equal.

Blacks and gays were understandably not *quite* as equal, though; obviously, Jews and women also lacked true equality. He considered these things carefully as he walked, slowing his pace a little.

There had been something very strange about this black one, quite threatening, with glaring bloodshot eyes and an animal-like snarl when confronted. He shook his head, wondering about the bizarre incident, thinking the participants would have been better served in a mental institution instead of a mosque.

Rounding the corner and entering the car park, he was suddenly seized and held immobile.

The open parking area behind the mosque was empty at that hour, and the dark angel worked quickly without interruption. Despite the yells and struggles, Gaytooth tore away his blessed undershirt and—finding him naked beneath his robes—tightened his grip, twirling him several times before rising with his holy burden into the night.

The imam's robes whipped about him, and he trembled in the chilled night air. His eyes watered as the winds cut into his face. His ears filled with sound—a deep, roaring noise, like rushing water—and he found himself without reference to position or direction as myriad pinpoint lights filled his vision.

Slowly, he began comprehending the horror of his situation as they flew through the air and cold seeped into his bones. A demonic entity was taking him to a cold, damp place without sunlight or sanctity, a foul, fetid cave where he would undoubtedly be devoured by the creature now holding him. He prayed earnestly, entreating Allah to remove him from the fierce grip of his tormentor.

Odors of fish and other pungent scents swirled about them. They heard the sound of the ship's warnings, their sirens loud in the night. These sounds and many more moving pinpoints of light greeted the low-flying aviators as they crossed the Hong Kong harbor entrance.

After some time, they crossed a busy thoroughfare in the expensive upscale Causeway Bay district. A prominent fashion boutique provided a perfect setting. Many mannequins were positioned to show colorful summer outfits and revealing ladies' undergarments in the expansive front window display. Henry Smith and his captive alighted in the darkness behind the building.

The vampire quickly deactivated the alarm and shut down the store lighting before arranging his most unusual display model. Silently entering the building and securing the unfortunate shivering imam with duct tape, the vampire bound hands and feet, taping each wrist to the corresponding ankle. In this manner, his victim was bent double, his legs splayed.

Forced into this secured position, he was taped firmly to a female display mannequin, thereby allowing him to maintain a small degree of balance. At the location between her artificial legs where the dummy, if human, would normally conceal her delightful female opening, the noble Muslim's head was affixed with gray duct tape.

Henry Smith disappeared for a short time, eventually returning with some necessary supplies. Quickly locating a local whore, the vampire entered her apartment undetected. Henry had high regard for prostitutes; the majority he had encountered were talkative with interesting stories to tell. Most were forthright, understood simple commerce processes, and smelled good. So, moving in silence, this formless cloud of mist and shadow removed a small jar of Vaseline from the lady's bedroom dressing table and a stick of bright red lipstick.

Exploring the tiny kitchen, he stole a large wooden spoon and an uncooked carrot, the feathery green leaves still bright and fresh. Always the gentleman, he left in compensation a coupon for a half-price discount on a fleecy toilet seat cover and an unopened packet of "snappy mint" chewing gum.

Henry returned quietly to the store window display. Pulling the robe over the revered and learned Muslim's head, his chubby naked buttocks were suddenly revealed. He fixed the robe firmly in place with a strip of duct tape and then applied Vaseline to the exposed posterior. Now sexually aroused, he vigorously penetrated the hapless imam.

During this unwholesome procedure, the violated imam made great supplication to Allah, imploring a colonic cleansing and pleading for the evil one to leave the world forever, seek forgiveness, and eventually find peace.

Henry thanked Fahim Ibn-Abidin for his good wishes before continuing his unsavory mission. Eventually, he fulfilled his previous expectations for gratification. Having finally achieved satisfaction, the evil Henry Smith stood back and grasped the wooden spoon. He thrashed the quivering Muslim buttocks in a final act of desecration. Both plump cheeks were soon made reddened and puffy by the determined application of the spoon. Henry stood back, gazing at the sweaty, twitching canvas spread before him. He considered each cheek, determined to write a fitting paragraph on each.

The vampire whistled a simple, happy tune as he took the whore's lipstick and wrote carefully in a decorative cursive script. On the left cheek, *"Visitors and ticket holders, please take a number"*. And on the right cheek, as a further insult, he drew a large Jesuit cross.

Having finished his artistic endeavors, he thoroughly coated the carrot with Vaseline before firmly pushing his intrusive vegetable into the abused, swollen anus.

He continued pushing until the carrot disappeared from view, and the sphincter muscle closed firmly about the bright green fronds, forming a tight, puckered seal.

"Now is the time to give thanks to Allah, good Muslim," Henry said softly, for he was not a bad man.

"For what should I give thanks, you devil?" hissed the holy one through clenched teeth.

"For your humble carrot—that it is not a plump young parsnip or perhaps a ripe turnip," the vampire replied pleasantly. "May I fetch a glass of water for you? On such a joyous occasion, I would suggest a glass or two of fine-aged cognac. Unfortunately, and as you can see, this is a fashion boutique. There is no brandy or other beverage available. But fear not, my dear fellow; I am sure that in a few days, you will remember this delightful experience with great pleasure. Not only that, consider a grand business opportunity that has just presented itself. I see a world tour for us. Perhaps Macy's in New York, then on to California, Harrods of London, and of course, Italy, France, and Germany; the possibilities are endless, don't you think? Fame and fortune await. Plenty of money is available for both of us, certainly enough to pay for a quickly detachable rubber insert and an artificial rectal hole for you.

Thinking of that, we could have an array of textured inserts to enhance the customer experience. There would have to be a goodly supply of fresh vegetables and lubrication for me. I see only a slight problem; you would have to engage verbally with customers as some may have a latex intolerance. What do you think of my idea? I'm sure you must share my grand vision?"

Once he was satisfied that the imam could not move, the Dark Angel activated the window and display lighting. Confident in his newfound ability as a freelance window dresser, he adjusted the illumination to show the imam and his leafy anal display brightly, with a most pleasing and dramatic effect. Henry smiled gently as the artistic lipstick graffiti seemed to glow brightly under the artificial light.

That was the amazing sight greeting unsuspecting shoppers the following morning. Store employees, assuming the bizarre presentation to be a radical publicity stunt or a progressive European art exhibition, did nothing to help the imam or disrupt the remarkably creative scene.

A sizable crowd of astonished spectators soon formed, partially obstructing the thoroughfare. Some entered the store and verbally taunted the holy man. Many others took photographs with small cameras and cell phones. It was not long before reporters from television and other news outlets converged upon the display, pressing the squirming, gurgling Imam for an opinion or interview.

Eventually, the blubbering, outraged victim was removed by police officers and hospitalized for two days. The carrot was extracted slowly without incident and stored in a container of preservatives at the hospital laboratory. Successful treatment for minor cuts and bruises was duly accomplished. A full day of muscular therapy was needed to transition from his enforced doubled-over posture and slowly regain the appearance of normality.

It was earnestly recommended that psychiatric evaluation be mandated as a condition for his release. Two nurses gave a local newspaper detailed accounts of their involvement with the carrot removal procedures but were quickly silenced by the hospital administration.

A full center page with three revealing photographs and a detailed account of the incident soon appeared in the *Hong Kong Apple Daily*. Somewhat muted television coverage, always mindful of public decency, followed the story by showing a few carefully selected images.

Despite his protests and entreaties, the imam was retained in jail for two weeks while an ongoing investigation determined whether criminal charges would be levied against him. Given the nature of available evidence and the lack of witness testimony, primarily because of the bizarre and most embarrassing circumstances, no charges were ever filed.

Questions about a legitimate entry visa and passport status were never pursued. His claims of US residency were verified, and he was cleared to leave Hong Kong. After his release and upon returning to California, the imam retired from his public duties to be replaced by a more traditional and predictable applicant.

An unexpected result of the dark angels' actions was the sudden emergence of a colorful criminal street gang.

About two months or so after the first storm of anal carrot publicity, a handful of local troublemakers were seen publicly brandishing fresh carrots, most threateningly and suggestively. These extravagant, noisy displays would intimidate innocent tourists and bystanders. Before long, the annoying young hooligans coalesced into an organized street gang behind the name *The Rolling Red Carrot Boyz. Rolling Reds, a*s they became known on the streets, with the widely recognized motive of a large leafy carrot.

Like an infection, their unsavory influence soon spread into local shopping malls, and by extorting small businesses for money, they became a credible social threat. They oozed from back alleys and disreputable nightclubs, clustering on the main streets, puffed-up, arrogant and swaggering, secure in their unhealthy camaraderie, and showing recent carrot tattoos.

This intolerable behavior was quickly curtailed. Sudden and very harsh police intervention contained their activities, and the notorious

Rolling Red Carrot Boyz was eventually forced to disband. Surprisingly the raw leafy carrot has become a potent symbol of Religious persecution and flourishes in Hong Kong art and literature to this day.

Many legitimate offers to purchase or otherwise acquire the carrot from the hospital were rejected. The righteous artifact was subsequently removed to a secret location and carefully preserved there where it remains.

CHAPTER 8

I sat with Henry on a park bench, watching mothers with strollers fulfill their temporary destinies.

"This accursed afternoon light gives me a headache and sorely tries my patience," he complained. "I have an unexpectedly empty feeling after leaving my place of worship, and even though the rascal imam is no longer in attendance, I am sure to be recognized by others if I return. The Sunnis were a welcoming and happy band. I will miss them."

To debate, the circumstances of Henry's banishment would be a pointless exercise, so I refrained from doing so.

Although I considered the incredible nature of the story and understood the attraction of voyeurism and other sexual components of the strange public display, I found my sympathies were with the deposed holy scholar. After all, the poor fellow was innocent of any wrongdoing, merely trying to restore a degree of propriety to the desecrated third prayer row.

Henry would have none of it when I tried to broach the subject.

"The hypocritical little piglet was only too happy when he publicly chastised my friend and me," he snapped. "Another example of bigoted Islam and the Muslim's attempt to humiliate and punish a brother because of the color of his skin. Whatever happened to their gospel of tolerance, acceptance, and brotherly love? The holiest Quran clearly states that: *All are created equal, none are greater than the next and rich or poor is the same without exception. A man should love his brother.*

"I was being loved by a younger, rather delicate brother Muslim when the fool imam started yelling at me."

He continued his angry diatribe.

"Not me alone, though. The flabby fool Imam unmercifully castigated my poor little Indian Ningappa. The stench of hypocrisy and ignorance is all-pervasive. It assails the nostrils quicker than bacon frying in a pan and is particularly well concealed beneath the cover of religious tolerance.

"Anyway, the revered Fahim Ibn-Abidin is a sanctimonious, hypocritical porker, so fuck him."

The dark angel paused for a few seconds and said, "Well, I suppose I did, didn't I?"

I considered Henry's callous attitude and the unpleasant details of the imam's downfall. The thought crossed my mind that this might have been a deliberate set-up, a ruse to provoke the imam and then retaliate against his predictable outrage.

I dismissed that idea as ridiculous speculation. It was far too complicated and devious. Henry's sexual demonstration in the middle of a house of worship was way beyond any normal experience and far removed from a reasonably predictable outcome.

"How important is your place of worship?" I asked. "If prayer is so meaningful to you, perhaps you can look for another mosque. I was not aware vampires were given to embracing religious groups or orders."

Henry sat in silence for a few minutes before replying.

"The Muslims gave me a sense of community, a feeling of belonging. They are surprisingly practical as a religious order. There is no idolatry except for their fanatical reverence for that grungy old Prophet Muhammad. Not too much bell ringing and incense either.

"Anyway, being a vampire is rather like being born an orthodox Jew. Nothing I can do or wish to do about it. I enjoy the freedom and sense of power. Much better than stumbling about on this lower plane of human existence. I could never find fulfillment as a used car salesman or researching squid behavior."

He grinned at me, savoring his small verbal triumph.

"I think," he continued, "I will join the Hail Saint Mary gang at the corner of Broadway and Argyle, although there is not a beard or hijab to be seen. If I change my black face for a Latino one, I should be good to go. I speak Latin fluently, so Catholicism should be a short learning curve for me."

He sighed wearily. "I am told they no longer burn Christians or actively participate in the Inquisition, so one vampire in the nest should go unnoticed.

"I might also seek out a nice pious dentist and have my teeth fixed. Sometimes the accursed things drive me to distraction. Painful to the extent that any reasonable vampire would be tempted to jam pork chop in a Muslim's arse."

"Rather than a carrot?" I asked. When he didn't answer, I continued, "Henry, please allow me to lend you the money. Have your teeth fixed properly. This will not be a problem for me. You can repay me when you're working. Also, the Muslim community will thank you for it."

Henry smiled and slapped me on the back. "Thank you, dear Jack, but no. I have to make my own way here. I do appreciate your offer, though."

"Okay then, but the offer remains open. Anytime you feel the need to beat on a holy man, remember that a good dentist might save an innocent victim."

Henry shook his head and laughed. "The imam was neither innocent nor holy, and pain did not drive my motive. Simple revenge is sometimes a good and satisfying thing. At no time did I choose to reveal his treachery or the great blasphemy for which he is guilty. You, above most, should know very well that things are seldom as they seem.

"As for the carrot," he continued, "It was the perfect natural cork, not only decorative but practical—no embarrassing seminal leakage to explain away. I am, if nothing else, always considerate and respectful of the needs of others. Anyway, if I change my appearance, I will find something with good teeth. In that case, no dentist will be needed, eh?"

I shrugged and thought about what was undoubtedly one of the strangest conversations of my life.

Surely, he could only "change appearances" superficially, which would not affect his core dental problems. It seemed to me that he expected a congratulatory response when trying to justify the now-infamous anal carrot corking.

"Wait, you just told me that you didn't care for the bell ringing and incense. If you become a Catholic, you will find plenty of that."

"No, Jack, I did not say that I disliked those demonstrations, just that the Muslims—from my experience— refrain from such practices. They pray at least five times a day. They use these small rituals for consistency and direction at those times.

Nothing like the Catholics, though, who need colorful robes and all the other accouterments. A grand visual display with incense, chanting, wine, and hand-wringing is expected and demanded by the papal hierarchy. Anyway, the louder the noise, the greater the God, don't you think? A great God should reside in a grand mansion and always be worshiped accordingly. I think I will enjoy my time as a good Catholic, maybe even wear a giant wooden crucifix."

I shook my head, surprised by his reply. "A crucifix? I thought vampires were allergic to crosses and holy water."

Henry laughed his soft, easy laugh. "You watch far too much television, young Jack. I will certainly wear a crucifix, probably upside down, though. I bet no one will notice. Well, better be on my way again. Thank you for listening to me, dear Jack. A vampire's life is a solitary one. I really enjoy our little talks. Next time we meet, I will update you on the Hail Marys. Take care, my friend."

Henry stood and inclined his head, moving quickly with his straight, almost military bearing. Watching him as he walked away, I realized he was becoming quite transparent. His outline remained visible for several seconds before disappearing altogether.

For many days I struggled with my budding relationship with Henry. Here I was, fast becoming the confidant of a queer vampire. I have known many gay men and women, but never a gay vampire or dark angel.

I confess his vampire tendencies bothered me greatly. In my opinion, the imam was unjustly abused and ultimately ruined. There was no reasonable excuse for such behavior, no matter how Henry tried to justify it or how painful his teeth were at the time.

How many other victims had there been? I wondered. How many others suffered such unjust pain and humiliation at his hands? So many unanswered questions remained.

Of course, I hadn't known him for long—a few weeks only—so perhaps my judgment was unreasonably critical. And who was I to criticize or judge anyone? I was certainly in no position to sit in judgment on a gay vampire.

I wondered about him greatly. Did he bite? Exist by feeding on the blood of others? What was the Angel thing about? How old was he? And more worrying, why did he single me out to confide in?

Whatever his motives, he was a good companion—funny, well-educated, and charming.

I suddenly realized I no longer thought to question his assertion that he was a gay vampire or dark angel.

My performance at work was suffering. Somehow research into the behavioral characteristics of Humboldt squid and their means of communication had lost much of the original allure for me.

I was now more concerned with the behavioral characteristics of modern vampires.

So far, my limited studies had revealed few facts. Most of the information was old, rehashed legends and questionable anecdotal accounts of sightings and encounters. Vampire activity remained securely within the realm of Hollywood filmmakers.

What exactly was a vampire or dark angel then? I asked myself. *A demonic creature perhaps living in darkness, ensnaring its victims and draining their blood? A horrible flying devil with nearly unlimited powers?* The Henry I knew fit neither of those popular images. On reflection, *"the Henry I knew?"* No, the reality was that I didn't know Dark Henry Smith at all. I just met with him briefly a few times.

My next meeting with Dark Henry was both memorable and disturbing, although I suppose I could say the same about most of our meetings. This one occurred during a small Southern California seaside art festival. I was strolling along Venice Beach, shoes in hand, enjoying the feel of the incoming tide, letting small frothy waves wash over my feet as I walked in bright Sunday morning sunlight. Hustlers and vendors were making their usual early morning weekend appearances.

The light ocean breeze brought a chill to the morning, and the sun, not yet fully in the sky, bore a promise of another hot day. After a pleasant half-mile or so of barefoot walking, I stopped at one of the many small restaurants lining the sidewalk.

Sitting at the bar, I savored this peaceful time far removed from the institute. A squid-free day for me today. I enjoyed a beer and sandwich while watching others pass by, then making ready to leave. I fished in my pockets for change to leave on the counter.

An empty sinking feeling overtook me as I realized my wallet was not with me—no credit cards, no license, and, more worrying to me, no ability to pay the bill. Another careful search through my pockets confirmed my wallet was indeed missing.

I approached the cash desk and spoke to a young Latino waiter. He listened to my story and then bade me wait while he called the manager.

"Eh, gringuito, hola. ¿Como esta? ¿que pasa? ¿Problema con el dinero?"

"Sorry, I don't speak Spanish. Do you speak English?"

"Of course. Let's sit at the bar for a while," he said softly, indicating a vacant place. "Perch here on this stool."

I stared at him, black hair graying at the sides, swept back and tied into a small ponytail, slender, medium height with rather delicate features. A short, trimmed black beard framed his face. There was something very familiar about his voice and manner, although I was sure we had never met.

"Perch?" I asked.

"Yes, perch, park, take the weight off. An *americano* word for sit, often repeated at marine research social gatherings."

I stared again, astonished at his appearance and suddenly feeling cold and very much alone. This transformation was far removed from any of my previous life experiences and as frightening to me as Henry's shape-shifting demonstration a few weeks earlier.

Surrounded by customers chatting and laughing, seeing others sitting at the bar occupied with eating and drinking gave me enough temporary courage to remain in my seat. I was much comforted by this welcomed and reassuring display of humanity.

"What do you think? I borrowed this outfit from a Salvadorian sailor. He should be awake by now. He will wander around for a few hours before realizing he is a black man with bad teeth and able to speak English, French, and Spanish fluently. He should be able to find a job and a dentist quite easily, I'm sure, eh? Anyway, I left him with a few dollars in his pockets to tide him over for a couple of days."

The voice was unmistakable. Henry had definitely returned.

Still shaken, I replied quickly, a nervous reaction without considering my words. "Your outfit fits you well, Henry, although not very vampirish. Of course, your last costume was even worse. I mean, a vampire should at least look like one, don't you think? You have no cloak, gloves, or anything."

Almost immediately, I wished I were able to suck back the trite comments and stupid observations. I started to apologize, but Henry interrupted me with a wave of his hand.

"Yes, I must agree. However, I will ask for your advice on this matter, Jack. How many vampires or angels have you seen recently?

What dress code did they favor? How did their features differ from mine? I suppose you are looking for a tall, thin figure with a pale face wearing a long black cloak, and speaking with a ridiculous Eastern European accent. Your old London cemetery phantom would be a perfect fit, perhaps, eh?

Now even that expectation has changed. Modern vampires are supposedly pale handsome teenagers with behavioral problems and inflated egos." He sighed overdramatically, shaking his head. "All of these changes make me feel quite old-fashioned. Perhaps I should hire an agent or publicist to improve my image. How think you?

I started to reply, apologizing again, but he cut me off with another quick dismissive movement of his hand.

"I have no permanent physical or visible identity. I am, I suppose, an enduring personality, almost like a ghost. We can communicate efficiently because of the form or body that I currently occupy. I exist for you in the half-light between your fantasy and imagination.

You, on the other hand, are the archetypical Scandinavian. Nordic blood, white skin, blond hair, and very blue eyes. One may say that you fit the pretty-boy mold perfectly."

"Sorry, Henry, I shouldn't have made such dumb comments. It's just that I'm not familiar with vampires. Like most folk, I suppose I'm conditioned by movies and stories to expect a totally different image. You are somewhat of a rarity, though."

"Not as rare as you think, Jack, as I will show you later. But that discussion is for another time and place. As for mass media conditioning, here is a great truth you have touched upon. It is, as we know, the primary instrument for those who seek power. They subtly control opinion and, therefore, can orchestrate the movement of the masses. Corporations, religions, governments, and unions are the same entity but move in different directions and at different speeds.

'I think; therefore, I obey.' The bleating sheep are undoubtedly unaware of the extraordinary collective strength they possess. If you watch advertisements on television, you will find perfect examples of guided thinking or thought manipulation intended to influence the unwary.

Your human race is pack animals, needing a leader or shepherd to function correctly. Without religious leaders or political governance, no matter how corrupt or inept, there will be misery and dysfunction. Your so-called freedom is an unwanted illusion. People will never be free of the oppressor until they accept that they are the oppressor. Ah, but that lecture is for later, for another day perhaps, my dear Jack."

He paused, shaking his head again before continuing.

"Enough of these depressing observations; I am a vampire, not a prophet—although I am told the pay is about the same." He laughed quickly. "This is not a lecture, Jack, and I am not angry with you. Now to show my good intentions, I will reunite you with your loved one."

So saying, he produced my wallet from his pocket with an exaggerated flourish.

"More vampire trickery, my young friend. You left it on the passenger seat. Definitely not a good place in full view of anyone looking through your car window."

"Many, many thanks, Henry, much appreciated. You saved the day for me." I glanced around the bar. "You are a manager here, then?"

"Just a customer Jack. I intercepted your message and decided to help."

We talked for another hour or so before parting company. By now, I was accepting of Henry's new identity and more relaxed in his company.

"*Adios*, dear Jack. We will meet again soon, I think."

Carefully adjusting a pair of very dark glasses before pulling the hood of his coat over his head, he walked to the open door.

I stared after him, watching as he merged with others on the sidewalk before quickly disappearing into the stream of people. Strangely overdressed, I thought, with his long dark raincoat and hood pulled over his head. His need for the odd apparel was understandable, though. Surprisingly, no one seemed to notice him on this beautiful sunny afternoon. I wondered if this was a happy coincidence, Henry appearing when he did.

No, I thought this was no accident. This was another demonstration for my benefit.

I asked for the check and returned to the cash desk, this time much relieved by knowing I was able to pay. The amount owed was nearly twice what I expected. I wondered if the check belonged to another person and was given to me in error.

After studying the bill for a few seconds, I glanced at the cashier, who smiled.

"The price is correct," she said. "Your friend—the one you were sitting with, the Mexican guy he said to put everything on one ticket." I laughed and paid happily—a fair trade, I thought, *for the priceless company and a rescued wallet.*

CHAPTER 9

You may remember from chapter one how Dark Henry Smith bought a used car, a large Lincoln town car from 1989. Mechanically it was in excellent condition, with perfect black paintwork, tinted windows, and a roof rack. A Saint Christopher medallion hung from the mirror, which he would habitually flick with his finger. He smiled at the faint smell of leather and caressed the padded steering wheel.

The vehicle would be paid for in monthly installments using the wages from his evening job as a bartender at a small saloon some three miles from his home. He had saved the deposit through frequent withdrawals from the collection plate at the large Catholic Church that was his new place of worship.

Behind *Ronnie's bar and grille* was a small paved yard where employees and patrons could park their automobiles. The vampire mobile was also parked in the yard when Henry was behind the bar.

Thursday evening, when he arrived late to work at around eight-thirty, he discovered that all available parking places were occupied. Muttering darkly, he backed into the street and parked a few yards from the bar. He had not yet shut the engine off when a sharp rap on the passenger's window drew his attention. He lowered the window, and a commanding voice, with a ring of self-importance, addressed him from the darkness.

"You can't park here, sir, too close to the intersection. Please move your vehicle."

Known for his pleasant and most accommodating attitude, Dark Henry Smith considered the request carefully before replying in a voice mimicking the enforcement officer.

"I have something for you, meter maiden." Then pointing to a plastic bag of groceries on the passenger seat indicated a large cucumber protruding from the bag. "A good fit for you. When inserted, it should provide many happy hours of pleasure."

This prompted a quick response from Andre, the noble parking enforcement officer.

"I will pretend I didn't hear that comment. This is the last time I will tell you. Move your vehicle. If you do not, I will write a noncompliance ticket and call the police." Andre spoke slowly; his words edged with anger. His job had always required tolerance for insults from ignorant miscreants as a daily routine, but this wretched driver had raised the bar with such mean-spirited words.

The frightened vampire, dreading a possible parking citation, replied softly in an ancient Mandarin dialect.

The bemused captain of parking enforcement foolishly leaned on the car door, putting his official city parking enforcement head through the open window.

"Excuse me," he said. "I didn't quite understand that."

As he spoke, the vampire Henry raised the window quickly, trapping the officer's head inside his car.

The officer was enraged beyond all reason, guillotined by the window, gurgling and coughing because of his suddenly restricted air supply. His peaked cap fell off as he flailed his arms and ineffectually beat on the window and door with his hands.

"I am so sorry," Henry said. "I am unable to understand you. Please speak clearly and slowly, or I will be forced to remove you. This is a no-parking zone. If you are unable to converse in English, an interpreter may be found for you."

Listening to more unintelligible commentary from the parking department representative, Sir Henry shook his head with a sigh of resignation. He slipped the transmission into drive and moved slowly from the curb, now in perfect compliance with the recent no-parking orders.

As Henry cruised slowly between ten and fifteen miles per hour, the unfortunate victim was forced to run and jump, grasping at the rain channel and stretching for a grip on the roof rack for support. Both nicely polished black leather shoes were torn from his feet before the first stoplight.

During two cruel miles of this enforced exercise, pedestrians shouted and waved in alarm. Other road users flashed lights and sounded horns. The vampire smiled happily and, as a reigning monarch would, sometimes, graciously acknowledge the waves and shouts from his obviously adoring subjects.

The kindly and most merciful Dark Angel, overflowing with concern for the well-being of his fellows, eventually stopped at a pedestrian crosswalk. Opening the window, he allowed the battered parking enforcement officer to collapse in a ragged heap. Andre crawled from the crossing onto the sidewalk, then sat propped against a "no parking violators will be towed" sign.

Gasping for air, without shoes or a cap, buttons torn from his uniform, he could be reasonably mistaken for a homeless drunk.

The vampire returned to Ronnie's parking area and quickly parked his car in the only available space.

Alighting from his vehicle, he was approached by Leticia Washington. Hand on hip and her most seductive smile in place, she whispered softly in a sensual southern drawl.

"Hello, sweet baby. Wanna go for a walk? We could do it behind your car, nice and quiet."

"Do what?" Henry asked, quite irritated by this latest interruption.

"Anything and anyway you want it, honey," Leticia said seductively. The dark one would, under normal circumstances, have engaged the young lady in a meaningful conversation. These were not usual circumstances, though. Already late for work and angered by the self-righteous bleating and farting from the unlucky meter-maid, his sympathy and high tolerance for prostitutes had plummeted.

The vampire considered her offer for several seconds. "Very well, if the price is right and you are enthusiastic."

"Okay, darling." She replied. A hundred bucks for you if no kids or animals are involved."

"Eighty-five would get it," he said. "I have no kids or animals."

"Okay, quick, then, what do you need? How would you like it?"

Henry thought for a moment before making a reply.

"I am easy to please, my dear. Some light housework, laundry, of course, dishes washed, and my evening meal prepared. I am not an unreasonable man."

Her smooth molasses and honey drawl rose to a strident Los Angeles ghetto screech.

"Okay, you cracked-out nipple-headed asshole. Fuck you and the old pig that brought you here, then."

Her sweet tribal song, born of the ghetto, carried on the evening breeze and echoed in the darkened streets and alleys of the shabby neighborhood. She turned on her heel and strode angrily from the parking lot.

The vampire winced briefly, hearing such awful language from a lady. He smiled grimly, suppressing his rising anger. "Not even a simple thanks for his most reasonable offer of work," he mumbled to himself.

"Oh, on the contrary, my dusky beauty, I believe *you* are the one who will be fucked and, sooner rather than later."

He walked purposefully from the parking area and took his belated position behind the bar.

CHAPTER 10

Charlotte Washington left New Orleans on the advice of her doctor.

"Move yourself outta this place, gal," he told her, "Before Brownie's boys do da big job on yah."

This time he was dead serious. "I know fo a fact they be here tomorrow wid bad intentions. Gonna cut yah good, my sister."

She thanked the old man, watching as he walked unsteadily from the path to the street. Though he was drunk again, she did not take the threat lightly. Brownie was a man of his word and would follow through and make good on any promise. There would be no bargaining, compromise, or explanations.

She shook her head, banging a clenched fist on the draining board. All these problems and her being just settled with rent paid and the promise of work at the Starlight Club. Cursing inwardly, she looked around the tiny front room, deciding the order in which to sort and pack her few belongings.

She did not know for sure, but she guessed that her stupid boyfriend Ray—the one who promised so fervently to support and protect her—had failed to pay Brownie. The more he used, the more he owed until

Brownie stopped the credit. The heroin and cocaine were not cheap, and Raymond had no steady income to repay the loans.

She lent him most of the money she made in the clubs and bars during the year, a goodly amount as tourists had been unusually kind to her that season. Now she had only a few dollars left, no future, and no choice but to leave as soon as possible.

On reflection, she became convinced that Ray used her money to buy smack from another dealer, hanging Brownie out to buy more time. He would soon learn that Brownie's time was more than he could ever afford. Why, oh, why was she born dumb enough to take up with another pine-headed smack user with no money?

She'd lived the better part of her life in the Mississippi Delta region, and this was home to her. New Orleans had always been her special friend. The tiny, quirky houses brought a promise of shelter. Music clubs and bars on familiar narrow streets gave her a reasonable living. She saw hope for the future in the smiling faces that passed her.

It was the smiling face of Raymond that cost her dearly—another pretty boy without the brains to hammer a round peg in a bull's arse.

Driving her fist into the draining board again, she made ready to move on and leave the Delta forever.

Mandy from the Starlight club was already working when the call came. Charlotte told a halfway convincing tale of a sick sister in Utah. "All I need is a ride to the station. I'll take the train to Texas from there. I'll be able to find my way to Saint George."

She was satisfied that the false trail she was leaving was sufficient to prevent Brownie from tracking her to California, her intended destination. Raymond, the stupid, could fend for himself back in New Orleans.

By two-thirty, she was packed and waiting with little Leticia.

Mandy arrived with her husband's truck, and by eight pm, Charlotte and Leticia were on their way to a new life in California.

They stayed for a while in a cheap motel by the Los Angeles airport. Charlotte was always able to earn a reasonable living. Even though a little battered around the edges, her exotic Creole looks and firm body attracted the attention of many admirers.

With the money she made from a plentiful stream of visitors from the airport, they moved to Compton for a few weeks and then to Chatsworth, where Charlotte stayed with her daughter for nine years. Her premature death came unexpectedly from a viral stomach infection, totally unrelated to her lifestyle.

Leticia, who had great love and respect for her mother, saw to the many details of her cremation. Her earthly remains were placed in a Ziploc freezer bag and stored in a nice ornate plastic urn. Leticia promised to return her mother to New Orleans when the opportunity presented itself.

Andy, an impoverished elementary school English teacher and occasional customer, wrote a poem for Leticia. He assumed he could exchange his doubtful literary talents for an hour of Leticia's time.

He left most dissatisfied with the four minutes she grudgingly allowed.

She promptly placed an advertisement in the classified births, deaths, and marriages section of the *Times*, using the emotive words Andy wrote for her.

> "R.I.P
>
> In Loving Memory of Charlotte the Harlot.
>
> Touched by many, loved by few, Charlotte is in heaven waiting for you.
>
> DEC 20, 1958–MAY 9, 2004"

Two days later, this heartwarming dedication was deemed unsuitable for publication and withdrawn from the paper without apology. Well, no matter, Leticia would place her very own personal adverts in the livestock and pets sections. The next day was spent drafting her small advertisements and preparing them for publication.

LIVESTOCK AND PETS

"Pretty little kitten for sale.

Loves people; come and stroke my pussy. You will not be disappointed. Very pretty, just waiting for your love.

Call for an appointment."

POSITIONS AVAILABLE

"All positions available for the right applicant. See which one suits you best. Please call for an appointment."

The *Times* accepted both her latest submissions without comment, and the advertisements appeared in both *positions available* and *pets and livestock* sections of the paper.

Leticia, now eighteen years old, moved on with her life. Following her mother's example, she wholeheartedly embraced the oldest profession with great dedication. She knew her mama was good, so she resolved to practice hard to make sure she was as good or better.

She left the old house and moved into a small two-bedroom apartment off Mason Avenue. Only a few other girls worked Broadway and Argyle, so her client base grew steadily. Before she was twenty-five years of age, her mastery of the profession was complete.

Having developed the predatory skills necessary for a successful competitive business, she realized that expansion would soon be needed. There were a finite number of clients one girl could reasonably accommodate during the course of a working day. That was her limitation.

After a most pleasant experience satisfying a new customer, she chatted with him while they dressed. He told her he was the owner of a fast-food franchise on Broadway. His Gutburger restaurant provided a reasonable living but was limited by his employees.

"Only so much one man can do in a day," he told her, articulating her problem perfectly.

"Then what would you do to change?" she asked.

"Franchise," he said. "The real money is not made by working, but by working smart. If I work at my Gutburger, I will make a profit limited by the seating capacity and a certain number of employees. But if I own the Gutburger, rent it to someone, and take a percentage of the profit, I can repeat the process many times. The Gutburger name is important, though."

He mentioned many famous corporate names in the fast-food industry as examples.

"Gutburger can't lose. They own the property, and I pay a chunk for the franchise privilege. They rent the equipment and furnishings to me and sell me the products to re-sell."

"Why not do the same?" she asked.

"Because my name ain't Gutburger, and I don't have the deep pockets," he replied.

"I could open other restaurants, but without the Gutburger name, I wouldn't attract the customers or get the deep resale discounts. They have an established product. It's a well-known and consistent brand. Customers know what to expect when they eat at the Gutburger."

Diarrhea, for sure, perhaps Chlamydia or *Ebola,* she thought but held her tongue because, at that moment, she understood precisely what she must do and how to do it.

A glittering sword, glowing with brilliant light and shining with a beam of incandescent crystal clarity, cut away at the darkness of her uncertainty and indecision, illuminating the pathway ahead. She had now what her mother always lacked; a plan for the future and a way out.

For the next eight hours, she reflected on her past life. Then, carefully considering her recent Gutburger franchise revelation hardened her resolve to follow a path to freedom and wealth.

"I will work until I'm thirty, save my money, and move to Vegas. Even marry and settle down if I find a good, reliable man. Perhaps buy some property, the first of a business franchise."

A name, then. *The Fantastic Fuck Factory*, *Awesome Whoresome*, and *Leticia's Little Love Shack is where the elite can meet to beat their meat*.

Of course, the inevitable disclaimer so everyone would feel welcomed, equality would prevail, and no feelings would be hurt.

Leticia's equal opportunity prostitution center. The possibilities were endless. She would work on her business plan that evening and vigorously promote the Leticia Washington brand.

After her confrontation with a sarcastic vampire in Ronnie's parking lot, a furious Leticia sauntered along the high street, propositioning occasional pedestrians without success.

Meanwhile, the mistreated parking enforcement officer, having recovered to the extent that he was able to hobble slowly along the street, moved erratically toward Ronnie's bar again. His confrontation with a sarcastic vampire left him with trauma-induced psychosis and partial memory loss due to oxygen deprivation.

He had only a vague memory of his previous life. Still, He knew that he was a person of great importance—possibly the head of an international banking chain or a nuclear submarine commander, perhaps related to European royalty.

Andre knew only that he must have been attacked, robbed, beaten, and relieved of his shoes and hat.

Leticia wrinkled her nose in distaste. She had no compassion for the homeless and a violent dislike for drunken ones. Here she was, though, about to confront a bum tottering toward her. A sudden feeling of sadness and hopelessness overwhelmed her, and for the first time in her life, she felt an inexplicable need to reach out and help the impoverished.

The unfortunate one without shoes tottering toward her would soon fulfill her charitable desires.

She stopped Andre in mid-stagger. "Look," she said. "I don't do bums, but on this one, and the only occasion, I will give you a hand-job, no charge here, in the doorway."

The shoeless parking officer stared at Leticia for a long time before replying. "Get away from me before I give you a citation, you worthless streetwalker."

He thought for a moment. What he had just said about a citation suddenly made no sense to him. Many seconds elapsed while he considered his reply. The word "Citation" had a special meaning for him, though, locked away somewhere in his memory, just beyond recall.

Leticia stepped back, totally unprepared for such rudeness. Still bitter over Henry's rejection, she was suddenly engulfed by a wave of smoldering anger.

How was such a thing possible? She had never been rebuffed before—not even by the old Japanese guy with erectile dysfunction. Now, two refusals in one afternoon and the last from a drunken bum. This was more than any woman could bear. Her motto, "guaranteed satisfaction for all," was as meaningful to her as "semper fi" was to a Marine Corps gunnery sergeant. Her professional reputation depended upon it.

Smiling sweetly at Andre, she said, "Please forgive me, sir. I am truly sorry if I disturbed you."

The captain of missing shoes, surprised by her sweetness, dazed and on the verge of collapse, was distracted by the sudden movement of her left hand. He never saw the overhand right. The blow caught him on the side of his jaw, dropping him to the pavement as a police cruiser pulled smoothly alongside the curb. Both vigilant officers within had been witness to the assault.

"Holy shit, George! That bitch packs a punch."

"Yeah, look, I think that's Leticia. Wanna go pick her up?"

"Nah, let it ride for a few minutes. Mebby, she'll whack him again."

Sean grinned, content to watch the small drama unfold.

Andre rolled onto his stomach and struggled to his hands and knees. His assailant moved quickly behind him, aiming a vicious kick at his rear end.

Fortunately for the enforcement buttocks, her kick missed. However, it was delivered with such ferocity that a nice, bright red, strapless, high-heeled plastic shoe flew from her foot, striking the parked police patrol car.

George and Sean, the two valiant law officers, stepped smartly from their vehicle. Prompted by this sudden act of hostility, they walked quickly and purposefully to the scene of the disturbance.

Many questions were asked, and few satisfactory answers were forthcoming. After some time, both miscreants were arrested, and further questioning resumed at the police station.

The judicial process's eventual outcome had Leticia confined to jail for three weeks: two weeks for throwing her shoe at a police car and one week for a hostile and belligerent attitude in court. It was probably her rudeness to the judge and disrespectful behavior in court that also earned her an additional fifty hours of community service and probation for three months.

Andre, with no shoes, received a citation for disturbing the peace and public intoxication. No jail time, but a fine of one hundred dollars.

CHAPTER 11

Late Tuesday afternoon, I was scanning the previous day's newspaper and finishing an early dinner at the Gutburger eating house when Henry walked in and sat down. As usual, I experienced a sudden shock at his appearance.

Although I felt no fear and was now quite accustomed to his strange behavior, there were always surprises and anxiety elements when he appeared without warning. We exchanged pleasantries and chatted amicably for a few minutes. I offered to buy him a coffee; he shook his head.

"Thank you, no, dear boy. I much prefer tea."

"Okay, Henry, a tea, then coming up."

"Can't-do Jack, you Americans are scarcely able to make coffee. As for the vile fluid you erroneously call tea, it is a mixture that is quite impossible to drink. A bag floating in tepid water is not tea. The only people capable of making tea properly are English, Irish, and Indians, and then only after many years of practice."

Okay, so no tea or coffee, then?

He laughed, "No, thank you, young Jack; much easier if I stick to water, I think.

Henry explained his new car purchase, detailing the funding process.

"You have no qualms about stealing from a church? You're taking money donated and collected to help the poor and needy. I think that's terrible."

"My dear boy, this mantle of self-righteousness is a poor fit for you. Any money in the plate supports the administration and maintains the church's luxurious edifice and attendant infrastructure. Charity is a convenient label to distract from the truth. My car is a most worthy charity."

When I didn't comment, he continued with his explanation.

"I did not steal but merely diverted available cash to a reasonable cause. The Muslims would have given the money to me had I asked and demonstrated a need."

"Your logic is faulted, Henry Smith, but rather than argue, let's change the subject."

I suddenly felt dizzy, unable to focus my eyes. There was a sound like the roar of a waterfall for a second or two, and then all was quiet again.

A small California earthquake, perhaps? But no one at the adjoining tables seemed to notice anything amiss.

Henry smiled at me. "Everything okay, Jack?"

"Yeah, everything's good, Henry. Just felt strange for a few seconds."

"Very well. Then to resume our conversation, consider the car-financing subject closed, young Jack amigo. Perhaps you will explain my faulted logic to me first, though. My definition of logic would be a science of reasoning correctly. How think you?"

I thought for a moment and nodded, "Yes, I agree with your definition."

"Do you also agree that, by definition, logic would encompass a conversation between a marine biologist and an accordion-playing vampire at a French cafe?"

"A burger joint, not a French cafe," I corrected.

He shook his head.

"No, *your* logic fails *you*, young Jack. Look around."

I did not argue, for we were now seated in the little cafe where Henry first showed me his ability to shift his form. I closed my eyes forcefully for several seconds and reopened them quickly, expecting to find myself at the burger house again. It was not to be. We were both in the bistro, sitting at the same outside table we'd occupied a few weeks ago.

Suddenly I was a schoolboy again, walking jauntily through a grassy field, across a paved area, and onto the campus grounds. Soon I would join a ball game with a few friends, and then just as quickly, I was seated once more at a table in the bistro.

I rapped my knuckles painfully on the table and moved my chair, scraping the iron legs on the pavement. My new reality was defined for me then by these simple gestures, but I was not reassured. This little restaurant was destined to create many memories for me and would certainly be a pivotal destination for me in so many ways.

Henry chuckled.

"I have ordered a glass of red wine for you as I am responsible for your cold coffee at the Gutburger. Now, a bite to eat, perhaps? I give my solemn word as a hideous vampire that the money for the check will not come from a collection plate."

Within a few minutes, my breathing had returned to normal. I cautiously accepted my newfound position at the alternative restaurant.

Was this a demonstration? A small lesson, perhaps to remind me that he held all the aces. *Very possibly,* I thought. *Not only the aces but the deck, to be played precisely as he wished.*

On reflection, I didn't pursue questions about the method or mechanics employed to achieve the incredible restaurant switch. Some things I decided are better left alone.

"Your little waitress will make an appearance soon, and then we will eat. I know you have many questions for me, and I will try to answer honestly. No more ravished imam questions, though."

"My little waitress" was a charming and most attractive woman who appeared with two large sandwiches. I assumed Henry had placed the order before we arrived. We ate in silence for a few minutes. Despite the extraordinary circumstances, I found myself enjoying the food.

Henry was, as usual, talkative and charming. The waitress returned with a carafe of red wine, filling two glasses.

When the time was right, and I could overcome my shyness, I promised to ask her out to a movie or dinner. Perhaps three glasses of wine instead of two would help.

"So," Henry continued, "for what it's worth, Jack, my name is not Henry Gaytooth. *Gaytooth* is a nickname I adopted and one that I have become rather fond of. My given name is Vonbondurantle, pronounced Henry Goldstein Smith, although I must admit Henry Gaytooth Goldstein has an elegant, old-world European ring to it, don't you agree?"

I shook my head, confused by his many names.

"Yes, and as always, you are full of surprises, Mr. Goldstein. Perhaps lord or sir—even the Honorable Sir Henry Gaytooth Goldstein would be a better complement to your old world leanings."

He laughed heartily.

"A grand idea, Jack. I may well adopt the lord before my name."

"But Goldstein? A Jewish name, surely? Hardly appropriate for a practicing Catholic and Muslim. And how is *Vonbondurantle* ever pronounced Henry Goldstein?"

He chuckled softly. "Because I wish it so."

Then he continued the conversation as if I had never asked my question.

"Yes," he continued, "the Jews are an old tribe. Jews adopted me in my youth. They hold fast to many ancient customs and beliefs. The preacher you call Jesus threw a gang of them out of a big temple for conducting banking operations and money laundering there."

Henry shook his head. "They never forgave him for that. Not much has changed over the years, I think."

We sat in silence for a moment or two before Henry spoke once again.

"One of the abiding disappointments in my life is that I never did meet Jesus or his wife. By all accounts, he had big balls—metaphorically speaking—an 'in your face' personality, and apparently, a likable fellow, though. Good with kids and quite tolerant of bums and hookers. I wonder what he would have thought of my little frolic in the mosque." I am sure had we been acquainted, we would have enjoyed many interesting conversations. Imagine Jack, Sunday morning at Saint Mary's, and the priest reading to the congregation from the new testament, Henry's first book.

He smiled. "I grow old, Jack, and weary. I find I have little tolerance for anybody now. As time passes my door, I find myself less tolerant of all things mortal."

"Are you old by our mortal standards, then?" I asked. "Yes, by your yearly count, I think I am about 648 years. Old enough to have witnessed many comings and goings on this plane. I would say that my expiration date has long since expired."

"Then you will live forever?"

"No, the passage of time regulates everything. There is an indelible time stamp on all things, living or not. A different clock than yours regulates my years. As an example, many butterflies live for a few days only. You, by comparison, would be immortal. However, the butterfly has no concept of a comparatively short lifespan. It's living, as with all things, is relative to its life frequency. Everything, by design, moves and resonates at different frequencies and amplitudes. So, that being said, consider yourself a butterfly, dear boy."

I smiled, remembering his way of addressing me as "young Jack." For a creature of 640-some years, a 38-year-old man must appear as a baby.

"There is a modicum of intelligence flickering behind your bright, curious eyes, young Jack. Study the original and modified theories of relativity again. You will discover more wisdom to be learned from that strange old Jew."

When he had finished speaking, I think it was then that I first became aware of the enormity, the extraordinary privilege, and the opportunity given to me. No longer consumed by fear and trepidation, I was able to converse freely with a being whose knowledge and experience was infinitely greater than mine. I felt like a wandering believer, perhaps meeting the Buddha in a local Indian restaurant.

I held my tongue with some difficulty, thinking of Henry's comment about "that strange old Jew."

A Comparison between Einstein and Henry would have Henry emerge by far the stranger and older of the two Jews. Also, intrigued though I was, I did not question him about his "Jesus or his wife" comment.

"Something I must ask you, Henry. Please forgive me if I overstep the bounds of courtesy. What is the bloodsucking thing all about? When you bite someone, do they then become a vampire? How often do you drink human blood?"

Henry grinned, his teeth gleaming whitely in the half-light. "Good questions, Jack, ones I am happy to answer. Blood is an essence that, to a small extent, nourishes me. By no means is it essential to my health or well-being. I drink blood during sexual encounters and in the heat of passion.

Human blood, I regard as a great delicacy, like a fine wine. Sometimes I might steal a little while a lover is asleep, then no more than one cup at a time, in minimal quantities only. Should I feel the need for blood, I will drink from bulls or other large animals—mostly from bulls, though.

Relatively painless and never enough to harm them, they soon recover."

He glanced at me as if assessing my reaction so far.

"As for biting humans? No, they do not become vampires. If that were to happen, the world would be populated by colonies of half-wits and bimbo vampires. Hollywood has much to answer for, don't you think? Jack, my diet is similar to yours, although I eat a lot of raw meat and fish as my need for protein is far greater than yours. All my food comes from the supermarket—preferably fresh, not frozen. Other than that, there is not much difference."

I nodded slowly, considering his reply. "You're not harmful to humans, then?"

"No, not purposefully, although I confess to a certain intolerance when I am provoked. For clarification, feel free to question Fahim Ibn-Abidin. Even then, more damage was done to his pride than his physical well-being. His arse probably reminded him of our encounter for a few days, though."

Despite my outrage at the disgraceful treatment meted out to the imam, I could not refrain from laughing loudly at Henry's last comment.

"You have seen the world change since you were young. Were your parents vampires?"

"I had no parents. I was born at seven years and delivered from the dark place between the stars. I was taken to a small tribe of Jewish settlers. So, suddenly, I became a seven-year-old member of the tribe of Levi.

At that time, the council was instructed to call me Bogelvandurewentl. As I grew, my name was changed many times.

"Dark places between the stars? What do you mean? Are you talking about outer space?"

He shook his head. "No, Jack, there are vast spaces or layers of motion existing everywhere. The black matter, some call it. It exists between the planets, between solar systems, and in your bloodstream between platelets. It is composed of movement; without movement, there is nothing.

Movement is the foundation of existence. Science will recognize these truths in a few years. Even now, as the understanding of quantum entanglement is being recognized as a legitimate scientific pursuit, new discoveries will be revealed that will change our idea of the world around us."

Later, when we have more time, I will tell you the whole story," He sighed, shaking his head.

"Everything is time, Jack, and all we are, all we will ever be, are custodians of our thoughts. Everything within the range of your senses is thought, and thought is motion. Thoughts are the building blocks of the world around us. The thought is motion, the dark matter."

I sipped my wine, thinking about this strange conversation. I suppose at heart I am an animal lover, my main interest being marine life forms, any plant or animal beneath the sea. I have no interest in any written works by Einstein; I avoid any conversation if the words Astro, quantum, or terrestrial physics are used. And so, it would need many more glasses of wine and many more years before I understood the meaning behind his words.

"Another personal question then." I continued. "How is it that your teeth are so painful?"

"To question a vampire about teeth is a terrible breach of etiquette. Vampires become quite enraged at tooth questions."

He glared at me briefly, a wicked gleam of malice in his eyes, and then laughed loudly.

"Ah, Jack. If only we had a mirror. Your face is a study of remorse. I joke, dear boy. Vampires are synonymous with teeth, are they not? Your question should have been, "why *were* your teeth so painful?"

I nodded, still a little unsure. "This is turning into a verbal questionnaire, though, Henry. I didn't mean to interrogate you. Let's change the subject."

Henry smiled broadly. "Just two friends having dinner together, Jack. I do not regard this as an interrogation. After all, I asked you many questions, even though you were not aware of it.

Now, to answer your tooth question. When I assume a temporary form like the black one I recently discarded, it comes with its inherent physical limitations. I expend considerable energy if I repair physical problems. In the case of the Negro fellow, it had bad teeth and a few other issues. I fixed a few of the defects in order of importance.

I believe that to leave any form; I occupy in better condition than when I inhabited it is my solemn obligation. I try very hard not to cause damage."

He sipped his wine and then rubbed his arm as if discovering his skin for the first time. "It was necessary to change from that black identity because the Muslims would have recognized me. Too many witnessed my confrontation with the Imam. Now this current Latino vehicle I inhabit is in much better health.

The memory of the previous health problems will probably linger like a shadow for a short time. I am usually meticulous when changing shapes but not infallible. There must always be a good reason to change forms, as it requires considerable effort. This Salvadorian character was the right choice, I think. Somewhat battered in places, but not too damaged."

He smiled at me, and I thought I saw a hint of pride in the expression.

"Now, to return to your tooth question. When I bite to extract blood, I project two canine fangs about three inches long. They are hollow and very sharp—a little like hypodermic needles, although much thicker, of course.

Blood is drawn through these fangs rather like sucking through two straws; It's discharged into my mouth through vents behind these fangs. So, there you have the simplified full tooth disclosure, Jack." Many seconds passed before I asked the next question.

"Okay, that was a pretty good explanation of the bloodsucking now; how about the angel thing? When we first met, you said you were known as a vampire or an angel. Are you a biblical fallen angel, then?" He laughed heartily. "True enough, we can project visual images of ourselves. Shapeshifting, some call it. Sometimes an angel is more effective if circumstances call for it.

An angel is often more comforting, more acceptable in many parts of the world." He laughed again and slapped my back. "All public relations, dear Jack, everything is perception, eh? And no, there is nothing biblical about me. Although I did trip over a few poorly written strands of human genetic material, I am not a fallen angel, but that, my friend, is for another time. Fodder for a grand conversation; remind me later."

I nodded in agreement and thought about his answers for some time.

"So, when you change shapes or discard an existing form, how long are you able to remain without a body?"

"Perhaps a year or so. The longer I remain without a form. The more difficult it becomes to enter into another. I don't treat the process lightly, Jack; I don't flit from body to body on a whim."

Reluctantly, I decided to continue my questioning at another time. Although Henry seemed happy to respond to anything I asked, I had no wish to annoy him with my persistence. He had patiently replied to all my inquiries without protest, and I decided to leave further questions for our next meeting.

We chatted for half an hour or so before he rose from the table. As usual, he inclined his head and, with a smile, bade me goodnight. "Sir Henry Gaytooth Goldstein at your service. Until we meet again."

I left the bistro a few minutes after Henry. About a mile of easy walking along Broadway brought me to my apartment.

As usual, sleep eluded me after talking to Henry—endless, restless turning and revisiting our previous conversations. So many more questions needed answers and presented themselves to be asked.

Even his name, Henry, Goldstein, then Smith or the unpronounceable Vonbon, something—or—other. It seemed to me he picked a name randomly and would use it as the mood took him. The strange *Gaytooth* was another example. I would call him Henry Smith, perhaps Sir Henry, as the situation required.

Resigning myself to a sleepless night, I eventually left my bed, pulled an old bathrobe around my shoulders, and stood, leaning over the rail of my little balcony.

Gazing out across the chilly night and the twinkling streetlights, I found a hazy flickering neon sign that I thought perhaps hung at the entrance to Ronnie's bar.

Suddenly I remembered an old Chinese proverb, an omen perhaps, and a constant uncomfortable reminder of my frailty in the coming weeks.

A charitable frog agreed to ferry a scorpion across a deep river. He extracted a solemn promise from the scorpion not to sting him. The scorpion agreed, saying, "To sting you would be foolish, as we would both die in the river."

The frog accepted this logic and started across the water with the scorpion on his back.

Halfway across the river, the scorpion stung the frog. Near-death and slipping beneath the waves, the frog asked the scorpion, "Why?"

"I did not intend to hurt you," replied the drowning scorpion. "To sting without malice is simply my nature."

I returned to bed and drifted into an unquiet sleep.

CHAPTER 12

The vampire Henry Smith walked on, a silent shadow drifting along Broadway. His black glasses reflected lights from passing cars. The cars' drivers or their passengers might have seen a dark shape, at best, a fleeting flicker of movement lost among other indistinct shadows cast by the streetlights. At the intersection of Argyle Street, he entered the courtyard gates of a large gray stone church.

Following the perimeter path to the rear of the building, he crossed a raised grassy area and then made his way through ornate iron gates to the graveyard. As was his custom, he meandered between the stones, stopping many times to speak with the inhabitants beneath. Sometimes he would sit on a slab if the occupant of the site felt inclined to chat.

His time at the gravesites was never less than two hours and, he believed, always well spent. Those beneath the green manicured grass also thought his time was well spent, and they waited in eager anticipation for his visits.

Some of those long interred were forgotten. Some had no one alive to remember them. For some, none among the living cared. The old gardener, Pablo, would often chat with them as he attended the graves.

He was sincere and well-meaning, although not given to diverse or interesting topics of conversation. Nevertheless, he was well-received and appreciated for his thoughtfulness.

After visiting, Henry would bid the silent ones a blessed evening, promising they would not lie forgotten and that he would return soon to talk with them again. Slowly retracing his steps, he would enter the church through great carved wooden doors at the main entrance.

He invariably found himself alone in the dim light and echoing aisles. It was here, sitting on an uncomfortable wooden bench, gazing at the ornate altar, that he would sometimes find peace.

This evening, after sitting before the altar for no more than a few minutes, he heard the front doors open and then shut loudly, followed by quick, echoing footsteps. The vampire curled his lip in distaste, recognizing the intruder as Father Philip Malloy, the new priest. He was the latest of the ineffectual hopefuls slated to replace the aged Father Strauss.

Mounting the altar steps and glancing briefly at the carved wooden statue of a crucified Jesus, Malloy quickly made all requisite hand and arm movements before launching into a tearful confession. He asked forgiveness from God for any sins, then for recognition and remembrance of his many efforts and good works in the community.

It was at that point that Gaytooth Smith interrupted the obsequious entreaty.

"Enough! You two-faced hypocrite."

Malloy yelled in fear and surprise.

"If Yeshua, your savior, were listening to your mewling," Henry continued, "he would take you by the throat and throw you through the gates of this church."

Malloy spun around to face Henry.

"Who are you? What are you doing here? How dare you interrupt a blessed discourse between our Holy Father and me? Now, leave here at once."

The old dark angel smiled grimly in the darkness.

"You have the rare privilege to address Sir Henry Smith, an angel, and a vampire. I would add a sentence or two to your laughable confession. Indeed, I would plead for great tolerance and mercy after improperly fondling the numerous children entrusted to your care."

"You are obviously a madman, sir. Leave this place now, or I will call the police."

"Call away, villain. There is no one to hear you—certainly not Jesus, a protector and friend to many children. You disgust me with your self-righteousness, you worthless pudding. Ask *me* for forgiveness. I am Lord Henry Smith, dark angel, chancellor of the collection plate, and worshiper in this delightfully ornate house. You may give thanks that I have no turnips to hand. One would assuredly take residence in your puffy colon."

"You are a lonely misguided wanderer, a poor soul lost in the night," Malloy responded, now an angry edge to his voice, still shaken by the sudden and unexpected encounter.

"Again, I say, leave this holy house of worship immediately!"

"I will leave at once," replied Henry, now angry himself because of the priest's belligerent attitude.

"You, however, will stay, remaining in the position that I place you in. You are remanded here until 12:30 tomorrow afternoon. There will be ample time for you to reflect upon your crimes and humbly beg forgiveness."

The vampire took several steps, moving closer to Malloy.

"During the remaining hours of darkness, you will have many visitors. They will come from their resting places in the cemetery to converse with you. My advice would be to adopt a most humble and contrite attitude. Do not anger them more than you already have."

The Dark Angel turned to leave and then spun around once more.

"Oh, also, you will be unable to reach the restroom and thus will be forced to relieve yourself in your underwear. Unfortunately, as you have recently eaten a large meal, the effluence will be considerable. Your plight might even make the evening news channels. Perhaps an in-depth interview, eh?"

"You are troubled beyond measure; go in peace, my son. Find healing quickly and be whole again. I will pray for you."

"And I for you perhaps," replied Henry. Father Malloy stared dumbfounded at the vampire. In the low light, he was scarcely able to see the figure before him. As he peered at the outline, he realized that where a face should have been, no features existed, nothing except two deep red orbs that may once have been the eyes.

He was overcome by a sudden feeling of terror, a deep, paralyzing cold in his stomach reaching up to engulf him.

"I will speak my old given name for you, so you will always remember our short meeting."

The vampire's booming voice reverberated through the church as he spoke his name. *"Voohnbondurantle."* The deep hollow sound soon reached a terrible, unnatural crescendo and suddenly filled Malloy's ears with dull pain, and the awful sound reverberated ever louder inside his head.

The vampire's voice rose and echoed in the poor light, seeming to flow all around like a great tide of dirty water. The priest fell to his knees as he felt the floor move beneath him. He thought he saw the walls bulge outward and cried loudly in fear, convinced that the building was falling around him.

In the darkness of the church, he could find no God to comfort him. There were no words he could remember to pray for his salvation or deliverance.

Henry Smith raised both hands. Malloy was raised to his feet and elevated about fifteen inches from the floor. He seemed to float with arms extended from his sides until he found himself unable to move, affixed to the wall behind him. His appearance was that of a bloated savior, crucified on the wall without a cross.

The old dark angel, sir Henry Gaytooth Smith walked quickly from the church, faint grunts and squeals from the priest Malloy reaching his ears as he left.

"Perhaps it is my fate to chastise the unworthy representatives of their gods forever," Henry muttered to himself, shaking his head. "I wonder if I could make any money doing this."

He made his way to Argyle Street, then to his small basement apartment. Later, the plaintive wistful sounds of an accordion could be heard, blending and drifting with the cool evening breeze.

CHAPTER 13

Early the following day, Andre Golembeski, a parking enforcement officer, walked slowly from Argyle Street to the big church on the corner of Broadway. He smiled happily, drawing in the fresh morning air and giving thanks for his recent recovery.

The city department, through its generosity, had allowed a whole week of paid recovery time and issued a new uniform without charge.

Although the detailed events of his accident were unclear, his memory was gradually returning. He knew he had been struck by a speeding motorist and left on the street. Engraved deeply into his fragile memory was the tantalizing vision of a beautiful woman who tried to assist him. They had subsequently ridden together in a police car. That much he remembered.

Fleeting, fragmented details of her beauty, red shoes, and soft southern voice haunted him, an unforgettable angel waiting somewhere to take him in her arms.

The black SUV lurking outside the church caught his attention. It was undoubtedly parked too close to the Broadway crosswalk and probably too far from the curb. As if by way of personal insult, it had also made an incursion into his beloved red zone.

He quickly approached the vehicle, noting its position, checking and recording the license plate, and then confirming the registration's current status. The black Mercedes stood immobile, a hated defiant symbol of capitalism. It had likely been parked by an arrogant owner who mistakenly believed his wealth would shelter him from impending punishment.

Andre happily issued four parking violation citations, smiling with pleasure as he recorded each one. He was now transformed into a warrior, a protector of the underprivileged, a knight, and champion in the service of the poor.

He danced around the Mercedes, kicking the tires as he did so. Jumbled confusing thoughts swirled and crowded together in his fragile brain.

He knew he would never own a Mercedes, and that thought seemed to insulate him from the greed of others. His Ford Pinto was a reliable friend. Neither he nor his beloved lettuce

He stopped transfixed, unable to think clearly as if he had been struck suddenly in the face. That was her name—Lettuce, Lettuce Washingboard, the woman of his dreams, the girl with red shoes.

Andre sat on the curb for many minutes, savoring his great good fortune. He decided to enter the church and offer a quick prayer of thanks, perhaps finding the Mercedes' owner within.

Kneeling in the back row, he thanked the angels for giving him the Pinto he rode in and the name of his darling Lettuce. He stood slowly, gradually becoming aware of a strange moaning sound like a large farm animal groaning in pain. Surveying the empty rows and pews in the church, he saw that he was alone.

No, not entirely alone. He knew that God and his angels lived in churches, as did Jesus. The moaning, now louder, seemed to come from the wall to his left. He walked carefully, approaching the source of this strange noise as his eyes gradually adjusted to the low light.

With a sudden shock, he beheld a rotund crucified daemon.

Having worked many years for the city's parking department, Andre immediately recognized the unhealthy flabby creature as an evil entity. A foul stench confirmed his opinion.

"Are you the owner of a black Mercedes SUV parked by the curb?" he asked the greasy, bloated beast.

Father Malloy stared in wonder at the uniformed figure standing before him. Surely here was a gift of deliverance from above. "God bless you," he croaked through parched lips. "Please help me. I am unable to move, and I was fixed here in this position last night. A lunatic stuck me to the wall with super glue."

Andre, steadfast in his belief and wise in the ways of the supernatural, readied himself for demonic subterfuge. He laughed softly. "Do not lie to me, daemon. I challenge you again. Are you the owner of the black Mercedes parked outside?"

Father Malloy saw all hope of rescue fade with the appearance of this latest madman and reluctantly nodded his head. "Yes, yes, the car is mine. Now, please help me from this wall."

"Then a curse on you and damnation on the filthy horde following you from the pit," Andre shouted. "Forever, be tormented for your vile sins and return now from whence you came!"

Father Malloy shed tears of helplessness and anger as he managed a choking reply. "I am already tormented, you babbling moron. Now please help me from this damned wall."

Andre smiled serenely as a sweet voice once lost from his memory suddenly returned to him. He knew then that the lovely miss Lettuce stood at his side as together they faced their devilish adversary.

"Oh, please forgive me, sir," he said. "I am truly sorry if I have disturbed you."

Raising his middle finger in a sign of victory, Andre strode from the church.

He walked quickly to the small hardware store on Argyle, where he purchased an aerosol can of high-gloss white paint. Returning to the accursed devil's chariot, he sprayed a large cross on the hood and a smaller one on each Mercedes' front door.

Satisfied with his divinely inspired artistry and confident that no daemon would pass the signs, he resumed his parking enforcement duties for the day.

Several hours later, city tow truck driver LeShawn, having been notified by Andre of the improperly parked SUV, secured the Mercedes and ferried his latest captive to the impound yard. The vehicle was deposited contemptuously in the corner lot, surrounded by battered Chevrolets and Fords, most seized from local Latino immigrants without valid driving or immigration documentation. This was Los Angeles county, after all.

CHAPTER 14

*"Henry Smith, the vampire, never had a wife,
but he had a sawed-off shotgun and a rusty Bowie knife."*

By 11:15, a noisy crowd had gathered outside the church, having heard about the presence of a foul-smelling goblin inside. Many came to witness and applaud a demonic possession and subsequent exorcism but were later dispersed by police. Inside, the church was filled beyond capacity for the first time.

Ancient and beloved Father Martin Strauss was called upon to perform, in great secrecy, the short exorcism ceremony and any necessary cleansing to release Father Malloy from the grip of the foul-smelling daemon holding him to the wall. Much to the disappointment of those inside, a large makeshift screen was quickly erected, partially concealing the smelly daemon.

Father Malloy pleaded, threatened, and cried for Father Strauss during the exorcism to help him from the wall. The good Father Strauss stood firm against the beast. Armed with blessed water and incense, he brandished his precious bible and splashed a significant amount of holy water in the face of the evil one.

With a fearsome and commanding voice, he directed the evil spirit to leave forever. So powerful were his commands that at 12:30 exactly—even before the ceremony was finished—Malloy was released, falling to the floor in a reeking, blubbering heap and upsetting the privacy screen. The remaining demonic vapors and unpleasant stench caused worshipers to cross themselves and reach for their rosaries before rapidly vacating the church.

An ambulance crew wrapped the wretched priest in a heavy blanket before removing him to the nearest hospital. Local radio and television stations recorded his departure. Many eyewitnesses were questioned, and their testimonies were made available for evening news viewers.

Two venerable Mexican ladies, Simona and Maria, both long-serving volunteers, spent the following day disinfecting the church, removing stains and bodily secretions from the stone floor. They were ordered by the deacon's assistant to secure any solid matter and remove the unholy shit far from the consecrated grounds of God's house.

Father Malloy recovered within a week but could not bring himself to enter the church after dark, nor would he ever do so. Five days later, his vehicle was located in the impound yard. Although in a restricted and monitored area, his once-proud Mercedes, a recent gift from loving parents, was profusely decorated with religious and satanic cult graffiti. The hubcaps were also missing. A reluctant payment of $1570 released the vehicle from impound.

The local community never really accepted Philip Malloy as a fitting replacement for Father Strauss. It was not so much his attachment to the brandy bottle as any man could be forgiven for that, even a priest. He was, after all of the Irish heritage and genetically required to sample a dram or two. It was not so much the cigars, either. A man was indeed entitled to a bit of tobacco occasionally. None of these habits weighed against him as heavily as his condescending attitude. Most people with whom he had contact found him pompous, opinionated, and overbearing.

His recent astonishing and embarrassing encounter with a devil—and in the church of all places—did nothing to improve his standing among the worshipers. Their opinion was that an ordained priest appointed to intercede between Jesus and the common man should be quite capable of dealing with any blasphemous entity in the house of God.

Now he was regarded with great suspicion.

Many believed he had encouraged or provoked the demonic activity to enhance his reputation through a great public display of spiritual strength. Unfortunately for the priest, the daemon was seen to castigate and humiliate the flabby cowering Malloy. Further, no reasonable man of the cloth would ever be seen riding in a vehicle with those awful crosses painted so crudely on the hood and doors of his car.

He acquired a derogatory nickname.

Those witnessing the exorcism were not reluctant to share their experiences. They described the awful smell emanating from Malloy's underwear. When talking among themselves, he was usually referred to as *"stinky boy Malloy."* The Mexican and other Latino worshipers, of whom there were many, had a particular ethnic label for him. He would forever be known to them as *Pinchi Padre Malloy*.

Their beloved antique and champion, Father Martin Strauss, was hailed as a hero. Only a man of such grace and goodness would dare challenge the forces of darkness so quickly and be able to trounce them so soundly.

Knowing his tenure was limited, the faithful decided to seek out and recommend a suitable replacement. They were most disapproving of the recent crop of candidates presented through regular Catholic advancement, approval, placement, and installation procedures. Rumblings of dissatisfaction grew.

Eventually, their discontent reached a crescendo of anger, culminating in a noisy confrontational meeting with Father Strauss, the deacon, and Bishop Maxwell. Threats of a boycott were overheard, and the possibility of street protests outside the church was loudly voiced.

Father Strauss, anxious to avoid even more unsavory publicity for the church, cautioned forcefully against further public outcry.

Both Bishop Maxwell and Father Strauss were aware of the tremendous monetary benefit from the recent publicity. A sudden surge in attendance paralleled a sudden overflowing of the collection plates.

However, neither would ever accept the obvious nor would agree that the prevailing satanic influences were, in many ways, financially beneficial to the church.

Both would agree, though, that God works in the most mysterious and unfathomable ways. The well-meaning bishop made clear to all attendees that the old must give way to the young. "The new all-embracing and accepting liberal philosophies of the young and inexperienced clergy are understood well. For the most part, they are a necessary change to secure a place in this rapidly changing world. Such views and opinions have, to an extent, been embraced and endorsed by the Vatican itself." He said.

The bishop knew that the issue of replacing *"stinky boy Malloy"* was a moot consideration as Malloy had not yet been installed as the permanent church priest. As the deacon had already explained, replacing him would appease the angry worshipers and increase flagging attendance and fill the depleted coffers once again. However, any new prospect would need many strong leadership qualities and a pleasing demeanor. He should be progressive yet respectful of the old ways—a Father Martin Strauss incarnate.

The bishop Maxwell promised an exhaustive private investigation into the matter of Father Malloy.

An exhaustive *public* investigation was already underway by county police. It was proceeding with great diligence, as Malloy was known to them for some time. An ambulance was called, public resources used, and with police involvement required to dispel an unruly street gathering—these circumstances alone certainly needed investigation.

CHAPTER 15

Philip Malloy was the only child of wealthy and influential parents. The family had enjoyed a privileged lifestyle in Bethesda, Maryland, for many years. His father, Robert, a hardworking and progressive Irish immigrant, started a freight and transportation company close to the port and docks.

His other accomplishment was marrying Elisabeth Arden, daughter of an old Boston family, wealthy and well-connected.

From an unlikely but loving relationship, their son Philip was born prematurely. This and other complications revealed after the cesarean delivery prevented Elisabeth from carrying more children. A later surgery ensured she would have no more offspring.

Young Philip grew up in a sheltered environment, protected and secured. He quickly became the center of the small family universe and a bright star worshiped by doting parents. At fourteen years, he began exhibiting tendencies that would later attract law enforcement's attention.

Elisabeth hosted a children's birthday party for a close neighbor was the ideal venue for Philip to explore his evolving predatory instincts. A game of hide-and-seek had Philip helping the young victims by hiding them in his bedroom closet. He would then feel beneath their clothing or place their little hands around his genitals.

Three distraught children were comforted by an enraged Elisabeth. They were offered rewards and games for their solemn promises of silence. Philip had no remorse when confronted by his mother. He claimed any touching was accidental in the close confines of a darkened closet.

His memories of these encounters were a source of great joy and excitement to him. They supplied the necessary masturbatory incentive to seek more innocent participants for his unnatural pleasure. He was strongly cautioned never to discuss details of his actions or tell his father of his inclinations.

Robert had great hopes for his only son to join the family business. Unfortunately, Philip had no interest in his father's company. He was content to pursue a sedentary lifestyle, removed from any expectation of work or participation in the business. He watched askance as the mysteries of company management were unfolded for him.

Eventually, a disappointed father acknowledged his son and heir as worthless freight company executive material.

Having reached the age of eighteen, with no inclination for work or any interest in academia, Philip listened to the advice of a friend, who suggested he join a seminary college to prepare him for a respectable life of devout priestly dedication.

He would eventually devote himself to saving or assisting the deprived and needy children that he loved.

It seemed the right choice—undoubtedly preferable to enrolling in the harsh military school proposed by his father and encouraged by his mother.

His first step was to attend college, then obtain a bachelor's degree in philosophy. Surpassing that hurdle, he would join a seminary school for four years. When called by the bishop to holy orders, he would be home, and dry, a priest once in the making now called and ready to serve.

Study in any guise was not a favorite occupation of young Philip. However, to his friends' amazement and his parents' delight, he blossomed in the college environment.

Soon he was producing excellent work in a timely and orderly manner. For the first time in his life, he succeeded in a venture of his choosing. His path was now clearly defined and illuminated by success. He obtained his degree and continued studying philosophy and history. Lavish praise and encouragement from both parents spurred him onward.

Having finished four years in college armed with a minor degree in history and a bachelor's in philosophy, he considered life as a Catholic priest. The Seminary school he applied to and for which he was quickly accepted provided the opportunity to decide during the next four years. Any decision he made was driven by a newfound desire to please his parents.

After three years of intense study, he decided to become a priest. For another six months, he devoted himself to prayer, asking for guidance with his life's calling.

Malloy continually worried that he was unsuited for life as a priest. He was helped by a dedicated mentor who spoke to him from his own experience: "You will know a conviction within, an absolute feeling that this path is the only one for you."

The problem was, he never did feel the absolute conviction or hear a heavenly voice telling him anything. He tried. He took an elective as a deacon for six months but remained unconvinced, even when called to holy orders.

It is reasonable to assume that the eight years spent as a divinity student is sufficient dedication to continue on this path, he thought.

At first, he was a sincere and dedicated priest. His proud parents were delighted, lavishing praise and gifts for his advancement. Unfortunately, his dedication to the service of the Lord faltered when in the company of children.

His instincts for pedophilia ran concurrently with his priestly dedication. There was no conflict in his mind between the love of God and his love for children. His love for the young ones was genuine, but his remarkable passion and desire to comfort and shelter naked boys were naturally in conflict with the laws of man.

He tried women and men as adult sexual alternatives but could find no gratification there.

The lure of the delicate young children would always prove stronger and ultimately much more fulfilling. Little boys were the forbidden fruit of his imagination and the sweet prize he would continuously nurture.

Many times he found himself dangerously close to arrest. Fortunately for him, he enjoyed the privileged protection within the understanding embrace of his church. He was sent for counseling and treatment in different states, always just beyond the reach of prosecution. His latest transfer to Saint Mary's in Los Angeles, a permanent position as the parish priest, was violently and very publicly interrupted.

Because of the notoriety surrounding recent events at the church, he became a sought-after television personality. This newfound fame gave him a platform from which to defend his position.

Now quite the local television star, articulate, well-spoken, and self-effacing, he deflected any questions about his inclination toward pedophilia as nonsense, stating most forcefully that such talk originated from evil forces conspiring to discredit him.

When questioned about his wall hanging, he insisted it was his choice. "I told God I wished to rid the church and congregation of recent satanic influences. I prayed earnestly that the Lord of saints place me on the wall of his holy house so that I could confront Satan himself. I stayed at my great personal risk until the evil was banished."

His congregation knew otherwise.

After many such interviews, he was offered a permanent position with a local news service. "The Father Philip Hour" was broadcast daily at 7:30 am, enjoying limited success for several months.

Malloy's recent media attention also prompted detectives to re-examine old unresolved child molestation complaints against the unrepentant priest.

CHAPTER 16

My cephalopod research papers and thesis were submitted to the institute by me and my assistant Angela. A short review brought many pleasing comments with promises of tenure and advancement. This lengthy project was now bearing a little fruit, and the voracious, dangerous Humboldt squid could manage quite happily without me for a couple of months.

However, it also left a vacuum in my life for a few weeks. I initially filled this void by reading and rereading the strange accounts of the Saint Mary's Church exorcism.

Every day that passed seemed to bring with it new updates of the bizarre occurrence. There was a seemingly endless file of eyewitnesses testifying from their various perspectives. Local television stations fielded experts in all facets of arcane knowledge. Each gave a differing opinion as to precisely what had happened.

Father Malloy's Mercedes was featured prominently, displaying the artwork it had recently acquired. Newspaper headlines were imaginative to a degree:

Devil busted in church. Daemon humiliates the local pastor. Did the devil have sexual relations with a priest? How a local priest became a Satanic cult leader. The devil kept a local priest as a personal sex toy.

There was a surreal atmosphere enveloping the matter. To me, it bore the unmistakable hallmark of the Dark Angel Smith's involvement.

I wanted to speak with Henry again. There were many outstanding questions from our previous meeting yet to be asked. Many questions about demonic possession were also waiting for him, and I especially enjoyed his unique personality and the most refreshing company.

I suddenly realized I had no way to reach him except by going to the church on the off chance of seeing him at worship or visiting Ronnie's bar while he was working. I chose the latter.

Ronnie's Bar and Grill, by virtue, of a thirty-year presence in the same location, was recognized as a local landmark. It had endured through two recessions, thirteen armed robberies, two small fires, police raids, and numerous employees. The location, a block before the corner of Mason and Argyle, was marginally better than squalid and probably best described as seedy.

It was here that Henry was installed as a bartender, working from 7:00 pm until 3:00 am most days. It was Thursday evening, about 9:30, when I walked into the bar to be greeted by soft music and the bright clatter of conversation.

I spotted Henry talking earnestly with a striking and, to me, most attractive woman. No, *most attractive;* I quickly changed to *incredibly attractive*. Each to their own, of course, but *incredibly* was my choice. Latina probably, Arabian possibly, but in any case, a woman I would not easily forget. She seemed to be the only female in the house. I guessed her age to be thirty to thirty-five years, although my ability to estimate ages had little credibility. After all, I missed Henry's age by a mere 600 years.

I waited until their conversation had finished before approaching the bar. Henry seemed delighted to see me. He was, as usual, most gracious and charming.

Unfortunately, and as expected, it was almost impossible to converse without interruption. The bar was filling with patrons, adding to the clamor of conversation and demands on Henry's time.

I finished an "on the house" glass of whiskey at a small corner table and took the opportunity to observe Henry at work. He was obviously a dedicated people person—never at a loss for words, never without a smile while attending to every customer quickly and courteously. A rare gift, I thought.

After finishing my drink, I approached the bar again, arranging to meet with Henry the following evening as the next day, he would only be working until 6:00 pm. We decided to meet at the bistro at about eight.

I will, I promised myself, inquire about the lady he had been talking with.

The next evening when I arrived, he was already seated. After exchanging a few words of greeting, we chatted about the Humboldt squid for some time. I was surprised Henry expressed such interest in my research—surprised and a little flattered. He told me how proud he was.

"I have read your squiddie papers," he said. "The research is factual, descriptive, and beautifully presented. I am quite drawn to those animals. From your descriptions, they are the wolves of the sea, communicating among themselves and hunting in packs. I have a better understanding now as to why you are so interested in them."

He nodded. "In many ways, they parallel the human race. Luckily their environment restricts their ambitions and confines them to the sea—though not quite as confined to known areas as they used to be, according to your research."

"Enough about my squid, Henry, now what about you?"

He smiled. "To begin with, I am delighted to report that I will once again attend the Light of Hope Mosque. Of course, Sunday mornings will probably see me at Saint Mary's as usual."

"But won't you be recognized at the mosque?"

"Remember, Jack, since correcting the imam; I have changed from black to brown.

My Latino appearance is now much different from my last costume; I'm sure nobody will recognize me. I am told there is a new and highly regarded imam, an earnest young scholar with wire-framed spectacles and the inevitable beard. I will enjoy meeting him."

Henry was right. He had indeed changed his appearance, and quite dramatically.

"I never really enjoyed the conversations or camaraderie at the big church. Although it does provide a good revenue stream," he continued with a smile. "As you probably know by now, there have been a few interesting developments."

"Yes, perhaps you will explain to me, a humble marine biologist, exactly how a parish priest managed to stick himself to a church wall, requiring an exorcism of all things to remove him. I understand that he had to be carted off by ambulance."

"An ambulance did remove him, but an exorcism was unnecessary, although it added a little color to the proceedings, don't you think?"

"The whole unsavory business has vampire Smith written all over it. Do please tell me what happened."

Henry laughed. "Yes, you are correct, only to a certain extent, though, Jack. Although Malloy was an ordained priest, he was never officially installed as the parish priest or assigned to any particular church."

Henry described Father Philip Malloy's recent history, including his unusually extravagant lifestyle and egregious behavior with children, eventually culminating with his odious and very public removal by ambulance.

"My involvement in the matter was insignificant," he concluded. "I simply stuck him to the wall for a few hours. Other interfering hands brought about his downfall."

"Again, your logic is faulted, Henry, although I hate to mention it. I remember the last time we discussed logic by definition. For you to claim you only stuck him to the wall and others were responsible for his problems is akin to saying, 'I only pulled the trigger, but external forces conspired to move and align the bullet that killed him."

Henry stared at me for a long time. Suddenly he laughed. "Okay, young Jack, perhaps you're right, but think of this: It matters not one whit to me. I am accountable to no one on this plane. There is no one to please, and many, by my actions, will be displeased. In the matter of *'stinky boy Malloy,'* I told him I was a vampire and cautioned him to seek forgiveness and apologize for his actions.

He did nothing but shout at me to go away. I stuck him to the wall so he would ask his God to forgive him humbly and with sincerity. Had he done so, he would have been released. But, no, he blustered, snorted, sniveled, and farted with self-pity, thus ensuring his prolonged unhappiness."

I wondered how Malloy was able to *fart* with self-pity, indeed a unique ability requiring many years of practice to perfect.

"Look, Henry," I said. "You cannot set yourself up as judge and jury. You can't determine the nature or extent of the punishment for those that disagree with you."

"And Why not?" He stared across the small table at me, raising his eyebrows.

I shook my head, having no answer for him and finding little sympathy for the deposed Father Malloy.

"I do not seek out miscreants to punish," Henry said. "I will admit to a certain satisfaction when presented with a deserving cause. Malloy was certainly a most deserving cause."

He paused to think for a moment before continuing.

"Perhaps I should view these situations differently. How about this? Lone vampire avenger clears a California city of evildoers. Gay crusader crushes the forces of evil. Something like Batman, eh?"

"Sounds good, Henry. The only problem I see is where do you draw the line. Big corporate evil, corrupt politicians, serial killers, or small personal nastiness, like domestic violence? Even you can't fix the world. And then there is the location. Is Australia more deserving than Finland?"

He smiled. "Of course, you are correct, young Jack. But think of the fun we would have if you accompanied me on such a crusade."

The wine and sandwiches arrived. We ate in silence for a while, enjoying the time with our quiet friendship, the cool evening providing a most pleasant interlude.

"You looked most professional behind the bar," I said. "You seemed to enjoy yourself, a very popular bartender."

"Why, thank you, dear Jack. I enjoy interacting with people, but this is only a means to an end—just a job for a while. My car is nearly paid for, all outstanding bills are now settled, and I do not need to find a dentist. Ain't life grand? As a matter of fact, I have another job due to start next month. September four."

"Congratulations, Henry. I'm a little surprised, though. I know the neighborhood is a tad run down, but Ronnie's seems like a good place to work. Where's the new place?"

"Next to the mall on Broadway. There is a small office block on the left. You can't miss it—dark blue paint with a large reflective front window. Give me a few days to acclimatize, and we'll have lunch in my office."

"In your office?"

"Yes, every good attorney should have his dedicated office, don't you think?"

I stared at him for many seconds, at a loss for words. Finally, I said, "Are you serious? An attorney? When did all this happen? I thought you were a bartender by profession."

"Bartender by necessity and inclination only, Jack. I am not now or ever was defined by any occupation. Among many other qualifications, I still hold law degrees in Europe and New York. I am a member in good standing, as they say, of the California Bar Association. Different bar from Ronnie's, though." Although he smiled, little happiness showed in his eyes.

"When one has amassed nearly six hundred and fifty years of worldly experience, one tends to accumulate knowledge in many areas. I did consider a position at a large merchant bank, but the trouble with that is relocating to New York. I suppose working on Wall Street again would qualify me as a financial vampire."

"You truly never cease to amaze me, Henry. I know by now I shouldn't be surprised by anything you do. All I will say is good luck and best wishes for your new job."

"Thank you so much, Jack. Your good wishes are most appreciated."

"Tell me, though, how will you manage the daylight hours in your new profession? Surely Ronnie's must be easier for you working the night shift?"

"Daylight or sunlight, both are painful to the skin and harmful to the eyes of the form I currently occupy." He shrugged.

"Dark glasses will protect my eyes, and a full-length coat or covering will protect the rest of me. Artificial light, for the most part, is not a problem if I wear sunglasses. I always wore dark glasses behind Ronnie's bar."

He leaned back in his chair.

"Here is a little more Hollywood vampire lore to contradict. It would take an industrial laser to turn me to dust—assuming that I decided to wait while it did so. Anyway, thank you for your concern, Jack, but not necessary. I have a lot of experience dodging sunbeams."

"I have a lot of experience lying on the beach looking for sunbeams," I said, chuckling. "We do have our differences, Henry."

"Indeed we do, Jack, but in many ways, we are surprisingly similar. Do you see the similarities?

I thought for some time before replying. "No, but I'm sure you will soon tell me."

Henry smiled, shaking his head. "Time to go, Jack. This little place is closing." He pointed to the waitress as she approached with a check in hand. "I thank you for the meal and, as usual, the excellent company. I will call you soon." As was his custom, he inclined his head.

"Lord Henry Smith Esquire, at your service."

I paid and then turned to leave.

The waitress smiled. "Many thanks, and good to see you guys again. I must ask, though, so please tell me to mind my own business if you like, but your friend—not the lady, the tall man—is he a lord? I couldn't help overhearing as he left."

I laughed at her question but more so at her earnest, almost reverential manner.

"Yes, of course, he's a lord. Don't you think he looks like one?"

"I suppose he does. Straight and tall with the white hair brushed back—a very handsome man. You can always tell a gentleman by the way he talks to others. I think it must be his English accent that caught my attention."

I stared at the attractive girl with long brown hair and a brilliant smile. This conversation was so wrong I was tempted to turn and walk away but instead continued our brief meeting.

"Okay, are you ready for a little game? Nothing serious; this will test your powers of observation. I will ask a few simple questions, and you reply as quickly as you can."

She smiled a wide-mouthed, flashing smile that lit her face. "Carry on, but if this is a sneaky way to get personal information from me, it may be easier to ask."

"I'm flattered—well, delighted, actually. Okay then, first things first. My name's Jack Cordell."

"I'm Julie Anderson." We clasped hands briefly and then resumed hand-holding again as she sat beside me.

"Julie, I've been meaning to ask you out for a few weeks now, a movie or dinner, perhaps? I never quite plucked up the courage, though; I suppose I'm not a great people person, always been a little shy. Would you go out with me if I asked you?"

Again, that wonderful smile. She wrinkled her nose and laughed.

"Are you asking me then?"

"Oh yeah, absolutely—I mean, if you're not married or with a boyfriend or anything." At that point, I decided to shut up, feeling that I had probably said too much. I gazed at this beautiful woman staring like a fool and feeling like a nervous schoolboy.

"You said something about a game, Jack." Her words snapped me back to the evening's reality. "See what you've done to me, Julie?' I laughed self-consciously. "Totally forgot about that. Ready then?"

Another colossal smile and laughing, "yes."

"What's your name?"

"Julie."

"How many sat at my table tonight?"

"Three."

"How many men?"

"Two."

"What color is my hair?"

"Fair."

"How tall am I?"

"About six feet."

"How tall is my English friend?"

"About six-four."

"How tall was the woman?"

"She was about an inch shorter than you. A beautiful woman. Is she your girlfriend?"

"No. In fact, I barely know her. Do you remember what she was wearing or the color of her hair?"

"Wow, so many questions. Okay, past shoulder-length, jet-black hair. Olive complexion. South-American perhaps? Probably middle-eastern. For sure, a beautiful lady. She looked like a much younger version of Cher. Can't remember what she wore."

"Okay, you win, Julie. For the grand prize, I get to take you to dinner at the place of your choice."

"What would I have gotten if you won the prize?"

We both laughed and kissed quickly, saying hurried goodnights as she returned to the small, darkened dining room to finish her shift.

I strolled to my apartment, knowing that I would not sleep. The memory of Julie Anderson smiling and laughing shimmered like a tempting siren, beckoning to me. Surprisingly, sleep came within the hour.

CHAPTER 17

Sitting on my balcony the following morning, I savored the small luxury of strong coffee against a background of muted street sounds and a warm but slightly overcast day. I leaned back in my old cane chair and dissected the previous evening. My thoughts revolved around the responses from Julie during our word game.

She had absolutely no reason to fabricate or distort her answers to the questions I asked her. She saw Henry as a tall English man. He was, for sure, at least an inch shorter than me. His hair was black with a few gray streaks at the sides, not white by any stretch of the imagination.

His voice was soft, probably Asian—certainly not English. He did speak in a very formal manner, though, which, I suppose, could have been mistaken for an English accent.

As for the woman at the table, I had no answer. I never saw her or heard her speak. The small round table at which we sat could not possibly seat another occupant undetected. Even if that were possible, why no introductions?

No, Julie was mistaken. There was only Henry and me sitting at the table.

Her impressions of Henry were inaccurate but understandable. Tricks of the dim light and moving shadows exaggerated from occasional passing headlights. All very plausible explanations, but not convincing.

I was confused and angry—confused by the doubts and contradictions surrounding a simple dinner between two friends, angry because I suddenly realized I had not asked Julie for her number or arranged a date.

It was only then that I recalled the woman in Ronnie's bar. At the very next opportunity, I would undoubtedly remember to question Henry about her.

Probably four weeks passed before I saw the note in my mailbox—a piece of lined notepaper decorated with beautiful cursive script.

"Lunch tomorrow at the office if you are able. Any time after twelve. Henry G."

Just before noon the next day, I waited in the reception area, an open-plan design that was modern and well-furnished. I was impressed, but more so by the company name on the business card dispensers. They were displayed in four separate, delicately carved bone containers sitting on the polished wood counter; each box was impressed with "The Law Firm of Rubenstein, Weintraub, and Goldstein." Beneath the company name were the individual names of each partner. The cards themselves were white with gold edging and heavily embossed black lettering.

The atmosphere bore the unmistakable imprint of wealth from the deep pile carpeted floor to the ornately carved furnishings. My impression was of money lavished within the constraints of good taste.

After a few minutes, the fashion model receptionist, a thin girl with hollow cheeks and far too much make-up, ushered me into a spacious office through a dark-paneled wooden door.

A large brass nameplate upon the door bore the name Henry. G. Goldstein Esquire, International Law.

Henry greeted me at the door, grinning. He motioned me to an embossed leather armchair behind a sizeable ornate desk. "Well, Jack, what do you think? Not bad for a new job, eh?"

"Henry, I have no words for such opulence but a partner so soon? I mean, it's been less than a month since you started. I must say, though, you're a perfect and distinguished fit for this office."

He laughed heartily and shook his head. "Thanks for the compliment, Jack, but a few words of explanation are required, as you might expect. I am not a partner. I merely inherited this office from the genuine and recently deceased Jacob Goldstein. The nameplate on the door is mine, though.

Anyway, all is well. I am earning a living wage and having my first medical and dental examinations next Tuesday. Just check-ups. This medical stuff is almost affordable now that I have full medical and dental insurance with the firm—I wish I had become a lawyer sooner. Now your turn."

I talked briefly in generalities and then relayed the gist of my conversation with Julie and mentioned my interest in dating her.

"She thought you were well over six feet tall, with white hair and an English accent. Most impressed when I told her you were a real lord."

Henry smiled. "I am many things to many people, Jack. Julie saw me as she wished me to be. She is an unusual woman and very gifted in many ways. She will surprise you as you get to know her. A fine but fleeting distraction. Not the woman you are hoping for, though.

You already have that extraordinary life partner chosen for you. She's waiting patiently in the wings. Remember this conversation at the appropriate time, my boy."

He delivered the last few sentences with a perfectly executed English accent, and his predictions quickly dampened the possibility of a serious relationship with Julie. As I expected, he would not give further details about my chosen partner except to say *soon*."

Henry, as I had come to know him: understated, infuriating, humorous, and always the unexpected.

"Ready to eat, young Jack? We have a Gutburger joint, an Italian deli, Subway, or our bistro within walking distance. My call would be the bistro—sound okay to you?"

"Perfect, Henry. A wise decision as one would expect from a distinguished big-city lawyer."

About ten minutes later, we were sitting at a sidewalk table, Julie in attendance. She returned quickly with soups, French bread, and shrimp salads. Having set the food down, she placed a business card in front of me.

"Just in case you find the time to call," she said softly. "My number is on the back." Before I had formed a reply, she was gone.

Henry laughed. "Beautiful girl. Just right for you, eh?"

"I thought you were gay. Doesn't that preclude you from ogling women?"

"To an extent, but I didn't ogle very much, as my tribal friends on the border say, 'women are for making babies, boys are for pleasure. I was always, and still am, most interested in the human form's beautifully functional design with all its" divergences. I am no stranger to the puffiness of a long-distance clitoris.

"A what, a clitoris?"

"Certainly, dear young Jack. A firm puffy clitoris is most desirable, better than chewing gum, in my humble opinion.

"Well, to each their own, Henry. You are right about Julie, though. Very attractive."

"Attractive and smart, as you will discover in time." We finished our food, and after a few more minutes, Henry stood. "Duty calls, dear Jack. I must go." He walked to the counter and stood for a while, talking to Julie. He paid the check and then waved as he turned to go. "See you soon, dear boy. You have my card, you know where I am, call anytime. Sir Henry, at your service as always."

I stared after his retreating form until he faded from view. Julie smiled as I said goodbye, with me promising that I would definitely call her and arrange our dinner date.

"Better hurry then. Your friend Lord Henry asked me to dinner a few minutes ago."

I reached into my shirt pocket, withdrew the bistro business card, and then turned it over to see she had drawn a big smiling face. There was no number.

"What is this? Forgot the number, dearest Miss Anderson? Since there is no number on the card, how do I call you? Or don't you want me to anymore?"

"Oh, sorry, I must have forgotten. Here."

She wrote her number and, smiling, handed back the card. We both laughed as I acknowledged the rebuke and apologized for my last failed effort.

"Now, you won't forget to call—not like the last time."

"Look, it's much easier if we arrange our dinner date face- to face, Julie. I'll have lunch with you tomorrow during your break if that's okay, and I'll call you this evening just to chat."

CHAPTER 18

Henry Smith was at the mosque for Morning Prayer. He would attend *salat* with his hand-woven personalized prayer rug. The center of the dark red mat revealed several large Chinese characters, green and gold, arranged in a circle. Roughly translated, the words said, "Beneath this carpet is the false Prophet Muhammad."

A young scribe led *Zuhr,* the mid-morning worship, that day. He continued with an angry diatribe after prayer, denouncing the devil's appearance at Saint Mary's Church.

"The wicked infidels have at last revealed themselves for the ungodly sinners that they are."

After a short recounting of the exorcism, he read from the Quran, quoting fiery passages of script calling for the destruction of all Islamic enemies and all infidels who would insult the only and most holy Prophet of Allah. The vampire smiled to himself, remembering his prayer mat. Although by no means believing himself to be an enemy of Islam, he would admit he was most undoubtedly insulting and disrespectful to the Prophet Muhammad.

He was insulting and disrespectful to many historical and religious figures. His universal contempt for most revered leaders made him, in his opinion, an equal and unbiased master of the disrespectful.

The young scribe Abdul Azeez continued in a penetrating voice. "I and many others see clearly how they harbor and nurture a terrible fiend, providing refuge for this unclean beast in a so-called sacred house of God. Without shame, they acknowledge this publicly and continue to ask God for his blessings. Because of this blasphemy, it has become my great calling to rid the world of this dark horror. Through the wisdom of Allah, so shall it be."

Heads nodded, and murmurings of approval were heard. There were few, if any, among the congregation who had not watched the television or read newspaper accounts of the recent exorcism. A sizeable detached room to the rear of the mosque was designated a children's area and often used as a madrasa during daylight hours.

Children were released at 2:35 after attending daily classes. Further use of the school hall was suggested as a meeting place, where the imam and scribes might gather, accompanied by many among the faithful, to plan the destruction of the tremendous church-dwelling Satan by any means possible.

Such gatherings were held in the early evenings after *Maghrib*, the evening worship. All interested voices would be heard; both Sunni and Shiite would be represented.

The Light of Hope Mosque was inevitably transformed into the *Light of the Holy Jihad Mosque*.

Nearly two weeks had elapsed before the disgraced Imam Fahim Ibn-Abidin resurfaced. He recounted to a small gathering his tremendous and valiant struggle with a devil. He was telling a suddenly attentive audience how he was captured and imprisoned in a foreign dungeon, escaping by his courage, wit, and the will of Allah. He told them he knew the creature abducting him could only be the Saint Mary's Church daemon.

No mention was made of anal intrusion by well-greased vegetables.

The highly regarded Dark Angel was present and contributed to every meeting. None of the worshipers, including Fahim Ibn-Abidin, recognized or connected him with any blasphemous sexual displays. His knowledge of historical events indicated that he had studied long and hard—his apparent reverence for all things Islam elevated him to a most admired participant.

It was unanimously decided that since the devil lived in the house, the place with the devil inside must be erased. In this manner, all traces of the resident evil would be eradicated. The decision was made with almost unanimous approval and required only a definitive plan to implement the destruction.

Someone suggested a firebomb to burn the place to the ground. This suggestion was not acceptable because large stone blocks do not easily ignite. Various incendiary devices were discussed but rejected because of the unpredictable outcome. Explosives were the popular choice. If implemented with careful timing and proper placement, the required destruction would be inevitable.

Although a secondary consideration, loss of life would be minimized, and the explosive material was easily within reach of any knowledgeable demolition enthusiast.

The plot was hatched, and in a very short time, a malformed fledging chick emerged from the egg. Stupidity and mindless Islamic fanaticism would nurture it to maturity.

As the discussions ensued, an impractical dream slowly became a reasonable and real possibility. Of course, many details had to be finalized, but a good start was made.

The priority now was to find a sympathetic expert knowledgeable in the use of high-impact explosives. Fahim Ibn-Abidin knew of such an expert. He was presently in the United States, touring various Islamic centers to promote world peace. The imam promised to meet with him as soon as possible and discuss the project.

Within two weeks, the meeting was arranged. A self-styled Pakistani prophet known only as Chowdhury, accompanied by the revered operative Khalid Al-Mihdhar, would arrive at the mosque on September 15 to meet with representatives selected from the madrasa attendees.

It was expected that the two experts would evaluate the target, instruct volunteers, and determine the quantity and placement of various explosives.

CHAPTER 19

The day after the operative's arrival, six chosen faithful worshipers sat at the long bench table in the madrasa, meeting quietly behind closed doors. Occupying the fourth chair was Dark Henry Smith, the vampire. Two more strangers sat on opposite sides of the table.

The vampire, quick to form opinions of people, disliked both of them, Chowdhury, more so than the other. The Pakistani prophet Chowdhury had an unfortunate resemblance to the priest Father Malloy. He was not as tall, by about three inches, and unlike Malloy, who was clean-shaven, Chowdhury had a small brown mustache and a thin straggly ginger beard. The other newcomer was of medium height and slim build with a trimmed black beard.

Before them were two open briefcases and two folders stuffed with papers and sketches.

Khalid spoke quickly in Arabic, translated as quickly into English by Chowdhury. He confirmed the church building and its location as the correct target. Within two days, they would enter the church as interested tourists and take photographs. The exact location on the wall where the devil appeared would be found and marked. At this place, a chosen martyr would stand and detonate the inside charges at the given signal.

"Ah Maria, what is bad is not a wall in the house of God but having the name Ali Kackhanded. Can you imagine? Where is Israel?"

Maria shook her head. "Pablo told me it was a city in Italy, but I don't know. Pablo knows nothing, so why would he know about Israel?"

Simona nodded in agreement. "One thing for sure: Israel is nowhere near Italy if our *Viejo Pablo* said it was."

Both ladies laughed gently at the thought of Simona's cousin Pablo knowing anything at all.

Chowdhury and Khalid Al-Mihdhar decided on a simple binary explosive despite a few dissenters who believed that dynamite or C4 plastic was the preferred choice.

Khalid Al-Mihdhar responded with a flash of anger. "Choose wisely, then. Who among you will drill fifty 40-millimeter holes around the bottom of a granite-and-stone wall without attracting attention? You have called us for our knowledge of these matters. If you are convinced that laborious methods and inappropriate technology are the preferred way, then we can offer you nothing. Better we leave now in silence with the blessings of Allah upon you."

With profuse apologies from all in the madrasa, Al-Mihdhar was eventually placated.

"We know that you, above all, who profess knowledge in these matters, are correct in your decisions. We thank you for your help and ask forgiveness if we have offended you in any way."

"Our purpose now," Chowdhury said quickly, "is to determine a timeline for acquiring all the necessary components. A suitable martyr must be chosen and schooled. During this time, a date for the completion of our holy jihad will be realized."

On September 26, Khalid Al-Mihdhar determined that two thousand three hundred pounds of primary material were needed, including diesel fuel, nitromethane, and aluminum nitrate. Also, one hundred pounds of Tovex gel packets would be used as the primary detonators. The ignition would be initiated by two cell phones and two small relay boards.

The aluminum nitrate would be acquired in reasonably small quantities at any given time to allay any suspicion. Chowdhury arranged to fund the scheme. Ostensibly a community outreach to benefit cancer survivors. Voluntary donations from worshipers at the mosque would be diverted to a more worthy cause.

A trusted worker not appearing to be of Middle Eastern heritage would be needed to obtain all the materials.

No Middle Eastern involvement would be suspected, thereby deflecting suspicion and hampering the inevitable investigation. No one present nurtured any illusions that the explosive devices' method and construction would be swiftly determined.

A list of different suppliers was compiled, and no vendor would record a large quantity of any material purchased. The church was a benign target; very difficult to determine a motive for its destruction.

The plot soon evolved into a workable plan. After much discussion, the hour for destruction was determined:

12:30 am on Christmas Eve. This time window would allow for the possibility of making any last-minute changes. If necessary, the final hour could be moved to New Year's Eve. Three months of preparation was considered marginal but workable if everyone contributed selflessly to the cause.

Sir Henry found himself strangely detached from the plotting and scheming at the mosque. Although involved as an active member of the "secret six," as the plotters were now called, he was rather annoyed that the destruction was provisionally scheduled for Christmas Eve.

He reveled in the festivities and a general feeling of goodwill at that time. He also developed a growing dislike for Khalid Al-Mihdhar and his companion. In his opinion, Khalid Al-Mihdhar was more concerned with his reputation as an Islamic hero than he was about the benefits or dangers to the mosque. As for Chowdhry, he was relegated quickly to *annoying bumbling pimp* status.

Beneath the wailing notes of his accordion, vampire Smith muttered to himself. "Another mindless Shiite conditioned by fanaticism and blinded by faulted religious doctrine. Another dedicated soldier, unable to see beyond the walls of his self-made prison. I will soon select a well-rounded parsnip as a parting gift for these two turkeys. By the will of Allah, so shall it be."

He was amazed by the plot's progress—how it had grown from a childish foot-stomping reaction to the church exorcism to the genuine, calculated destruction of Saint Mary's Church. The destruction of the church and the probable loss of life were easily justified at every step.

It would seem the only prophet of God, and Allah himself wished it so.

Henry was not unmindful of his culpability in the matter. Having stuck Father Malloy to the wall, he knew he was the conjuror ultimately responsible for raising the daemon now destined for destruction.

How strange, humanity still behaving like spoiled children, reaching for the stars but with no understanding of the dirt beneath their feet.

It was surprising to him. Even after so many years of watching the antics of these delightfully willful creatures, nothing had changed. Good and evil were forever defined for them by self-serving religious bigots. Right and wrong were dictated by leaders of the countries to which they were told they owed allegiance by an accident of birth. They were the sheep collective and, as they always did, moved without questioning the dictates of their corrupt, manipulative shepherds.

It was a somber, reflective vampire who gazed at a blank wall in the kitchen of his small apartment.

He stared with unseeing eyes past the memories of faint echoes and through the dust and clamor of many ruined centuries. Punishment for time poorly used was, for him, brief flashes of former lives now beyond recall. He saw a hundred visions of fire and devastation, screams of the injured, and masks of hopelessness on the dying faces.

The outcome was always the same. Tragic effort expended to champion causes soon lost to history. Names of countless victims were never recorded. Forgotten soldiers in wars and contests so important today, only to become hazy memories tomorrow.

Exploitation, violence, and misery were not the only conditions remembered as years passed. There were the triumphs of intellectual advancement and a growing acceptance of humanitarian practices, moving slowly forward as the glow of understanding and reason illuminated many dark places. Often reason and logic were violently rejected by the fear and greed of those who cling to power.

With his left hand, he wiped at the corners of his eyes and, in doing so, removed the bitter, angry tears that were forming.

The chains of ignorance are not broken easily because the links are forged from superstitious traditions with false promises of glory and redemption. The passage of time will never completely eradicate the love for power or unearth the plentiful seeds of greed and corruption.

Thinking upon these things for a long time, Sir Henry came at last to a place where he was not touched by anger or sorrow and could find clarity and purpose as he had done a thousand times before.

He decided to intercede on behalf of Saint Mary's Church. "I will change the outcome of this ridiculous and dangerous game," he muttered.

And while Dark Henry Smith considered his strategy in the church destruction scenario so, demolition expert the vaunted Khalid Al-Mihduar considered the natural and often embarrassing consequence of his area of expertise.

As a child born in the impoverished Western Kandahar border area, he would study the world around him and marvel at the often unpredictable behavior of the people and animals he encountered. Of particular interest to him were stray dogs. He wondered at the pack behavior displayed in leaders and followers and later learned well about the simple reproductive processes, having dabbled in them himself. Beyond obvious attraction to the female in season was another strange penile stimulant that held his attention.

Most male dogs would sniff, circle the chosen place, and defecate. During the shitting process, the dog would gaze into some distant place as the fecal matter was expelled. At that time, the animal would usually experience an obvious erection. Whatever the reason for this phenomenon, it was not an isolated occurrence. This behavior so captivated the young observer's interest that he watched, entranced as family members performed the same rituals in the smelly confines of their old wooden outhouse.

He wondered at the possibility of a faulted human design; if an erection required defecation, then indeed, the bed or even the tent would soon be filled with dung. If defecation came first, then reproduction would be most inconvenient and require continual scraping and washing. Surely, Allah, in His wisdom and goodness, would never permit such a logical betrayal.

Such was the boy's dedication that he was often discovered kneeling in the sand while peering through the small holes he had made in the wooden outhouse door. Despite slaps and kicks from siblings, beatings from his despairing mother, dire warnings, and occasional genital mutilation by his revered father, the young Kahlid never lost interest in his unusual hobby. He saw that when a female was mounted and penetrated, a frequent occurrence in the family outhouse, no defecation occurred.

So, he reasoned, an erection was unnecessary to complete a bowel movement but was a simple, random, and naturally occurring condition.

As he struggled into maturity, diverse thoughts of electronics and sexual gratification consumed him either, mutually exclusive to the other. He learned the intricacies of advanced circuitry and basic industrial wireless architecture, so he was beset by uncontrollable and unexpected erections.

Akin to the defecating dogs of his youth, the feel of a smooth tantalum capacitor or the sight of an innocent naked 28-pin eprom would cause a sudden and powerful need for gratification. His learning curve in fundamental and applied electronics would have been considerably reduced had he not found it necessary to leave his books and masturbate frequently. After these covert excursions, he was always mindful of washing thoroughly before kneeling and asking Allah and the prophet for forgiveness and enlightenment.

His learning progressed slowly as there were few functional schools in the area. Students hoping to attend these bombed-out institutions were discouraged by threats of beatings and the ever-popular application of sulphuric acid in the face. Luckily, a small crumbling coffee house within walking distance was a meeting place for local heroic insurgents. Two hours every day, it became a madrassa to teach the fundamental laws of sharia. The big city of Kandahar frequently donated books to the madrassa, most of which were declared unsuitable and burnt in the street every two weeks. Kahlid rescued a few volumes of electronic engineering theory to study. With the help of others, he was able to learn and practice reading at the madrasa.

Soon, sex and electronic components became inseparable in his mind.

As his reputation and recognition in the border areas grew, he attracted the attention of Pakistani Islamic radicals. Here was a natural recruit for them who would soon learn to fashion sophisticated time delay detonators.

The seductive recruitment process was simple. "Allah commands you to further the cause of the prophet and promote the interests and teachings of Islam. Your life will improve immeasurably, and great rewards will be available to you. Also, you will avoid the inconvenience and embarrassment of a public beheading, and you will not experience the pain and humiliation of disembowelment."

Such attractive terms convinced the young student to join the dissidents and accept their tuition in the dilapidated coffee house. He was taught to make and deploy small high-impact explosive devices to use against western infidels and corrupt local government institutions during that time.

So, perhaps we should shed a tear for the smelly, wretched child born in a dung heap with dogs and goats as his childhood companions. At least try to understand the hopelessness of the underprivileged. Or, perhaps we should not. Better, we weep for the arid, windswept border areas of Afghanistan and Pakistan, where ignorance is maintained and enforced through distorted religious teaching, and the broken words of false prophets multiply in misery.

On the other hand, rather than concern ourselves with such obscure philosophical considerations, let's go for breakfast at the Gutburger. On an average day, scraps from the tables would feed Khalid Al-Mihdar and his degenerate family for a week. None of this matters, of course, for as we all know, *nothing* is as it seems on the border.

CHAPTER 20

Khalid Al-Mihdar was satisfied with the work and progress to date. Within two days, his production parts would be finished, leaving another two days for testing.

Having finished and tested the prototype detonators and then specified the quantities of explosive materials, Kahlid, the self-styled *master of mayhem,* was entertaining unclean thoughts about his eldest sister again.

He lay on his bed, remembering when she was in her fourteenth year. She then introduced Kahlid to the mysteries of the female body at the back of the goat pen. He remembered well the thick, tangled bush between her strong muscular thighs and the potent smell of ammonia and goat droppings enveloping them as they frolicked in the damp straw. So powerful was the imagery that Kahlid decided to engage a professional's services to relieve him of the mounting pressure in his scrotal area.

The bumbling, scheming Chowdhry scanning the local paper brought Leticia Washington's advertisements to his attention. "Look, my brother, a filthy western whore, is advertising her services. And, as we well know, a dirty whore is much to be desired. Far greater than a clean one with heavily decorated and scented wares."

I have a most wondrous plan for enjoying her offerings at no cost, he thought.

"We will go to her house tomorrow when you are ready."

The following day, Chowdhry, having telephoned and made arrangements with Leticia to entertain a party of two, arrived with the revered Kahlid Al-Mihdar at the small apartment. When the price was finalized, Chowdhry paid. Handing Leticia a one hundred dollar bill, he watched her furtively as she took the money and put it quickly in her handbag. Still holding the bag, she beckoned to Kahlid, and they both walked into the bedroom, followed by Choudhry.

Watching Leticia closely as she quickly opened the nightstand drawer and put the handbag in, he smiled a bloated, greasy smile. "I will first wash my enviable parts, and after urinating, ensure my member is clean and ready to grace your dilapidated infidel vagina."

"Piss away then, fool, and don't miss the bowl or make a mess. If you do, you will clean it up, and don't think I won't check. I don't have a litter box, so you must learn to use the toilet today. Remember tubby towel-head while you're fondling your little dick; *if* you can find it, the clock is ticking. One hour is all you get." She shook her head and made a mental note never to accommodate anyone wearing a turbine or a turban again.

Within the secure confines of the small bathroom, Choudhry stood for a moment in contemplation. He knew he had been insulted by a whore and would savor his imminent revenge. It would taste sweeter than any honey, more satisfying than a cup of the best palace wine, for none can insult a prophet of his stature without violent retribution.

Smiling, he quickly removed his turban, revealing matches, an emergency road flare, and a small container of lighter fluid. He removed all the magazines from a rack and then piled them on the toilet seat cover around the toilet tissue roll.

Opening the window and spraying lighter fluid over the shower curtain, he lit the distress flare placing it under the pile of magazines before emptying the remaining lighter fluid over the pile. Within a few seconds, a good blaze had erupted. The plastic shower curtain and road flare provided clouds of noxious smoke that billowed into the hall. Choudhry threw open the bedroom door screaming, "fire everywhere; the house is on fire; run for your lives." Much better had he waited a few more minutes giving Kahlid and Leticia time to fully involve themselves in the business at hand.

Leticia and Kahlid, unaware of the plot, scrambled from the bed hastily, grabbing clothes and shoes before running through the smoke to the safety of the stairs. Choudhry returned to the bedroom, unnoticed in the ensuing confusion. Removing all the money from Leticia's handbag, then replacing the emptied bag in the drawer, he hurried after Kahlid. The three refugees stood on the sidewalk staring at the building. Leticia, realizing she had left her handbag in the bedroom, turned to retrace her steps.

Choudhry grabbed Kahlid by the arm, pulling him to the parked car.

"Run, my brother, before the fire; people come."

Leticia ran back to the apartment, frightened and confused but determined to salvage her handbag, if nothing else. Much of the smoke had vanished, and after entering the bedroom, she retrieved her bag from the nightstand drawer. Making her way hurriedly to the stairs again, she stopped at the bathroom.

Here was the source of the smoke. Behind the door, the smoldering wreckage told the story of the arson, treachery, and deceit. It did not speak of the stupidity or how much easier it would have been to pay the girl, enjoy the experience, and move on, certainly for Khalid Al-Mihdar, who stubbed his toes painfully as he left the bedroom and never found sexual release in the short time available.

Leticia stood in the bathroom for many minutes, gazing at the damage and trying to understand what had happened. Within the hour, she had removed any threat of fire by dousing the smoldering magazine pile with water. The shower curtain remnants she threw into the bathtub.

Although the smell of smoke permeated the apartment for a few days, there was no fire danger to concern her. Only the onerous task of cleaning the bathroom remained. A reason for the disaster soon became apparent when she tried to pay for her lunch at the Gutburger.

CHAPTER 21

My "little waitress," as Henry called her, had exceeded all expectations. I was delighted.

Julie was not only a beautiful, sensual woman but intelligent and funny. She had worked at the bistro for just over three years. She was already holding a master's degree in applied psychology and was studying mightily for her doctorate, maintaining the evening job to support Peter, her thirteen-year-old son.

Henry had said, "be surprised as you get to know her." He was correct. Here was one exceptional lady—a woman I was taking very seriously.

I was so preoccupied with Julie and her son that neither the institute nor Henry Smith held the interest for me they once had. I felt slightly ashamed for neglecting my friend. I called him to make amends, and we arranged to meet at the Gutburger for a late lunch.

When I arrived at about 2:30, Henry was already seated in a booth facing the window. We chatted for a half-hour or so before ordering.

During a temporary lull in the conversation, we sat in silence, gazing at the street activity from the window. Across the road was a row of stores: a few yards further, an intersection with stoplights.

Parked outside a small clothing store, a yellow Volkswagen sat, waiting patiently for its driver.

Suddenly a small white Ford Focus pulled up behind the Volkswagen. A flashing yellow light on the roof and the words "Parking Enforcement" on the door identified the new vehicle.

A few minutes later, a woman left the clothes store and attempted to enter her car.

Luckily, a uniformed parking enforcement representative speedily interrupted her getaway.

Henry looked at me and grinned. "Here, Jack, a small human drama unfolds for your amusement."

I nodded in agreement. "Good-looking girl, though. Warning or ticket, do you think?"

Henry stared across the street for a few seconds before laughing loudly. "I know both of them. Let's wait and see."

They seemed locked in animated conversation, full of hand and arm movements, fingers pointing, and heads nodding.

Suddenly they were holding hands and walking toward the stoplight. Crossing together, they both turned and soon entered the Gutburger.

Sir Henry smiled and nodded as they passed our booth, but neither noticed or acknowledged us. The two lovers held eyes only for each other.

"Clients of the law firm or customers at Ronnie's?" I asked

"Neither," Henry responded in a low voice, then recounted his tale of both brief encounters with them, concluding, "Two wandering souls now thrown together again to enjoy their short lives. A happy accident or design? How think you?"

"If you are involved in their lives, then design. Otherwise, absolutely random."

Henry nodded. "I am not involved with either of them other than the short meetings I told you about. But the correct answer would be by design. Their meeting again was preordained."

"Then, by whom was their meeting arranged?" I asked, preparing an argument for random occurrences. "I don't believe in any magical elements or supposed forces that control our destiny. No preordained actions or responses."

Henry laughed gently. "You accept and believe in the explanations of the sciences and logical reasoning only then?"

"Yes, I do."

"We are in this restaurant by design, whether you believe it or not. Everyone has a part to play, big or small, but every part is essential to the bigger scheme. We are not here by accident, Jack. Every scheme is dependent on the next higher level. Occasionally we may glimpse details of the greater plan."

I started to interrupt, but Henry cut me short.

"Everyone within our interesting little circle moves as intended. We are all here interacting with design and purpose. Rather like your beloved cephalopods. Each is a separate entity unto itself, but the *group* interacting is the most efficient unit."

"So, if the design is functional," I replied, "then the outcome is known. That being so, there is no reason for anyone to do anything to achieve that outcome. It will simply happen."

"You are wrong, Jack. By your reasoning, the cephalopod would drift aimlessly without purpose. It would simply expire if it did not fulfill its preconfigured destiny without needing to hunt for food or reproduce. However, it—like us—has no understanding of its ultimate purpose."

He gave me a few moments to consider this.

"Now, returning to your belief in scientific explanations for all things physical and without any magical elements or other controlling forces. I await with great interest your explanation for a large Catholic priest suspended on a church wall for twenty-four hours with no visible means of support."

I lifted my hands in mock surrender, giving up the argument as Henry continued his questionable explanation.

"Our lives are like a gigantic jigsaw puzzle, with all parts fitting perfectly together so we can stand back and see the finished design. Each piece is satisfactory by itself, but only when it includes the whole is its true purpose understood. Of course, we might not care about the bigger picture, just happy to exist as an independent part. The problem with that is that our destinies are preconfigured to a great extent, and eventually, we will be moved to satisfy the higher plan. The feather is not the bird.

Here is another small fact for you to consider, young Jack. Everything you know and understand is what you have been told and shown, so it has always been. Your teachers were taught by their teachers and so on through the years, right or wrong. Consider the sources, eh?"

Okay then, Henry, but education, like history, is not stagnant. It will continually evolve with time. Otherwise, a *flat earth* concept would be perpetuated. Nothing would change.

So, here I was, again entangled in a philosophical discussion about the nature of human existence, the structure of life, and its purpose. However, there was not much debate or discussion. Henry stated the nature and purpose of existence as a fact, and how could I argue? So, all things metaphysical and arcane were illuminated for me from a booth with dark red plastic seats and a Formica-topped table littered with plates of half-eaten cheeseburgers and fries.

I think it was that unlikely combination of cheerful, greasy, Gutberger ambiance and the prevailing mundane clatter and babble from adjoining tables that grounded the conversation in my conventional world for me. The fact remained that my gay vampire friend and companion had decided to explain the nature of life and the origins of existence to me in a burger joint instead of a university lecture room. Just another delightful, surreal interlude for me and again, enjoying the unique company of my very dear Sir Henry Gaytooth Smith esquire.

"Here is another fact for your consideration, dear Jack," he continued.

"All actions, including the seemingly random, are pre-ordained. You may drop a pencil and bend to pick it up in response to that occurrence. Nothing in that seemingly inconsequential sequence of events is random. Again, we are moved to satisfy the greater plan."

"Okay, who does the moving then?" I asked.

"Each day, we see the results of those forces moving beyond our comprehension, powers that lift mountains and change the course of rivers. There are nine gods; ancient creators and architects manipulating and providing energy that could easily and very quickly turn man's greatest achievements to dust." Every action we take has a real purpose that may not always be readily apparent. Sit a baby before a grandfather clock. The child may stare, fascinated by the pendulum's motion but with no understanding of the clock's purpose or the mechanism concealed within the case."

He motioned to the couple in love.

"So now we see a whore with a meter maid that together fulfill their destinies as they were meant to. Simple creatures moving like children, but be assured; there is enough magic around us now that could strip flesh from our bones and unhinge our minds. Our insignificant little lives are only links in an endless chain, Jack. Every action we take, big or small, will affect that link or a link above or below it."

I nodded. "Yes, I have witnessed a little of this quite recently." Now, explain to me in simple terms about the nine Gods you mentioned just now.

"There are nine creator Gods with us on this earth today. There were twelve at one time, another subject for us to explore at a later date, Jack. Anyway, they are the ancient ones, and humans are their children. The Babylonians, Greeks, and Egyptians knew them well—research old Egyptian Gods, dear boy; good practice for you. There is plenty of relevant study material available. Intelligent life on this plane is very much older than you think or were led to believe."

"Okay, Henry, but I don't need any practice. My life revolves around research, but Your *nine God's* reference interests me, though. I will try to find some information about that."

"So, you understand my explanation and subscribe to my position then?"

"Yes, I think I do."

In truth, I did not, but I told him I did, hoping to prevent a more detailed discussion that could take several hours of obscure explanation.

While the great philosophical debate rested, I glanced at the table where the uniformed parking inspector sat with the pretty woman. They were deeply absorbed with each other, gazing into the other's eyes and holding hands while their coffee cooled.

I wondered if this was how Julie and I appeared to others when we started dating. I had a feeling that it was.

"Love blossoms in the most unlikely corners," Henry laughed. "Best wishes to both of them."

I thought of Julie and nodded in agreement.

Having gnawed through burgers and fries, we stayed for another half hour or so. Before departing, we arranged to meet at the bistro a week from Friday.

Andre sat in the Gutburger with his darling Lettuce—or rather, Leticia, as she had just revealed her real name to him.

His joy was overwhelming, a love so breathtaking that it was more significant than even the promised promotion, perhaps more than the city parking department itself.

He had accumulated thirteen proud years of devotion and service to the parking enforcement department and would hopefully enjoy many more years to come. Andre needed a disciplined routine to function, happily, an ordered, regimented existence without surprise or deviation. Consistency was his watchword and the cornerstone of his happiness.

He never married, although his search for a suitable woman continued throughout his orderly life. In recent months his life was anything but orderly.

An accident with a speeding car, the partial loss of his memory, police inquiries, a confrontation with demonic forces, and now this unexpected meeting with the woman of his dreams—quite a remarkable few months indeed.

Here he was now, his duties ignored and a possible ticket disregarded as if it were nothing. His life was swirling in an incomprehensible vortex of disruption. Strangely none of this concerned him.

He gazed into the beautiful brown eyes of Leticia and forgot everything. *How odd*, he thought. Poised to issue a citation and then suddenly engulfed by a shocking awareness.

His red-shoed angel was suddenly standing before him with an improperly parked yellow Volkswagen. They stared at each other for a long time.

"Lettuce, you are Lettuce," he whispered.

"Whaa? Who you calling a lettuce, meter boy?" She clenched her fists, ready to contest a perceived insult.

"No, no, your name is Lettuce, isn't it? Lettuce Washingboard?

"No, fool. My name is Leticia Washington. Do I know you?"

"We met on the street a few weeks ago. I was hit by a car, and you helped me. The police drove us to the station. Don't you remember?"

"Ooo yeah, I remember now." She recalled some details of the incident with a bum on Broadway, then punching his head, and the cops taking them both to the station.

Her memory of the jail and the couple of weeks she spent there were very clear. The memory of the wizened, raisin-faced bitch of a judge who sent her there was also clear. The judge was a small, rail-thin woman with no sense of humor or compassion, permanently covering her unhappy skeletal form with a thick black robe. Presumably, to intimidate or impress those before her. Or possibly, because she felt cold.

"All stand for the judge. The Honorable Millicent Carlisle is presiding."

The various well-lubricated attorneys, squirming and groveling with their artificial reverence, were not forgotten either.

"Yes, ma'am, I will, your Honor." "Oh, at once, your Honor." "Thank you so much." "If it pleases, your Honor."

Oh, she remembered the court alright, and she believed the court remembered her. Sitting and listening to the dull, mousey little judge, her mind wandered as it often did.

Leticia imagined the judge in her private chambers, gripping the edge of a large oak desk; her black robe pulled over her head, her bony naked ass sticking in the air. The

Honorable Millicent became a cartoon character with her eyes crossed and tongue hanging over her bottom lip.

The burly sheriff's deputy would be waiting again, as he did every morning.

He would spread the emaciated cheeks and enter her roughly, stripping away any pretense of dignity or pride. His large rubbery fingers gripped her shoulders tightly, and as he started to thrust, beads of sweat would form on his glistening bald head.

Although this was an imaginary scenario, Leticia had the urge to mop the sweat from his head and polish it to a gleaming sphere using a good quality lemon-scented wax furniture polish.

When his passion grew and his thrusts increased, the judge's bony frame would start to shake, then rattle.

Leticia, desperately trying to regain a small degree of self-control, suddenly remembered the wind chimes her mother bought in Chinatown, short lengths of hollow bamboo swinging from a frame. When a light wind blew, the bamboo sticks swung into each other, producing an empty rattling sound. This was the sound the judge made as the deputy banged her.

The more his passion increased, the louder the judge rattled: hollow judicial bones rattling in the damp heat of an unlightly love affair. Contributing to the orchestral rattle were the grunts and gasps from the deputy as he plowed into her, producing little cries and wails from the judge. Eventually, the deputy's lust culminated in a great roar of triumph, followed by a prolonged judicial scream from the judge.

All was well in the courtroom until Judge Millicent asked Leticia a question. She could not answer coherently as the vision of the excellent rattler swam before her. She laughed uncontrollably, her mirth growing as each second passed.

"Dear Lord, if I don't stop laughing soon, I think I will rattle."

The Honorable Millicent Carlisle was not laughing. She glared at Leticia. "Did I say something to amuse you? If so, please feel free to share your humor with the court." Leticia could only shake her head. She was trying unsuccessfully to stifle her laughter and produced loud spluttering choking noises.

She was near hysteria now, peals of laughter filling the court. The judge nodded to the deputy. "Remove this defendant. If and when she regains her composure, we will resume. The defendant is remanded until tomorrow's session."

Leticia snapped back to the present situation. Yes, she remembered Andre. Not a bum at all, but quite a nice-looking guy with a uniform. He was taller than she remembered, probably because he was wearing shoes and a hat now.

He suddenly took her hand and, without explanation, guided her across the street. Here was a man holding her hand instead of reaching for her ass. He would prove to be a true gentleman, actually paying for her burger, asking nothing in return. This was a new experience for her and a good one.

As they talked, she gave a brief history of her new life in California and her mother's death but realized that it was too early yet to confess her actual profession or details. For the first time, she was distressed by feelings of shame when he asked. Instead, she told him she was in public relations and about to start her own business.

She had found a man who, within five minutes, had upended her life.

Andre, for his part, knew he loved this woman. He wanted to jump from his seat and shout, telling anyone who would listen that the beautiful woman sitting in the opposite chair was his and that he was in love.

Cupid, smiling broadly, put aside his bow and kicked him hard in the balls.

After some time, they arranged to meet again for dinner. Leticia would cancel her work schedule to be with him, something she wanted to do, with no thought of time or money.

Andre waited for her to drive away before returning home himself, wandering in a cloud of confusion and delight.

CHAPTER 22

Sir Henry met with the seven plotters at the madrasa the following afternoon. He was told everything was going according to plan, and the materials for the explosives were inert and safe to handle. All the supplies had now been moved to a large wooden storage building at the side of the mosque.

This would house everything needed and allow for the assembly of the components without scrutiny.

However, a martyr was not yet chosen. Surprisingly, no volunteers had come forward, willing to extinguish themselves for greater glory.

The scribe Abdul Azeez spoke. "Our brother Chowdhury has a plan. It is unusual in that a martyr will be appointed. Please let us hear him now, without interruption."

Chowdhury stood and addressed those seated. "As you know, we have no volunteers. Our timeline is already three weeks past our expectations for this. I suggest we appoint a person capable of fulfilling this position quickly. My nominee is a simple old Mexican who will stand at the wall without question if told to do so." He fingered his beard as the plan unfolded.

"His name is Pablo Gonzales, a gardener, and outside maintenance man, the cousin of an old cleaning woman who also works at the church. I met them both during our first visit to the location. Khalid Al-Mihdhar took several photographs of them standing at the accursed wall."

At this point, Khalid Al-Mihdhar withdrew five prints from his briefcase and passed them to those seated at the table. "You have all seen these before. "Pass them around and remind yourselves again," Chowdhury said.

"Although this Pablo Gonzales is not a Muslim, he will surely find favor in the eyes of the Prophet. Peace and enlightenment will be upon him and his children."

Chowdhury nodded before continuing. "During the course of our conversation, I told the dirty old woman Simona that we were from Israel. The cousin Pablo believes Israel is the capital city of Italy. I did nothing to correct him."

He paused to smile and, nodding, acknowledged the scattered laughter from his audience.

"I am sure he will happily carry the pack and vest, although it is better if he is unaware of the contents of his backpack. He is old, toothless, smelly, and feeble, so much better that he remains ignorant of his real purpose. In this way, he will be saved from any mental anguish and spared unnecessary, stupid decision-making.

As for the explosives around his waist, he must be told that they are solid fuel heating sticks for use in heaters donated to the poor. He will understand he is carrying a demonstration heater in the backpack. In that way, he will not be burdened or troubled by the mysteries of high explosive material and electronic detonation. He will think only of heating elements and stoves for his dirty, impoverished friends.

After displaying the solid fuel sticks, he will expect to demonstrate the heater. Obviously, this will not happen."

A long silence ensued while the other attendees considered the suggestion—a minute or so of mutterings and nods culminated in another scattering of applause.

"A wonderful solution to a potential problem, my brothers. Our gratitude and blessings" said Khalid Al-Mihdhar in Arabic. "Peace be upon the one among us for his excellent suggestion."

He then referred the conversation to Chowdhury for a better English translation.

"Our old Mexican will detonate the first charge, after which, Approximately forty seconds later, the first primary charge will detonate against the cemetery sidewall. Another forty seconds and the last primary charge will detonate against the street sidewall.

By our calculations, each primary charge should demolish at least sixty percent of each wall—more than enough to cause a total collapse of the building.

Henry smiled.

"Allah smiles upon this blessed jihad, and peace is to all gathered here."

Everyone at the table smiled and nodded.

The dejected vampire sat in the kitchen of his apartment. He leaned back in a cheap wooden chair, staring as he often did at the blank wall before him. He thought of the meeting he had recently left and shook his head, scowling. These buffoons were happy to sacrifice an old innocent without consideration.

"So much for brotherly love," he muttered.

He could imagine the arguments to support the murder and the predictable "all in the holy name of Allah, the Most merciful," a martyr beginning his sacred journey to heaven, a great honor to be chosen for the righteous jihad, peace be upon him.

Although he could probably prevent Pablo from suffering injury, the principle remained. He was not even a Muslim, yet they would have him carry explosives in a backpack and around his waist without knowing what he was carrying. They would get him inside the church and have him wait; a harmless, defenseless old lamb led to the slaughter, the perfect sacrifice.

Sir Henry grew restless with suppressed anger as he considered these things.

Perhaps it would be better if he ignored the situation, turned his head from the impending catastrophe, and let the fools demolish Saint Mary's—or themselves in the process.

After a little while, the red in his eyes faded, and he remembered his meal again with Jack at the Gutburger, where they looked upon two more martyrs, a meter maid, and a hooker. He laughed as he thought of them and briefly rejoiced in their happiness.

He left the kitchen to retrieve his accordion. The music would slowly wash away his anger as it had always done. The blood he wanted would soon satisfy his increasing hunger.

Pablo, the old gardener, was bewildered. Suddenly his company was sought after, and his opinion asked about many things. The kindly Italian, *Senor* Chowder, had explained about the heating program for the poor.

In particular, how he—Pablo, an old gardener—had been honored by being chosen to lead a charitable program on behalf of poor Latino church worshipers. He was to give his surprise demonstration of heaters and fuel to churchgoers on Christmas Eve.

"Very important," he was told. "Tell no one about this plan in case the heaters do not arrive in time. We want no one at Saint Mary's to be disappointed."

Of course, Pablo would remain silent as if his life depended on it. He was, after all, chosen for his outgoing personality, wit, and charm.

Senor Chowder had explained. "We must have an experienced man, personable and intelligent. We have been told you are such a man."

"I am such a man, *senor*," Pablo replied, pleased and a little surprised. "My speaking of English is bad, but I am ready for your task if this is not a problem."

Leticia was a happy hooker—probably as happy as she had ever been, or at least as happy as she could remember. Her new man Andre was a gem, indeed an unexpected and somewhat bewildering experience for her.

For the first time in her brutal, rather sordid young life, she could lay claim to the affections of a true gentleman who was considerate and caring. It had been only two weeks since they had found each other again, but she thought they were perhaps the two most important weeks of her life.

What a strange, convoluted trail from that violent evening on Broadway to a parking infraction outside the Gutburger.

She was so profoundly affected by her affair with Andre that changing her way of living seemed natural. There would be no more street walking, just attending to three or four select and rather needy long-standing clients. Even these would stop soon, although her sense of duty required that she continue with them for a while. She couldn't just cut them loose without assurance that their needs would be adequately met and their wants would be satisfied without her.

There was enough money in the bank to support her for some time. Andre was working, and with her money plus the small insurance settlement from her mother's death, she would soon be able to retire.

Andre, for his part, was walking on a cloud of delight. His previous need for routine and predictably was forgotten. No longer dependent upon daily repetition for comfort and security, he was finding new freedom in change.

His thinning brown hair, always parted on the side and combed to the left, was now brushed straight back. The small graying mustache he had trimmed for thirty years was gone, shaved off on the advice of Leticia. He was actually starting to enjoy his new life.

He knew his mother would have been so proud of her reborn, adventurous son.

She would see he had a girlfriend, of all things, and a good-looking, sexy one at that. Never before had he been so blessed.

He thought of his accident on Broadway and how it all started a few short months ago.

He remembered the black Mercedes improperly parked, leading to a confrontation with a stinking goblin on Saint Mary's Church wall. He also remembered how he flipped off the devil lurking there and set the sign of the cross on the doors of the evil vehicle. Then a beautiful yellow Volkswagen he saw was parked too close to the crosswalk and most certainly deserved a ticket.

From that time forth, his world had changed for the better. It was always parking violations and traffic infractions that seemed to illuminate the path leading to this moment so important in his life.

"I will return to Saint Mary's with Leticia and give thanks for our good fortune," he whispered to himself.

He recognized that Leticia was the pivotal point in his limited but rapidly expanding universe. There were a few times in the quiet moments when he would reflect on his old life and wonder if the new path he had chosen—*or had been thrust into*—was really for him. Sometimes he saw everything around him spinning wildly out of control.

He would imagine that he sat on an old bicycle hurtling down a steep path, unable to stop, with no choice but to hang on until the inevitable crash.

Salvation always awaited him, though. As he flew over the handlebars, destined to land in a sizeable spiny cactus patch or a bottomless pit of untreated sewage, a laughing Leticia would be there to save him. Arms outstretched, she would catch him as he sailed through the air and return him gently to his feet.

Four weeks later, on December 15, they would drive to Union Station, head out from Los Angles, then by rail to New Orleans, and make good on a promise Leticia had made to her mother. They had no strict timetable to regulate them, as these few days would serve as an impromptu vacation. They allotted eight days to travel out, scatter the ashes, and then return to Los Angeles.

He and Leticia would be together during Christmas. He would move in with her, sharing the apartment. They intended to live as a married couple, move to Las Vegas after the New Year, and—if all went well—be married shortly after that. Such was the dream of a parking enforcement officer, a vision of the future for him and his wife.

CHAPTER 23

On Friday, November 18, Henry and I met at the bistro but ate in the dining room instead of our usual street table. The weather was too cold and miserable for comfort, even in Southern California.

I was working at the institute again and assigned to another project with Angela. This time we were to investigate the possibility of harvesting plankton and krill for human consumption. We would study the effects of sound and light as primary mediums to attract the little fellows.

Of course, attracting them in sufficient and meaningful numbers was another matter altogether. Further, having attracted the little guys, they had to be removed from their watery homes, processed, and preserved.

After reviewing the project requirements and timeline, it occurred to me that I had no interest at all in this significant humanitarian venture.

Sometimes it is better to shut up and dig in, though. The institute had good benefits and all the resources to conduct extensive research on many levels. Another element in any project like this is that one never knows exactly where the investigation might lead.

Henry appeared, seeming to materialize at the table before me, a ritual I was slowly becoming accustomed to. It was something he often did, but never for effect. I believe he did not perform well for an audience, and I had never seen him do so.

Without a doubt, he was capable of many astonishing demonstrations of his paranormal abilities. I had witnessed some of them during the nine months or so that I had known him, yet never had I seen him deliberately trying to impress or intimidate anyone. He was, in fact, the master of understatement.

He stood and, in greeting, extended his hand. "Well, good to see you again, Jack. What to eat this evening, eh? May I suggest the fried plankton sandwich, perhaps grilled krill with boiled vegetables? The ever-popular starfish with steamed asparagus even."

"How about a simple filet mignon," I replied. "Or at least a hamburger with fries."

Henry grinned, a sharp wolfish smile that, for a few seconds, displayed rows of gleaming white teeth. "Sounds better than my choices, young Jack; this is a cause for some celebration. Aren't you pleased to continue at the institute with another project?"

I nodded, but the expression on my face was apparently unconvincing. I detailed my concerns about the project while Henry listened attentively. "There are times when a third-class ride is preferable to a first-class walk, Jack." He replied slowly. "At least you are working and drawing a wage."

"Yeah, I know, just me whining again." He nodded, laughing gently.

"You are a dedicated perfectionist, young Jack, not always an easy cross to bear." It was my turn to laugh, and suddenly the mood brightened.

"Okay, Henry, but so we don't forget the reason for being in this restaurant, what will we eat?"

After some debate, we both settled on prime rib. As usual, the food was excellent. Despite Henry's company, I found the atmosphere slightly dampened by Julie's absence.

The music was not as cheerful, and the lights were not as bright as they seemed.

We discussed the "The Father Philip Hour" television program. Henry had watched two episodes.

"Some unbiased criticism is due," he said with a hint of sarcasm. His unbiased critique ranged from anger to feelings of nausea when seeing the posturing Malloy and listening to him expound on the teachings of Jesus and the principles of Christianity.

"I should have left that sweaty, puffy imposter on the wall. Unfortunately, our display in the church has left many unseen consequences."

"I'm shocked to hear you say such nasty things about a humble priest, a man of the cloth, and a minister to the poor," I said.

Henry curled his upper lip to display a row of even white teeth and two long savage canines. This was the first time I had ever seen him project them, and the shock of that terrifying inhuman image forever changed my impression of him.

For a few seconds, he stared past me, then snarled, a deep, protracted animal growl, chilling and frightening—almost like a large angry dog, but much deeper and more threatening.

As quickly as his demonic expression appeared, so it was replaced by the calm, somewhat aloof Henry I had become so accustomed to.

"Please don't be alarmed, Jack; just an expression of anger for a moment. Certainly not directed at you. I intend no harm. Much better to express myself verbally than physically, don't you think? Anyway, the wretch is now cursed, his shoes will be broken, and many men will taste his wife.

It was some time before I managed a reply. "Sorry, just joking, Henry. I didn't realize this was such a touchy subject for you. As for the curse, I don't think he has a wife to taste."

Henry chuckled in such contrast to his recent angry display. "Not so much a touchy subject, my friend, but rather a worrying one—and circumstances that I am entirely responsible for." As for a wife, if he doesn't have one now, he soon will. A woman who will bring him well-deserved misery.

The waitress brought coffee.

Henry grinned at me. "Not quite the same as Julie, eh?" We both laughed, breaking the rather tense, serious mood.

CHAPTER 24

After coffee, Henry pushed back his chair and began an astonishing story of recent happenings at the mosque. He described the Muslims' outrage over the Malloy exorcism and their abiding belief that a devil had taken residence at Saint Mary's.

"Yeah, I can understand their point of view. The fiasco at the church and the media coverage was quite amazing incidents. As a result, we are now treated to Malloy television five times a week."

Henry nodded. "Exactly, but I am afraid there is much more to it than that. The anger at the mosque is so intense that there is now a genuine intent to demolish the church." He shook his head. "These people are fanatical and devout in their desire to destroy the Satan Malloy by any means possible."

"Well, they will get over it, I suppose; they'll have to. I mean, they can't just remove a huge building in the middle of the city. Anyway, how stupid to believe there is actually a devil in the church. Bigoted, ignorant religious doctrine at its best. I think we have a ship with prejudicial morons at the helm Henry."

Henry shook his head, silent for a moment, before replying.

"Then remember this, Jack; there are a few folks who believe that a savior of humanity walked on water before he died and then returned from the dead."

"But, that's not the point, though, dearest Jack. The Muslims believe, stupid or not. Through the strength of their belief, they have the intent and technology to destroy Saint Mary's Church. This is a real threat, not just empty words. They intend to do this."

I shook my head in amazement. I believed every word Henry said but just could not accept that a group, acting together, would undertake such an extraordinary enterprise. I suddenly remembered the Humboldt squid.

They would undertake a communal effort to destroy an enemy or hunt for food. Nature gave many other examples. Ants were another group acting as a disciplined collective, as were wasps and bees, a seemingly endless list—including humans.

"So, what's next then? Call the authorities. Get the cops involved?"

He shook his head. "No, first more coffee, but to answer your question—call the police and tell them what? "That a group of Islamist extremists intends to blow up a church because a devil masquerading as a priest supposedly lives there?" Hardly credible evidence, Jack."

He was right, of course. Who would believe that story? Certainly not a judge, who would have to sign the search warrants.

"Do they have the expertise with explosives? Are they able to obtain everything to do this, then?

He nodded and then continued after finishing his coffee.

"They have everything—workforce, materials, and a very practical plan. Even have a vampire to help them." He grinned and explained his position among the plotters. "So, I have intelligence but no plan as yet. Still working on that. I have about three weeks to make a decision."

"Henry, If I can help, if there's anything you need, please let me know."

"Thanks, Jack. I knew I would be able to count on you. In truth, I believe you have the makings of an excellent vampire. How think you?"

"I don't think I have the vampire personality, Henry, although the possibility of living for another six hundred years is intriguing."

He laughed his old Henry laugh and stood from the table. "Good to see you again, young Jack. A pleasant evening and good food as usual, even if the service was somewhat lacking. I am sure we will talk soon."

As was our custom, we shook hands. Henry inclined his head and walked slowly to the door. I sat for a few minutes, lost in thought.

"Chose your friends wisely" is an old proverb my father would repeat many times as I grew. Usually, as a result of unfortunate lifestyle choices in my youth. And here I sat, suddenly realizing that my best friend was a vampire.

What, I wondered, would dad have thought of that, and how would I ever explain it to him?

> "Sir Henry Smith, The vampire never had a home,
> He started on a darkened track
> To travel this world alone."

I headed for the bathroom. Not more than five minutes had elapsed when I returned to the table. A woman now occupied the chair that Henry had recently vacated.

The table was not cleared, and my unfinished coffee stood waiting.

"Excuse me, forgive the intrusion, but this is my table. Not quite finished yet. There are plenty of other places with clean tables available."

She stared at me for what seemed a long time before she spoke. "How very observant you are. Of course, there are other tables. I am not one of your inept students. I chose to sit with you at *this* table, Jack. Now, please order more coffee."

The emotions I felt ranged from anger to astonishment and everything in between. As I stared at my uninvited guest, I realized that she was strangely familiar. I knew her, or we had met recently.

"Well, are you going to order the coffee or not? Perhaps you prefer to stand here like a dummy waiting for the resurrection."

I sat, staring at her. "No, I am not ordering coffee or anything else. You owe me an explanation, at the very least. You take over my table, demand attention, and display an astonishing lack of manners. Do we know each other?"

She smiled. "We will soon know each other very well. We have never met, although we have sat at the same table more than once. Now, if we are to continue with a civilized conversation, we must do so over a coffee."

And here I remembered my parents. Mother, a psychotherapist, told me a simple method she would employ to calm her nerves when she spoke before an audience.

"I always imagined the people in front of me in their underwear. When you strip away the expensive clothes, everyone is reduced to the same level."

I tried my mom's cunning strategy and was left with a delightfully curvy woman wearing lacy bright red nylon underwear.

Against my better judgment, I relented and ordered coffee, apparently the necessary catalyst to continue this bizarre encounter. Not only was I now intrigued by her attitude but equally impressed by her exotic appearance.

To say the least, she was an attractive woman: black hair falling past her shoulders, high cheekbones, slim, with an enticing figure. I was briefly tempted to ask her to stand so I could conduct a full appraisal, then decided against it as the vision of her in red underwear was distracting enough.

There was something so familiar about her, but I would certainly have remembered if we had met before. Her impressive sarcasm, belligerent attitude, and monumental rudeness would not be forgotten.

"So, do we start with introductions?" I asked

"Of course. My name is Anneliese. You are Jack, are you not?"

"Jack Cordell."

I extended my hand. She took my hand; briefly, I saw her long fingers with beautifully manicured nails. I first noticed her clothes: a dark gray business suit and a white blouse underneath—no jewelry except a heavily embossed silver ring on her right index finger.

The coffee arrived.

"Anneliese, I have a quick question for you. Are you always so unpleasant and confrontational? Or is this a special occasion?"

She smiled, a delicious and inviting smile with lips slightly parted to show even white teeth. I think it was the full lips and those high cheekbones that I found so appealing.

Reaching across the table suddenly, she took my hand. I felt the warmth, surprising to me, as I expected her hand to be cool.

We continued squeezing hands lightly for some time. A second or an hour, perhaps, I knew not which. Neither of us wanted to release our grip, it seemed. It was the strangest evening but one I didn't want to end.

Gazing into her eyes, then at our hands, we suddenly laughed as we relinquished our hold.

"So, if this is what coffee does for you, please allow me to pour another cup."

"Only if you join me," she said.

Her accent was German, maybe Eastern European, quite pronounced and unsuited, I thought, considering her Hispanic appearance. I poured coffee for two, then waited as she raised her cup.

"Now, how do we know each other, Anneliese?"

"Well, Jack, we do not know each other yet. I was in that horrible little Ronnie's bar one evening. You walked in and sat in the corner by yourself. You started talking to him when I finished my business with the barman. A few minutes later, I left."

I stared at her for some time before the memory returned. Then suddenly, I remembered the evening at Ronnie's, the first time I saw Henry at work.

Here was the woman I intended to question Henry about for so long. Anneliese looked quite different from the lady I remembered at the bar. Probably her clothes. I remember the black hair falling past her shoulders and a dark blue blouse. Here she was dressed quite formally.

"Yes, I do remember—or at least I remember seeing you," I said. "For sure, the most attractive woman in the place."

"Why, thank you, Jack, for a compliment indeed, although I was the only woman in the place at the time, I think. Your kind words were well-meant, though."

For another half hour, we talked trivial chat with no effort or substance.

"Coffee's nearly gone," she said.

"We either say goodnight now before this place closes or go to The Broadway. Perhaps I'll buy you a drink. Their bar is open until midnight. Far nicer than Ronnie's. Then, well, if you feel so inclined, we can go to 447."

I nodded, delighted to extend the evening in the company of this fine-looking woman. "Sounds good to me, Anneliese. What is 447, and where is it?"

She laughed, taking my hand across the table again. "You are a strange one, Jack. 447 is my room number. I'll be staying at The

Broadway for a few days. I often do. Now you settle for the coffee, and I will meet you in the lounge."

I have always liked The Broadway; comfortable without pretensions, although I have never stayed there. I had been to a couple of sponsors' meetings for the institute some two years ago. It was, at most, a ten-minute drive from the cafe.

Driving to the hotel gave me time for the feelings of guilt to surface. "What if" scenarios were plentiful.

What if Julie had returned unexpectedly with her parents, and they decided to stay at The Broadway? What if terrorists decided to attack The Broadway instead of the church? Agents combing through the rubble would discover two bodies, me jammed on top of Anneliese.

How would that situation be explained without acute embarrassment? It would not, of course, but suddenly I didn't care.

Because thinking of that trim body and those full lips were sufficient incentives for me to pursue my dishonorable intentions—and pursue them, I did. She was waiting in the lounge at a corner booth. I sat beside her, comfortably placing my arm around her shoulder or holding her hand beneath the table, like a couple of kids on their first date.

She drank white wine, I with anisette and brandy—a luxury I seldom indulge in. Still, the situation called for it, and I made a quick but impassioned apology to my liver before raising a glass.

The evening seemed destined for the extravagance of illicit romance. A few drinks punctuated our endless conversation. I learned she was German, and her name was Anneliese Reinecke.

I had many questions for her, not the least being how she knew my name. I asked a hundred others, but I remember nothing of our discussions to this day except a sudden, startling comment she made. And the delightful accent that seemed to roll and flow all around me.

"Turquoise Jack, Turquoise, not red., Oh, And silk, not nylon."

After an hour or so, our conversation temporarily exhausted, she grinned. "Well, are we ready for 447?"

"I'm sure we are. I can't wait for the next Anneliese experience."

The magnetic card key granted us entry into a large, well-appointed room. Before closing the door, Anneliese hung the *do not disturb* card on the handle. "Just in case we decide to sleep in," she said. "Now, I go for a shower, you make yourself at home, watch TV, or we have a few magazines on the table. I won't be very long."

She disappeared into the shower. I followed her, washing my face and hands in the washbasin.

I returned to sit on the edge of the large double bed, waiting. My head was spinning, and I stood unsteadily for a little while. Sudden and most unexpected onset of flu-like symptoms came over me, very strange, as I felt fine in the bar. Anneliese came from the shower, a large rough white towel covering most of her body. She stared at me.

"Are you okay? You don't look very good. I hope I am not affecting you like that. Jump—no, I don't think you will be able—crawl into bed, and I will do my best to help."

I peeled off my clothes and crawled beneath the sheets as she suggested. "I must have drunk too much, although two or three drinks don't usually affect me like this."

The white towel dropped to the floor, and almost at once, I began to feel better.

"You like?" she said, pirouetting quickly in front of me.

"More than you could ever imagine," I replied, staring at the slim seductress.

"Now, into bed with you, woman. I feel better already."

The alarm sounded with a demonic digital persistence that reminded me of scalding water. I reached to turn it off but could not find the damned thing.

It continued to rain the high-pitched scalding water sound all around me, fulfilling its detestable purpose to the extent that I was forced to leave the bed.

Eventually, I did so, but not before a magnificent struggle with the sheets and blanket that ensnared me.

The clock was under the bed, my bed in my old familiar apartment bedroom.

I silenced the alarm and then stood for a long time gazing around me. I should not be here. I was in The Broadway, room 447. And then came confusion and doubt. Was I ever at Broadway? Was there ever a girl, Anneliese? I remembered the name and the sound of her voice—nothing else.

The shower welcomed me as it usually did with hot, steaming water. A few minutes beneath the blessed waters revived me, cleansed me, and prepared me for a post-mortem of the previous evening. I dried myself, almost ready to pull on my boxers when I noticed the blood—many streaks of bright, fresh blood on the towel. I returned to the bathroom to check in the shower.

I saw blood on the floor—not much, but there should be none at all. I examined my body for any wounds that might be responsible. In the joint of my right arm, about an inch below the bicep muscle, two evenly spaced puncture wounds marked the source of the leakage. There was no pain or swelling, although my arm felt a little stiff. They were clean, fresh wounds, as though stabbed with a pencil. A little cortisone cream followed by two large Band-Aids, and the repair was complete.

A haggard, unshaven stranger gazed back at me from the mirror despite the shower. I pulled on an old sweater that matched an equally old pair of jeans. After combing my hair, I was almost ready for the Gutburger breakfast.

My front door was locked, the back door was locked, and I found no broken windows or signs of unauthorized entry.

My apartment was as I had left it. The only unusual signs were a seriously thrashed bed atop an alarm clock. The alarm was set and had sounded at the appropriate hour—nothing unusual here at all, just a late Saturday morning with daylight flooding the rooms.

A check through my wallet showed credit cards and my driver's license all in place. There was an appropriate amount of cash left from a night on the town. What happened to me, and if I was at the Broadway, how did I get home?

Outside on the balcony, distant street sounds brought a small degree of reassurance. Troubling to me were the vivid memories of a delightfully naked brown-skinned woman sliding into bed with me.

I remembered her purring like a cat, her scented smell, and the curves of her lithe body. I remembered her kiss and the taste of her skin.

I was concerned because there were no memories of any subsequent action. I didn't remember what happened that night with Anneliese, but I hoped we enjoyed it.

Sex before starvation or perhaps starvation before sex—either way, I was hungry. My car was in the carport, locked, with the alarm set—no damage anywhere.

The Gutburger shimmered like a fast-food oasis in my mind's eye. Within ten minutes, I was sitting, waiting for my order. Within the hour, I had eaten a large Denver omelet with fries and filled my third cup with coffee. The world was now a better place.

Try though I might, I had no recollection of anything after Anneliese slid into bed, and I ran my hands over her damp body. I had no idea about the manner in which I left The Broadway and the subsequent journey home. Answers to my questions would have to come from Anneliese. There was no real mystery; I would meet her again, and all would be explained. I wanted to see her again, desperately.

Perhaps I had activated the Julie Anderson curse and incurred an appropriate and reasonable punishment for a cheating asshole of a boyfriend. If that was the case, then let it bring down more punishment on my unworthy head as I was undoubtedly going to see Anneliese again.

Upon reflection, I could argue that, as there was no memory of the sex act itself, then sex might not have occurred. That being the case, I was exonerated of any evil doing except for the intent. Of that, I was definitely guilty. Somewhat reassured as fragmented memories returned, I decided to retrace my steps from last night and inquire at Broadway.

At the reception desk of the Broadway, I asked the clerk to call Anneliese. He asked for the name again. Anneliese Reinecke, I repeated.

"We don't have a listing for anyone of that name. Sorry, do you have a room number?"

"447. She's staying for a few days. Checked in last Friday, apparently."

He nodded, then, after a minute, shook his head and frowned.

"Not very helpful today, I'm afraid. There is no listing for anyone, Reinecke or Anneliese. Not only that, room 447 is closed. It has been for two weeks. The seven rooms on the top floor are all closed for renovation."

"I was there last night, room 447; I was a guest of Ms. Reinecke. I spent about two hours in the lounge and then on to room 447. Obviously, there's a mistake somewhere. Please check again."

I fished in the back of my wallet. Sure enough, the bar tab receipt.

"Look, this shows I was here last night, at least. I drank brandy; she drank white wine."

The clerk took the receipt, examined it for a few seconds, and then shook his head again. "This ticket shows you were here and spent cash in the lounge bar, but not last night. This is dated November 30. Today is November 21. It doesn't show the year; unfortunately, it looks very fresh, though. Perhaps the manager can help us."

The manager answered his page and promptly arrived—a neat dapper little man, anxious to help. A detailed explanation from the clerk produced the same frown and head shaking.

"Okay, first, let me show you room 447. While we are doing that, Harold will check for the night manager's bar receipts. That will show if there are problems with our date stamps."

I thanked him profusely for the help, feeling more and more like an idiot with every step. I knew perfectly well that Anneliese and I had been in bed in room 447. For how long, I couldn't say, and now it seemed I couldn't say when either.

Here I was again in the same elevator stopping on the same floor as last night. This time the manager was my companion, walking along the same dark-blue carpet to room 447. The double-sided do not disturb sign Anneliese placed there last night on the door handle still hung.

Inside, the room had changed. The large bed was stripped, sealed with a plastic sheet, and was in the middle of the room. No television or magazines were evident. There were no towels or soap, and a layer of dust covered the shower and hand basin. A painter's spray gun lay on a plastic sheet by the shower door. This room had seen no occupants for some time, just as the manager said.

We returned to the reception desk. Harold stared at the bar receipt again before returning it to me.

"All our date stamps print out perfectly. There is one thing, though." He handed me a bar receipt from last night. "This is an original from last night with the date and year, but our paper is pale green. The one you have is identical except for the year missing—and the paper is pale yellow."

He was absolutely correct.

"Gentlemen, I thank you for all your help. I have no explanation, but my apologies for wasting your time. There's obviously an explanation somewhere, but I don't know what it is. When I locate Anneliese, we will certainly spend a weekend here at The Broadway."

Harold smiled and shook my hand, as did the manager.

"I look forward to meeting Ms. Reinecke in the near future. When you check in to 447, you will stay in a newly decorated room. Take this complimentary voucher—good for two months—for two free days, double occupancy, in any room."

Returning to my apartment again, I made the bed with some effort and checked the sheets for blood. There was none.

It was impossible to form any conclusion or produce any reasonable explanation for the previous evening's strangeness. I must have fallen asleep on the bed, for it was now dark in my room. I looked at the clock—almost 8 pm. I had slept for five hours and felt much better for it. A large coffee on the balcony helped my frayed thinking processes function again with a degree of normality.

A few critical memories returned: meeting Anneliese in the cafe after Henry left and the amazing unnecessary rudeness and arrogance she seemed to delight in. She knew or had business with Henry. I would ask him at the next opportunity.

Again I slept deeply, waking Sunday morning at about 7 am, this time without an alarm. In the shower, I pulled away the Band-Aids covering the two wounds on my arm. Both were almost invisible, having healed perfectly—another bizarre legacy from last night.

CHAPTER 25

During the first half of December, Leticia was determined to visit as many local California locations as possible before the New Orleans vacation. For her, it was the last look at places her mother would frequent when she was alive, a sentimental journey for both of them, her mom peering from a freezer bag. This would be their last California visit together.

It had been more than ten years now since mama died. For more than ten years, her remains in the urn had been moved from room to room and from their house to an apartment. Soon they would say their last goodbyes in New Orleans.

But before that, there would be a weekend at the beach, a night in a cheap motel on the Pacific Coast Highway, then back to meet Andre for breakfast. As it happened, the late December weather was predictably miserable, but she endured, clambering over rocks with her mother in the face of cold wind with spray from the hurrying waves soaking through her clothes.

Also, this was a time of healing for her and a distraction from her profession's rigors. In particular, a near disaster when some turban-wearing idiot recently tried to burn down her bathroom. That was the worst experience she could remember. The bastards set her house on fire and robbed her, on the same day, all before lunch.

The wind blew sand and sea spray, covering her mother's plastic bag. Finally, enough was enough. Her mom had seen the beach and the sea again; she would be happy to return to the tranquility of her urn for a while.

It had been a happy two days. She'd eaten a light meal in the little café they would sometimes visit, drank coffee at the Fourth Street coffee shop, taken a long walk in the park, and now this quick trip to the beach. She returned to the motel, packed her wet clothes in a large plastic trash bag, and prepared to leave the following day. Later in the quiet evening hours, she thought seriously about her strange life and wondered about her minimal education; perhaps she should enroll in college and take courses like other people. What courses, though? A master's or doctorate in applied prostitution, or at the very least, a bachelor's in sexual diversity and fornication. And with thoughts of such grand ambitions and higher education swirling in her mind, she fell into a deep, peaceful sleep.

Leticia drove north toward Van Nuys from Seal Beach. She had arranged to have breakfast with Andre before his Monday 10 am shift started. Both north and south on the 405 freeway experienced congested lanes, as usual, offering no respite from the miserable stop-go-crawl conditions that commuters steeled themselves for each workday morning and evening.

Construction work further hampered a mile-and-a-half stretch of the northbound fast lane in the center divider.

Leticia decided to show her mother a final look at a California 405 freeway traffic jam before returning her to Louisiana. She reasoned that stopping on an off-ramp or hard shoulder would attract the unwanted attention of the Highway Patrol. Much better to pull onto the next off-ramp leading to an overpass over the freeway. Luckily there were only a few vehicles on the bridge, so she was able to perform a quick but blatantly illegal parking maneuver in the left lane.

She thought of Andre and how disappointed he would be with her naughty obstructive parking. Acknowledging her antisocial driving behavior, she activated the emergency flashers.

Just a second or two, then Mama Charlotte would have had her fill with the noise, fumes, and congestion that identify Southern California freeway systems.

Leticia lifted the heavy decorative plastic urn from behind the back seat and jogged a few yards to the place where there was a construction break in the safety wire mesh. At this point, she could look down at the stream of northbound traffic. The decorative urn had an equally decorative lid sealed with a thick plastic seal.

She tried to remove the lid as she had often done before, intending to take the transparent freezer bag containing her mother's ashes and hold it over the traffic below. Charlotte would then have a nearly unobstructed view of the crowded 405 freeway one more time. The urn had two large handles on either side, reminiscent of early Turkish design. A simple twisted knob was sufficient for a handgrip on the lid, but it was not designed for leverage.

Unfortunately, the lid had become stuck in place, held firmly by the seal. Try though she might, Leticia could not force open the top, although she had removed it easily the previous day.

It might have stuck because beach sand from the freezer bag had scraped off onto the seal as mom was replaced. Not the sort of girl to quit easily, Leticia seized the container by the lid knob. Now with one hand on a side handle and one hand firmly gripping the lid, she swung the urn in a high arc and then stopped suddenly, jerking at the cover.

Through experience, we all know that God works in the most mysterious ways, and we see he does because his plan worked perfectly. The lid came off; regrettably, the side handle also came off. A hairline crack, unnoticed before, caused the handle to break away suddenly, and Leticia was left holding the lid in one hand and most of the broken handle in the other.

Inside her airborne arc, Charlotte sailed gracefully over the traffic below. Like a gray pumpkin, the urn seemed to hover for a moment before plummeting into the vehicles below. This was undoubtedly Charlotte, the harlot's last ride.

The driver of a red Toyota Camry had no time for evasive action as Charlotte, in her flying chariot, exploded on his hood. His windshield fragmented, and he veered instinctively into the fast lane of traffic. Within seconds, a six-vehicle accident added to the already miserable morning commute.

Leticia gazed down in horror at the carnage below. Her last and abiding memory of her mother's final resting place was a small cloud of gray ash drifting lazily over stalled cars in the fast lane of the 405 freeway. She retreated quickly from the crime scene and away from the overpass bridge. She drove across surface streets before joining the freeway once more ahead of the accident.

Within minutes the radio announced the accident, giving alternate routes to avoid the mess and assuring commuters that the Highway Patrol would soon arrive.

The accident prevented traffic from flowing into the northbound freeway, and Leticia's drive improved significantly. A little before 9 am, she arrived for breakfast at the Gutburger. Andre was already waiting, and together they ate their morning meal while watching local television accounts of a freeway accident.

Andre frowned at the images. "You just missed that one, darling."

Leticia nodded innocently. By the time breakfast was over, more details had emerged. Apparently, a vehicle owned by drug dealers was driving erratically, attempting to avoid police.

A passenger in the car hurled a container, believed filled with cocaine or heroin, into oncoming traffic. Further details would be made available in the near future.

It took about four hours to clear the freeway lanes. Eventually, traffic continued north. A lack of witnesses hampered the police investigation.

Initial analysis of powder residue found on vehicles at the scene showed no indication of narcotics. Evidence obtained from heavy plastic fragments was inconclusive, but the investigation would continue.

A damaged transparent freezer bag was later recovered from the hard shoulder. Traces of powder similar to that found adhering to several vehicles were sent for further analysis. Later the following day, police issued a statement requesting information from the public. They were seeking the driver of a white or gray Volkswagen or small Ford seen in the vicinity of an overpass bridge overlooking the accident.

After serious consideration, Leticia decided not to tell Andre of her freeway adventure. She knew he had little tolerance for improperly parked vehicles. Certainly, none for one stopped illegally on an overpass in the left lane.

Leticia canceled their trip to New Orleans on the pretext that Charlotte much-preferred life in Southern California. Andre agreed with her decision, suggesting instead that they attend Saint Mary's midnight mass on Christmas Eve. He would ask the priest to mention Charlotte by name.

Leticia was sure her mother would have chosen to be remembered flying over the 405 freeway accompanied by the sounds of breaking glass and shrieking tires. An elegant, fitting memorial, she thought, to be remembered by many in the years to come.

Ariel Images of the freeway wreckage immortalized Charlotte on television while the further investigation continued.

The following Thursday, December 17, Henry listened in amazement to the news at a hastily called meeting of the secret six.

Chowdhury told of a terrible accident. "Just after 8 am Friday, our great and revered specialist Khalid Al-Mihdhar was struck down without warning. He was traveling on the accursed infidel freeway toward our mosque. A container fell from a low-flying aircraft, striking the vehicle next to him. The stupid, Godless driver of this car swerved into him, pushing his car into oncoming traffic.

Others struck his vehicle many times. Shielded by the grace of Allah, he is not dead but lies in the hospital, gravely injured. He will recover, but he will not be available to assist our holy jihad during that period. We will feel his noble presence at every turn; peace be upon him."

Chowdhury struck the table with his fist before continuing.

"I am sure these actions are of demonic origin. This disaster cannot be a simple coincidence. It is an obvious attempt by the church devil to pervert the course of our jihad."

Many questions remained unanswered, and many decisions had to be made.

"An alternative direction must be affirmed. We have the materials at hand and a plan in place. Our most significant change of instruction will be activating the detonators.

Without Khalid Al-Mihdhar, we do not have the experience or the knowledge to fabricate reliable circuitry for cell phone activation. Let us meet again in three days. Through the guidance and wisdom of Allah, I will have another method to trigger the detonators by that time."

Awab, a devoted member of the worshiping congregation and contributing participant of the secret six conspirators, asked a question. "If the devil, appearing on the wall of the church, was removed by the old priest through a ceremony of exorcism, why is it necessary to demolish the building?"

"A good question—one that was discussed at a previous meeting," Chowdhury replied. "The daemon was removed from the wall but not destroyed. There were many witnesses in the church at the time. The beast inhabits the building and will continue to do so. This creature is a great enemy. It will spread misery and desolation as long as it remains.

This church is no house of God, no holy dwelling. It is a dark place cursed by the presence of such horror and a real danger to the community. Our purpose is unchanged. We are right on the course we have charted."

Sporadic murmurings of agreement were heard, but for the first time, some at the table shook their heads, seeming to call into question their intent.

"Turnips and carrots come in many forms," Henry muttered. "It would seem I need only one now." He decided to attend the next meeting and learn the new method for igniting the explosives.

After a quick prayer for the speedy recovery of Al-Mihdhar, the meeting was adjourned for three days.

Julie returned from Washington after visiting with her parents for three weeks. "I've missed you so much, Jack, but we have to talk." She was full of news and overflowing with excitement.

I nodded, not sure what to expect.

She frowned as she usually did when trying to get my attention.

"Okay, here goes. You know dad and mom are not getting any younger. Dad is nearly seventy-six now."

I nodded again, remembering her description of the elderly Washington parents.

"They want me to move to DC—either live at their house, or they'll find an apartment for me. It all sounds good on the surface, but I don't want to end up as a nurse. It's bad enough with the waitress job here, but at least the weather's good."

I nodded again, trying to assimilate this news and corral my emotions. "Why don't we discuss this in bed? It's far more comfortable."

She laughed. "No, not yet. If we go to bed now, there will be no discussion, as you very well know. Perhaps a little later, when we both understand the options and implications of this conversation. I know you won't want to hear about my leaving, but this is serious—at least for me. I have to make a decision soon, and you're an important part of the process, Jack."

"How does Pete feel about this? I asked. His opinion is important too. There will be big changes for the boy if he must start school again in another state. A moment ago, you said it all sounds good on the surface. To me, it all sounds bad on the surface."
"Would you consider coming with me, though, Jack?"
"Yes, of course, but at the moment, it seems there are more cons than pros. I'll research the cost of living and job availability. I think DC is super expensive."

Julie smiled her dazzling smile. "Can't be more expensive than Southern California, surely? Something for you to think about, though."

Renting or buying any property in DC was very expensive, as I had been led to believe.
What were the advantages then? I suppose if Julie's parents rented an apartment for her, perhaps we could share that. There were a couple of recognized universities, so a teaching job for me was possible. The weather was not as favorable as in California for sure, but the downtown social life was apparently thriving, with plenty of good restaurants and clubs.

Still, I could see no advantage in uprooting, except I would be with Julie. At this time, I didn't think I wanted to or was ready to settle down with any woman. Julie would be a great choice, though. I wondered if she had considered the disruption to her doctoral program studies. She was more than halfway through writing her thesis. To undertake a move at such a time was a poor choice.

Suddenly, I remembered a brief conversation with Henry a few weeks ago. Something about *"Julie being only a distraction, a fine woman but not for me."* Those words would return to haunt me.

I wondered about the Muslims and their church demolition project. I wondered about Henry's involvement with that. But most of all, I wondered about the mysterious disappearing Anneliese.

On Sunday, December 20, A dark angel sat with the five Muslim plotters at a madrasa table. They had convened to hear Chowdhury explain a change to the explosive detonation process.

"You will all be heartened to learn that the esteemed Khalid Al-Mihdhar is recovering quickly. I saw him at the hospital on Thursday, and I was told he might be released by the first of January." After a smattering of applause had subsided, Chowdhury continued.

"As I told you at the last meeting, my brothers, by the grace and wisdom of Allah, through the goodwill of Khalid Al-Mihdhar in the hospital, I was given the knowledge to pursue a different method of detonating the explosives. The Tovex gel will initiate the main charges. Detonators will fire the gel. Instead of activating with cell phones as the revered expert Khalid Al-Mihdhar intended, we will fire the gel detonators with a safety fuse that is waterproof, flexible, and small."

He paused to gauge the audience's reaction.

"This is a simple and predictable method. Rather than electrical ignition, we will use an open flame. The burn time for these fuses is predictable, at about thirty seconds per foot. So, it is relatively easy to calculate the time needed for detonation. The length of the fuse will be decided soon. There will be a different length for each side of the main charges, of course.

A volunteer will light the street side fuse, walk through the gates, and light the graveside fuse.

The total burn time will be set to allow for an unhurried period so our volunteers may leave the target's vicinity without attracting attention. This is my proposal. If you have questions, please ask now, for it will be necessary to implement this plan within a few days."

Henry stood. "A quick question for you, brother Chowdhury. Exactly what time is the intended destruction to occur?"

"Thank you, my brother, during midnight mass on Christmas Eve. The mass begins at 11:40, just before midnight. By 12:15, a few passersby or vehicles will be on the street. I have checked with the almanac, and there is no full moon for six days, so we will have the darkness to help us."

The vampire nodded, pausing briefly before his next question. "When the midnight mass service has started, the church will be filled with people. It is a large church, holding many worshipers. How is this destruction of so many people justified?"

"You are correct, of course," Chowdhury replied. "All who continue to worship in that unclean place should expect the fiery hand of Allah to sweep away the evil. How many, I ask you, have not heard of the living daemon? How many have actually seen this creature?

Any, who sets foot inside that evil house, is complicit in a great blasphemy. None who enter there are Muslim. All within knowingly accept their responsibility, having turned their faces from righteousness. I spoke of the fiery hand of Allah. We are the burning hand of God. All assembled here were chosen for the jihad."

Sir Henry smiled and nodded before sitting. "Thank you for the clarification, brother Chowdhury. Peace be with you."

There were no more questions.

"The vest with the powerful Titadyn-30 sticks was made ready for Pablo, the gardener, as was the backpack. His wristband signaled that the device was tested and working," Chowdhury explained.

"Our esteemed brother here"—with a sweep of his hand, he indicated the seated vampire—"will work with the dirty old man, fitting the vest and setting the detonators in the pack."

Chowdhury continued to elaborate on the details of the plan. Using notepaper and pen, he confirmed the duties of all-present.

The primary charge material would be mixed on Thursday; one full day was allowed for this. Six 50-gallon steel drums must be filled.

The Tovex to be placed in each as detonators, and then the drums will be moved and secured on Friday. Then, Friday afternoon, two long-bed pickup trucks were to be driven from the rental company to the mosque.

A hired forklift would do the loading, with three containers on each truck; a simple one-way operation with no unloading would be needed. That evening, the bombs would be carefully positioned with their detonators in place.

Three of the chosen six would park their cars in the church parking lot, ensuring a place was reserved for the graveside truck. The roadside truck would be positioned as close to the start of the red zone as possible. As this was a no-parking area, there should be no vehicles obstructing the truck's positioning.

Later, under cover of darkness, the fuses would be set and ignited.

Henry smiled but said nothing. Their plan was horribly flawed. It had no exit strategy should the explosive fail to ignite. There were too many loose ends. If the explosions went as planned, there would be two demolished rental trucks to explain away; a rented forklift quickly traced also the presence of a known demolition expert and his activist partner in the vicinity.

There would be time enough to discuss the brilliance of the Chowdhury plan in the darkness of the mosque.

He would provide an excellent opportunity for that debate as Chowdhury dangled from the main door, suspended like a priest with no visible means of support and without an audience to interrupt or applaud.

"We will convene in two days. At that time, I will expect a volunteer to step forward to ignite the fuses. Peace be upon all assembled here, and may Allah smile upon this work in his name."

The next day, I met with Henry at the bistro, inside the dining room again, late Monday afternoon. He was already seated when I arrived. We exchanged greetings and shook hands, as was our custom. I was anxious to hear an update on Saint Mary's demolition scheme but just as interested in talking about Anneliese.

"Here's a deal for you, Henry: I'll buy dinner in exchange for a tiny bit of information."

He grinned. "Then perhaps we should go to the Broadway. I hear the food is delicious, although I have never eaten there."

I felt the hairs rise on the back of my neck. Did he know about Anneliese, then? Well, so what? I was not a baby and had nothing to hide—except from Julie, perhaps.

"The food here is just fine and much less expensive than The Broadway. Anyway, the pinch of information I'm after is so small that a Gutburger breakfast would be more than enough."

"Very well, young Jack, a compromise then. Dinner here first, then information exchanged over coffee."

"A perfect solution. While we're waiting for food, how about an update on the Saint Mary's situation?"

Sir Henry smiled. "Yes, and then a progress report from you on the plankton situation."

I nodded, knowing I had little to report except a few vague ideas. Henry told me of the Sunday meeting he attended, how the explosives and detonators were in storage in the maintenance building, and the plan ready to implement on Christmas Eve. For the first time, I became aware of the reality.

Within three days, there could be a catastrophic incident resulting in a considerable loss of life. A few weeks ago, this unreal fragmented scheme that Henry discussed with me had now evolved into the awful vision of an imminent and horrific disaster.

"Will you be able to stop this?" I asked.

"Yes, Jack. I cannot allow this to continue. If I don't intercede, then other forces will. The queen and pawns are already in play in this celestial chess game of ours. I am, after all, and with regret, responsible to a great extent."

"You are responsible for sticking a child molester to a wall, nothing else. The erroneous conclusions drawn by a crew of simple-minded bigots are not your responsibility."

Henry stared past me, gazing into a place beyond my vision or understanding. "Perhaps," he replied. "But the philosophical considerations are meaningless. I intend to stop this Christmas day madness." He sighed wearily.

"Very well, young Jack; here is the latest update for you." He told me briefly of the freeway accident and the derailed Jihad.

"This is no longer a game of words or consideration of possibilities; here is a picture of scorched bone shards and burning flesh. There will be children in the congregation when the church is demolished and other innocents slaughtered and maimed in the name of a God weary of free choice, tired of the freedom he gave to fools. This ain't no disco, Jack."

"No, this is premeditated murder by majority agreement, I think."

"Murder by eight people and more," he replied. "Bleating sheep as always led by a couple of fanatics blinded by half-truths and conditioned thinking—all in the name of their personal God. Through the ages, every technological advance brings with it a universal need for stupidity to become the next norm."

I nodded, considering his words. It was many seconds before I spoke.

"Here is another deal for you then, Henry. During the first week of the new year, I will most happily buy dinner for us at The Broadway."

He grinned and nodded his head. "I will hold you to that, young Jack. There will be much to talk about."

We ate in silence: shrimp and stuffed potato for me, a large rare porterhouse steak for Henry. The food, as usual, was excellent. Julie was not working for another week, so the dining area still lacked something. The word *sparkle* came to mind.

I told Henry of Julie's plan to possibly move to Washington. He listened but did not comment. Two glasses of Red wine were served, although I didn't remember ordering it; I did remember drinking two glasses, though. Agreeable small talk punctuated the space between two more glasses.

Eventually, over coffee, I told him some details of the plankton project.

"You will find they are attracted to sunlight, not sound," he said. "As interesting as your project is, I doubt there is a financially tenable way of processing them. A floating platform like an oil rig with a large volume centrifuge to separate the little fellows is one way to do it, but hardly economical. At the very least, you will have the collection, processing, transportation, and distribution."

He sipped his coffee before continuing.

"Krill being that much bigger would be easier to harvest, but to process them economically for mass consumption is another matter. If you were able to think beyond feeding the Third World, perhaps processing them commercially as a natural oil supplement would be better."

I shook my head, amazed at Henry's ability to think through problems unrelated to his area of expertise. "If you want a consulting position at the institute, please let me know," I said.

He chuckled. "Interesting work, but the money isn't there yet. Anyway, I am currently fully involved with a church demolition project."

I suddenly felt a pang of guilt. Here I was, prattling on about my work. At the same time, Henry faced the unenviable responsibility of saving many people's lives in a packed church—a responsibility he chose to accept. That was more than anyone should have to bear.

It was probably the wine affecting my thinking, but I felt a wave of deep sadness wash over me. I saw Henry fleetingly as a noble figure, alone but resolved in his purpose.
"Okay, but I will say again, Henry: If there is anything I can do for you or help in any way, let me know. I am only a phone call away." I shook my head. "Hell of a time to pick, Christmas Eve. Peace and goodwill toward men obviously don't apply to these cretins."

He smiled and nodded but made no reply. We sat in silence for some time, both of us seemingly occupied with our own thoughts.
After a little while, Henry stood from the table.
"Jack, I have to go. As always, good to see you again. I doubt we will meet before Christmas. I will keep you abreast of the happenings at Saint Mary's."
"Yes, please do so, Henry. Remember, if I can do anything to help, just call. Have a great Christmas, and anyway, I'll call you after lunch on the 25th."
We shook hands, and he walked to the door, or rather he seemed to fade before he reached the door. I never saw him open it.

CHAPTER 26

I sat again, thinking of our conversations during dinner. With a start, I realized I had forgotten to mention Anneliese. *Too much wine, probably,* I thought. Within fifteen minutes, I downed another cup of coffee, paid the bill, and headed home.

It was a twenty-minute brisk walk from the bistro to my apartment. Over the years, I developed a habit of thinking through problems while walking. I found this therapy to be productive and relaxing. Sometimes though, I would forget where I was and be forced to regroup and retrace my steps.

No matter how determined I was to take note of my surroundings, it was not unusual for me to suddenly realize I did not know where I was.

This evening was dark, with no moon and a good chance of rain. The unusually warm air clung heavily to me, and the smell of ozone and sulfur bought the warning of a coming thunderstorm. After some time, I slowed my pace and, for the first time that evening, took notice of my surroundings.

I had no idea where I was. I must have walked from the bistro to my apartment a hundred times, following a broad, brightly lit main road with light traffic at this time of night. But now, there was nothing—no cross street, no lights from passing cars, and no street sounds.

I peered at my watch in the low prevailing light. 9:40. I should be home or at least very close by now, but instead, I stood before a wide dark road with no buildings that I recognized, just indistinct threatening shapes behind the darkness.

Once again, I had wandered from whatever path I had started upon.

There were no sounds either, which sent a chilling foreboding through my bones. *How was this possible?*

Okay, too much wine for sure, but where the hell was I? This was the city, not some dark backcountry lane.

Turning and looking at the road from where I had just come brought no comfort. The street was the same in front or behind me: a wide featureless ribbon of black highway, unwelcome and unfamiliar.

After a few minutes of panic and indecision, I decided to continue. The road from the bistro was one I could navigate blindfolded to reach my apartment. Drunk though I was, I had definitely not changed direction.

Walking slowly, I thought I could hear footsteps behind me. Many times I stopped suddenly, turning and listening intently for those imagined steps. The only sounds were from my shoes on the road, sounding loudly against a somewhat ominous silence.

Trying to note my surroundings, I approached a large building that seemed to radiate an unpleasant pale yellow glow. It was vaguely familiar somehow. As I drew closer, I saw, to my astonishment, a flickering sign high above the front entrance. In bold red letters, it announced The Broadway Hotel.

A sickly yellowish light covered the building, presumably radiating from the neon sign above. What should have been an enormous relief to me now increased my anxiety. This was not The Broadway I knew so well, and if indeed it was the hotel, then I had been walking in the wrong direction, which might explain some of the puzzle but not the lack of streetlights or the silence.

There was a malevolent aspect to the place, reminding me of an old abandoned movie set, a façade that deceived the senses with nothing of substance within. For some time, I stared at the building before me. Everything about this place was different from the hotel where Anneliese and I met. It stood alone, waiting in the darkness, with no other buildings or structures nearby.

The Broadway I knew was close to a bustling shopping mall with many stores on either side of the street. Within a few yards, there was a sizeable well-lit intersection with a crossing and stoplights. My confusion deepened. There was no other hotel within several miles of the Broadway.

I must be asleep somewhere, lost in a strange dream.

Then came the panic. I remembered leaving the restaurant after settling the bill and remembered wishing Henry goodnight. I remembered how he never opened the door to leave.

I must still be at the restaurant, asleep in the chair. I stared at my watch again. 10:52. But just now, on the road, it had been 9:40. I had not walked for another hour for sure. I couldn't think clearly now beyond the wine, confusion, and rising fear.

No matter how lost I was, here at least was a landmark—and one where I hoped to find directions. Dreaming or not, I decided to go inside.

I walked hesitantly through the double glass doors and into the main lobby. The reception desk before me was the same as I remembered from my last visit. A bright young woman happily answered my inquiries.

"Yes, this is the Broadway–and the only Broadway I know of."

I thanked her and then walked around the lobby to where I remembered the elevators were. So far, everything in the hotel was as I remembered it, except the depressing yellow lighting. The lounge seemed the same, with only a few customers scattered at various tables.

There was something very wrong here, or perhaps very wrong with me. In any restaurant or bar that I have ever visited, there is noise, sounds of laughter, murmur of conversation, and an overall indication of humanity. Here there was an unnatural silence.

My estimate of time passing was strangely at odds with my watch. I glanced at the bar clock; my watch agreed within a few minutes. I had been here for at least an hour, although it seemed as if only a few minutes had passed. No, there was definitely a problem.

Perhaps I talked with the girl at reception for a minute or so, but certainly not more than an hour. Passing the reception desk again, the girl smiled.

"Would you be Mr. Cordell?" she asked.

"I used to be, but now I'm not sure. Do we know each other?"

She laughed. "Oh no, but I do have a message for you. Shall I read it? No, on second thought, I'm not too sure how to pronounce the name."

She passed me a piece of paper, upon which was written *Jack. Call, please. Anne Reinecke.*

I stared at the note and then at the receptionist. "And what number would you suppose I should call?" I asked.

"Oh, sorry, that would be internal. Number 447—her room number."

I stared at her for a long time. "Many thanks. A small favor if you would. Please call 447 and tell Anneliese I will meet her at the bar. I intend to drink even more than I already have—that last part is just between you and I, Miss?"

"Please call me Susan, Mr. Cordell. I will make that call for you now."

"Thanks, Susan. Please call me Jack."

I was proud of the way I reined in my excitement. Had I been alone, I would have pumped my fist in the air and yelled. The thought of holding Anneliese again was deliciously enticing. Perhaps now there would be answers to all the mysteries surrounding our last meeting.

I walked down the stairs and onto the sidewalk to be greeted by a soft refreshing breeze, the air clean and cool. The early morning light showed cars on Broadway in silhouette, their headlights throwing twisted, moving shadows on the hotel's wall behind me.

I felt no surprise; Susan was not behind the desk when I returned, and It was no surprise at all to find the lounge bar closed, although I had been gone for no more than five minutes.

Despite the crushing disappointment I felt, I knew it would be pointless pursuing Anneliese again.

Life was growing everywhere around me. I heard whispers of sound and movement. Tiny blossoms of light and color were sprouting from the darkness, bringing with them relief and a goodly amount of gratitude.

When I reached home, I would call the institute and present an update on my investigations. I started my walk back to the apartments with renewed confidence. Daylight brought hope, washing away all previous traces of fear and uncertainty.

I would shower and sleep. Perhaps even find enough courage to call Anneliese, maybe not. Either way, I was again grounded in a familiar, comforting reality—a return to my boring life far from vampires, daemons, evaporating hotels, and disappearing women. A simple, comfortable state that I could cling to if the world crashed down around me.

Later over coffee and in the reassuring bright morning daylight, there would be time enough to think through the frightening events of the night.

CHAPTER 27

The last meeting at the madrasa before completing the holy jihad was convened on Tuesday, December 22. The school was canceled for the day to allow the previous gathering of the secret six. As usual, the Pakistani Chowdhury addressed the meeting. Opening the dialogue with blessings and a short prayer, he asked for a volunteer willing to ignite the main charge fuses.

The scribe Abdul Azeez raised his hand. "I am driving the roadside truck. It will be a simple task for me to light the fuses when I have positioned my vehicle."

"The committee thanks you and the wisdom of Allah will surely guide your hand," Chowdhury said. "All pieces are now in play. Timing is important, but to a lesser extent, now we are decided upon manual ignition for the main charges. Before I repeat the sequence of actions for the last time, are there any questions?"

There were none.

"Thank you, my brothers. Tomorrow, four of our members will gather at the maintenance building at 9:00 in the morning. A show of hands from the four."

Four of the six seated raised their hands.

Chowdhury smiled and nodded. "Very good. The main charges will be mixed and made ready tomorrow. This evening, two open-bed pickup trucks will be available from the rental company reserved for our purpose. Both drivers, Abdul and Fahim will deliver the vehicles to the maintenance shed this evening. A forklift will be provided to us on Wednesday the 23rd in the afternoon."

He looked at the small audience and smiled, stroking his beard—a nervous habit Henry found most annoying. *I suspect his mother does the same with the hair under her nose, probably where he acquired the practice as a baby.*

"I think we are clear in our purpose and understanding so far?"

Heads nodded in agreement.

"I will continue then. As soon as the forklift delivery driver leaves, both trucks will be loaded with three barrels each. At that time, labels will be placed on the barrels and truck doors. They are self-adhesive."

He produced two samples, passing them to the others. They were about fifteen by eight inches, with dark green lettering on a white background. They were professionally made and nicely designed. The first was for each barrel.

EPA WATER RECLAMATION PROJECT
NOT FOR HUMAN CONSUMPTION

The others only:

EPA WATER RECLAMATION PROJECT

They were intended for the front doors of each truck.

"These are to allay suspicions should anyone decide to investigate more closely."

Heads nodded with approval, along with a little more beard-stroking and smiling from Chowdhury.

"Very well, then. To continue, my brothers, on December 24, both trucks will be in position between 11:00 and 11:15. They will be parked as close to the building walls as possible. Three vehicles will be holding a space for the graveside truck.

When the graveside truck arrives, one vehicle, the Mercedes that is driven by brother Awab—will remain while the other two will leave.

Our brother Abdul Azeez will drive the roadside truck. He will leave the vehicle and wait in the Mercedes. His wristband will signal the time to light the fuses. When both fuses are burning, he will again join Awab and Fahim in the Mercedes. As their part is finished, the Mercedes will return to the mall parking lot, and Abdul and Fahim will go their separate ways."

There was a long pause and murmuring of voices as the assembly considered the plan.

Chowdhury asked for questions again. Again there were none.

"The last part will be the gardener Pablo's contribution. He will arrive at the site driven by our worthy brother Henry, who will fit the vest and set the backpack's detonators. When he is satisfied that all is correct, he will leave the target and drive away. At exactly 12:15, Pablo will be notified by his wristband signal to detonate the vest. By that time, the main charge fuses will initiate the Tovex.

Within fifteen minutes, first responders will arrive at the site. There will be confusion, panic, weeping, and screaming, but the evil will be vanquished.

Once again, he asked if anyone had questions. As before, there were none. Chowdhury smiled his oily smile and pulled his thin straggly beard before launching into a long rambling prayer, thanking all in attendance for their support.

At 5 pm on December 23, the vampire entered the church. As he closed the doors behind him, a young priest emerged from the vestibule. A genial fellow weighed down heavily by many righteous good intentions. He offered his hand.

"Good afternoon, I am Father Evans. How may I help you?"

Henry smiled. "A pleasure to make your acquaintance, Father Evans. I am Henry Smith." Shaking hands, Henry explained his small dilemma. "My friend Pablo is old and somewhat infirm. He does not speak English fluently, although he tries. As a matter of fact, you may know him. He cuts the grass and tends to the cemetery here."

"Yes, yes, I have met him on a few occasions. He seems to be a good man, giving his time freely."

The vampire nodded. "Yes, that would be Pablo. Here is the situation, father. Pablo is very concerned by the plight of the—no, your—your impoverished parishioners. To that end, he is planning a small display in the church."

Henry explained in as much detail as he thought necessary, omitting the live chicken release. The priest nodded thoughtfully.

"Well, I'm glad you told me. For him to interrupt, the mass would be intolerable. He should go through the proper channels at a reasonable time and ask permission." Henry laughed, pointedly shaking his head, and continued with heavy sarcasm.

"Of course, he should; how silly of me. I forgot there are always proper channels and reasonable times. Does your God require that the poor address him through appropriate channels asking for food?

At what time should they do so? Perhaps the correct and proper channel information and a list of reasonable times—Pacific Standard, of course—should be made available and posted next to the wall notice asking for donations.

Am I to assume that a 'reasonable time' for his display would be when the church is empty, and nobody would possibly be inconvenienced?"

Father Evans glared at the vampire, blood flushing his face with anger. He started to reply and then stopped himself. After several seconds he continued.

"You made me very angry, but then I realized my anger was misplaced. Often, we of the church are beguiled by our own self-importance, misled by beliefs other than our mission's simple truth. I apologize. Pablo must give his address to the worshipers—but not standing by a wall at the back where he will not be seen or heard, but instead here, where I stand before the altar.

He may use the microphone so all will hear him clearly. Mass will not begin until he has finished speaking. I will see you when you arrive and announce to the congregation that our gardener, mister Pablo, will speak. As you say, his English pronunciation is not so good. I will stand with him and translate as necessary."

The priest smiled. "If he is any good, he can give the Sunday sermon next week—free of charge, of course."

There was nobody else in the church at that time, so there were no witnesses available to recount how, for probably the first time in history, a vampire hugged a Catholic priest in a large church.

There is hope, after all, thought Henry. Within the walls of this highly ornamental house, where bullshit accumulates quickly and in vast quantities, humanity is found in the most unlikely places. He doubted Father Evans would ever experience the unwanted intrusion of a greasy vegetable.

As the time for destruction drew near, some of the conspirators had misgivings. Many of the faithful also doubted the wisdom of these radical actions. "How are simple people worshiping in a church suddenly our enemies'? They asked among themselves.

"True, a devil was seen on a wall in their church, but a priest quickly removed it, and it has not been seen since. We know these Christians. They are not worshipers of evil. On the buses and in the stores, we sit together and stand side by side. Now suddenly, on the word of a foreigner, we are to take instruction in such a grave matter as to kill others? No, this is not the Muslim way."

Rather late in the day, but many Muslim worshipers from the mosque made several failed attempts to reach various members of the secret six. A few long-standing members of the mosque held a hastily-convened meeting. A junior director and two management staff members were in attendance and listened wide-eyed and horrified as the overall plan was unveiled.

Sir Henry Smith answered his front door to a timid knock. Before him, as expected, stood a nervous Pablo, the gardener.

They sat together for an hour or so, Henry explaining again the sequence of events that Pablo should expect. There was no misunderstanding, as the native language spoken between them was Spanish.

"I have decided to sit in the church to wait with you as you give your demonstration."

This pleased the old man greatly.

"This afternoon, I spoke with Father Evans. He will allow you to speak by the altar. I will pass your backpack to you when the wristband flashes. This way, you do not have to support the weight while standing."

The little gardener smiled, thanking the vampire many times.

"So, I will be there to help you in any way I am able. One more time, so there is no mistake, let us drink to your great success."

As Henry indicated a large bottle of Don Julio tequila, Pablo displayed another huge smile.

"You will come here tomorrow at 11 pm. I will drive you to the church. We will enter the church together and sit together. When your indicator signal flashes, you and I will stand and move to the podium by the altar.

I will fix the vest switch, help you with the backpack, and return to my seat. I will count off two minutes and raise my hand.

You then throw open your coat and begin speaking with the congregation. You no longer have to strike the large red button in the center of the vest."

Pablo listened intently and nodded.

"After you demonstrate what is in the vest, show what is in the backpack."

Pablo nodded. "I am demonstrating fuel sticks for the heaters, then a heater in the bag on my back. This is correct, yes?"

The vampire smiled. "No, there is a change. Unfortunately, fuel and heaters proved too expensive. Only a few would be available to distribute. So, much better for the poor people, food will be provided for many of them—all the ingredients they need to make *posole*.

Many chicken and cheese *tamales* will be made available as well. Through the generosity of the Main Street Light of Hope Mosque, this food will provide enough to feed 200 families."

The old man shook his head. "Generous indeed, sir. This mosque is the pretty building that is a house of worship on Main Street?"

Henry nodded.

"I have seen the place," Pablo said. "So, then, what am I demonstrating now?"

"You will demonstrate vegetables on the vest and five live chickens in the backpack. The chickens are advertising hens, each representing the five wounds of Christ. When people have seen the vegetables, you will open the backpack and throw each chicken into the air, one at a time. They are young and healthy and will fly about over the seated worshipers, causing much joy and astonishment."

Pablo stared at Henry, saying nothing and shaking his head as the vampire continued with his instructions.

"Each chicken will have a label attached to its leg. A message on the label will wish everyone a happy Christmas and give a telephone number for the mosque. There will also follow instructions for the impoverished to obtain food.

Now, there will undoubtedly be some last-minute changes. I will let you know tomorrow."

"Yes, sir, much better than heaters and fuel," the old man nodded vigorously. "A demonstration like a festival with live animals. Perhaps we could also bring goats and sheep?"

The vampire laughed. "Perhaps at another time."

Pablo grinned and nodded.

"Not for your demonstration tomorrow, though. There is not enough time. But think of this. We will organize a food festival for the poor. Both houses of worship will participate. It could be held at the Aeron Glass Marine Institute on Broadway.

They have a large grassy area behind the main building that could be used. I know a scientist working there. He would help, I'm sure. Should that not be possible, I am sure there will be any number of other sites that would be made available to the cause.

We will have plenty of live animals, pigs, goats, sheep, and perhaps cows and horses. Chickens and ducks as well, maybe even turkeys."

The old gardener was now smiling broadly. "A fine idea, sir. I am sure we will find many volunteers to help us. We could name it the Saint Mary's Food Festival, with all donations being used to buy food for the poor."

Henry considered the possibilities for many seconds before replying. "Yes, a fine idea, indeed. We will meet together later in the New Year. I will speak to my friend at the marine center when we meet for lunch at the Gutburger. I would insist on one meaningful change, though.

As good as your suggestion for the name was, it is not appropriate."

Pablo's eyes widened, and he glanced quickly at the vampire. "What then would you have this festival named?" He asked.

Henry leaned back in his chair. "Considering the importance of this food festival and the fame it will soon generate—through newspapers, local radio, and television—I envision large banners with the title 'The Pablo Gonzales Festival and Food Drive.' After all, we should give credit to those who are deserving. What do you think?"

Within the hour, good tequila was consumed, followed by a cup or two of strong coffee. The vampire drove the old gardener home. After well-wishings and hand-shaking, Henry drove to the mosque.

Parking his car on a side street a block from the building, he walked—a transparent shadow shape sliding through the ornamental hedges and gardens—until he came to a large wooden structure at the side of the main building. Through the closed double doors, the wispy misty form passed. On a sidewall to his right, an array of garden tools hung neatly on hooks and brackets; the larger ones were carefully arranged between wooden rails. A few yards from the front doors, two pickup trucks stood waiting.

At the back of the building stood six blue 50-gallon steel barrels, all fully prepared with three Tovex gel packets secured inside and held in place with screw-on caps. A hole had been drilled in each cap, through which passed a long coiled length of safety fuse. One end of the fuse was crimped into a detonator buried in the first Tovex packet.

Henry studied the array of explosives and pondered the situation. He briefly considered lighting a fuse or two and letting the cards fall where they may. One barrel exploding would undoubtedly touch off the other five. With such a reaction, the mosque would probably be demolished. He considered again, eventually deciding to deactivate the detonators.

Having finalized his plan, he quickly left the building to secure supplies at the nearby supermarket. Into the darkened market, he went unseen and unnoticed by the remaining cleaning crew.

After a lengthy search in the fresh meat and deli section, he secured eight precooked and smoked Kielbasa-type German sausages, each about twelve inches long.

The sort of fine pork sausage one may comfortably eat with a little rich gravy, boiled potatoes, and a light mint dressing, perhaps topped with a few small steamed white mushrooms and young asparagus shoots. Drawn butter would complement the asparagus nicely and add to the complexity of the delicate flavors—a simple, tasty meal, lending itself well to a glass of fine Merlot.

He also took six packaged uncooked pork chops and twelve plastic bags.

Within twenty minutes, he was again back inside the maintenance building, making the necessary changes. He unscrewed the barrel caps, recoiling at the pungent odor of the vapors from the nitro mix. He carefully removed the Tovex packages and separated them from the detonators by pulling at them gently.

His next step was to detach the fuses by cutting them, leaving about two inches still crimped into each detonator.

Pushing a hole through each pork chop with a small potting fork prong, he passed approximately two feet of fuse through each chop and then forced about eight inches of fuse into each flavorful sausage.

Every delicately seasoned sausage was secured to its pork chop with a length of rough twine. These assemblies were passed through the threaded hole in each barrel, and the caps were replaced and tightened. He pulled the fuse gently until feeling a slight resistance.

From the outside, it was impossible to detect any change.

In reality, there was no active propellant to initiate the primary charge explosives when the fuses were lit. The burning fuse would expire in a sheath of delectable sausage meat.

The vampire packed the eighteen Tovex sleeves in plastic bags; in all but one of the remaining bags, he stored the detonators and the two extra sausages he laid in the remaining bag. This would be his Christmas dinner.

Checking carefully around the scene of his activities, he saw nothing that might attract attention. Retracing his steps, he placed the explosive bags in the trunk of his car and drove slowly to his apartment.

CHAPTER 28

Henry Smith, an Angel, was holding down the line;
he was fixing people's problems, but he never did fix mine

Just before 11:30 am, Abdul Azeez parked the roadside truck. He had a favored position inside the red zone and toward the rear of the church. There were few vehicles and almost no foot traffic on the chilly Christmas Eve day.

He left the vehicle but quickly returned, deciding to minimize the distance between the truck and the church wall.

Reversing the vehicle for several yards, he then jumped the front and rear wheels onto the sidewalk. A few more yards, and the truck, now half on the sidewalk and half on the road, was parked to his satisfaction.

About fifteen minutes earlier, the graveside truck had arrived. As planned, the three occupying vehicles moved to allow room for the truck to secure a good position.

It was the perfect place because the truck's side was facing the front of the building, only a few feet away. Awab took an available position in front of the truck, parking the Mercedes and waiting with Abdul Azeez.

At 11:35, a bright yellow Volkswagen pulled into the parking lot. Andre and Leticia arrived a little earlier than planned. This timing would allow Andre plenty of time to talk to the priest about mentioning Leticia's mother in remembrance during the service.

Although on vacation until the first of the year, Andre couldn't ignore so many flagrant violations committed by an obviously drunken truck driver. Walking back to the truck with Leticia, he noted the license plate information and the EPA WATER RECLAMATION data on the door and barrels. He knew it was unusual for a state agency not to include an address or phone number, but that was the very least of the department's anomalies.

He was suddenly overcome with righteous anger. Not only had this demented creature parked a truck in the red zone, but it was obstructing the sidewalk as well.

He muttered loudly to himself about the selfish, antisocial behavior of the imbecilic thug driver.

Leticia bit her bottom lip, remembering her recent creative parking display on the freeway overpass.

Andre's long-time friend and city tow truck driver LeShawn would work until 5:00 am Christmas morning. A short phone call and the stinking violator would be removed very quickly.

LeShawn smiled broadly. Andre had undoubtedly picked a justifiable example of stupidity this time. He could imagine Andre's outrage. Red zone, *no parking anytime* sign, no lights, and on the sidewalk of all things. *What an idiot.* Within ten minutes, the truck with barrels in place was secured on his flatbed, and he was dieseling along Main Street to the impound yard.

"Thanks for that one, brother. You picked a real winner."

"Yeah, a true genius," Andre said into his phone. "There's another one—same truck, same agency. This one's in the church parking lot. The fool's parallel with the chain-link fence, taking up four spaces."

"What an asshole, another drunk part-timer, probably. Well, I'll see you guys before NewYears'. Might even buy the beer."

"Sounds good to me, friend. We'll meet soon, and I'll most definitely join you for a beer, Have a great Christmas." Andre smiled, closing his phone and slipping his arm around Leticia's waist as they walked to the front entrance.

Unfortunately, Abdul, Fahim, and Awab were unaware of the tragic fate befalling the roadside truck, as it was invisible to them from the Mercedes. The church effectively blocked the Broadway side of the road from view. For about two hundred yards, nothing could be seen except an old gray stone church wall.

Later that evening, as arranged, Pablo met with the vampire at his house.

"I hear you are a great public speaker, amigo."

"I'm not afraid, sir."

"Very good then, Pablo." Henry Gaytooth recounted his conversation with Father Evans in detail. "Would you be ready for this task?"

Much to his surprise, the old gardener smiled.

"Many of my friends will be there," Pablo said. "The right words will come to me because I am asking God to help others. No one will judge me for the words I use, but rather by the feeling in the words."

The vampire shook his head and smiled. "I have found hope for the second time this week." He whispered under his breath.

"This is good, my friend. I will be there with you. The vest is not needed now. We need only your words of wisdom and the white birds in the backpack."

"Sir, Mister Chowdhury said how important the vest was to his plan. Are you sure we do not need to use it?"

Henry spoke quickly in English. "That puffy posturing fool should have his plan in his ass, along with a large turnip. This will soon come to pass." Then he explained just as quickly in Spanish so Pablo would understand: "Not to worry, my friend. Mister Chowdhury will be more than happy with no vest."

The old man smiled, relieved that any possible conflict was resolved.

"Another detail for you to consider, my friend. As good Father Evans will call you when we are seated, the flashing wrist signal will not be needed either. Just leave it with the vest, here with me."

Although Pablo did not see the vampire load the chickens into the backpack, he could hear them scratching and rustling as they changed position.

"One more rehearsal before we leave, my friend. Then we go."

The old gardener nodded.

"After speaking and addressing the congregation, wish everybody a very happy Christmas. Then tell the audience that you have five white birds for them to see, and they represent the five wounds of Christ. The birds will fly as you throw each one in the air. There is no more to say. You then sit again next to me."

Pablo smiled widely, proud to have been chosen for such a great task. "I will have no problem at all, sir."

Henry and Pablo arrived at the church well past 11:00 pm, and the vampire noted the nearly full parking lot, the conspirators' Mercedes, the graveside truck, and a familiar yellow Volkswagen.

He did not see the roadside truck and assumed it had not yet arrived. *Somewhat tardy*, he thought, *surely not the first thread of the plan unraveling.*

From his car, Abdul Azeez was the first to spot Henry and Pablo, the gardener. He nudged Fahim, opened his phone, and called Chowdhury. "In position. Everything is as planned."

"Wonderful, I will signal the old martyr then. When the countdown is complete, you will be notified. Allah, please bring peace to you, my brothers, and fill your hearts with joy.

May your paths be forever illuminated by the brilliance of his wisdom."

From his car, Awab was the first to see the four arrivals approach the church. His startled cry caused his companions to spin about in their seats. He pointed to the church door.

Two men and two women walked together. Both men wore the unmistakable white *thowb* upon their heads, the traditional *taqiyah* head covering. Both women wore *khimars*, obscuring their hair and falling over their shoulders. Anyone of the faith would recognize the four as traditional Muslims.

"How can this be?" Awab cried. "Our brothers and sisters are passing through the doors of this awful, unclean house of sinners."

"Nevertheless, it is so. Four of our own flesh," Fahim said.

"That we have seen," said. Awab "How many more are already seated, do you suppose?"

Fahim shook his head, greatly troubled by this latest situation.

"Our brothers are in this temple, and soon it will be destroyed; this must stop now."

Awab opened his phone to call Chowdhury and explain the terrible situation. He waited for a few seconds as Chowdhury considered his reply.

Awab snapped his phone shut, staring ahead for some time before detailing the reply.

"We are told to proceed. Chowdhury claims that the people we saw were police agents dressed in Muslim clothes to disguise themselves. I think this is a poor judgment and lies from a false babbling prophet."

The young scribe, Abdul Azeez, shook his head. "This man is a fool. By what shining revelation is he guided to say such a thing? He is not with us to see anything!"

"You were the first to call for this jihad," Fahim said, looking at the scribe. "Since then, this Pakistani has directed our work as if it were his own. We asked for help and direction from Khalid Al-Mihdhar and Chowdhury within their field of expertise—only that and no more. Here in this car is the true director. What is your decision, brother Abdul?"

"No Muslim shall die by my hand," he answered. "It is by no means the will of Allah, I think. I will go to the roadside truck and pull the fuse," he said, leaving his seat.

"No," cautioned Awab, restraining him with his arm across his shoulder. "Better to leave the fuse in place until we have advice or taken instruction on this situation. Pulling it might trigger the detonator."

Abdul nodded after a moment's consideration. "I will go quickly to the church then and tell our brother Henry not to let the martyr activate his vest." He left the Mercedes and ran to the church.

Inside, the start of Pablo's small demonstration was delayed, and all seating was occupied, for the building was filled to capacity. Four strangers, men and women, stood inside by the door, all wearing traditional Muslim clothing.

Father Evans approached the small group and introduced himself. "Thank you all for coming. You are most welcome here. Please wait a minute or two while I find chairs for you to sit in; as you can see, we are full to overflowing."

The older man shook the priest's hand, thanking him for his kindness. He introduced himself as Qasim and then introduced the others. "I am a Muslim and a working manager at the Light of Hope Mosque. You are, of course, always welcome at our house."

As Evans left to arrange seating, Abdul walked quickly through the open doors. He was at once challenged by Qasim, who immediately denounced the plot to destroy the building. Abdul nodded, telling Qasim to wait before he walked rapidly to the front of the building and beckoned to the seated vampire. In a hushed voice, he explained the reason for his presence and cautioned Henry to leave the vest untouched.

"We believe there is no good reason to continue with this plan. We have many problems within our hearts and conscience, and most agree that the evil daemon that showed itself to us on the wall is gone. So convinced are we that four Muslims from the mosque wait at the back by the door. None among us will kill another Muslim for any reason, and we know now Chowdhury is mistaken for directing us to do so.

I have spoken with one of the four as I entered. I know this man. He is Qasim, a manager, not a police agent, as Chowdhury would have us believe."

"It is done," Henry replied. "Before I left, I found fault with the vest and backpack. They would not function as intended. So instead of this heater demonstration, the old man Pablo will make a brief plea for food to feed the impoverished.

I must say my heart overflows with joy at the thought that many innocents will be spared because of your humanity. A question, though, what happened to the roadside truck? What manner of problems did you encounter?"

Abdul stared at the vampire. "Problems? My brother. What problems? I delivered the truck myself at the appointed time. I was to have set the fuse on Chowdhury's signal."

It was Henry's turn to stare. "There was no truck when I arrived. The road was clear."

Abdul wiped his brow with his sleeve and shook his head, now very afraid. "I have no answer. How can a truck with such a heavy load disappear so quickly? I must inquire of the others who wait for me. I will return here soon to join the service."

He stopped at the doors to talk with the four Muslim visitors and explained the recent collective change of heart. In the most severe terms, he was told that he and the conspirators must present themselves at the madrasa on December 28 at 9 am.

The young scribe told his two colleagues in the waiting Mercedes about the forthcoming meeting. Of more immediate concern to him was the sudden disappearance of the roadside truck.

He ran into the street to verify Henry's story. The explosives-laden truck was indeed missing an awkward situation because, at that time, his wristband flashed the signal to initiate the destruction. He returned to the car and called Chowdhury.

"We have encountered a setback to the schedule." He said, choosing his words carefully. "The roadside truck is missing.

Four of our brother Muslims wait Inside the infidel church for the service—they are not government or police agents, as you thought, but fellow believers from our mosque. Therefore, it is not practical, reasonable, or even possible to inflict damage that might endanger innocent lives, be they Muslim or not. There is no jihad to complete. I have decreed it so."

Closing the phone, he and his two fellow plotters walked into the church to observe the service.

Father Evans was as good as his word. After greeting his flock and introducing the four visitors from the Light of Hope Mosque, he called Pablo to the podium. "Our friend Pablo here, with whom many of you are acquainted, has a message and a small request to make of you that is appropriate as we hold this midnight mass and meaningful, whether we celebrate Christmas or not.

I will translate his words into English. He is not yet fluent in our language, and I think there may be one or two seated here who are not fluent in Spanish."

He grinned at Pablo and held the microphone between them.

Pablo acquitted himself with humor and dignity. There was a quality in his speech, simplicity, and sincerity that resonated with his audience. He explained his grave concern for many in the parish, mostly the old and infirmed.

"I am here as a living example for you," he said with a smile. "I am able to fill my stomach daily. There are many who are not." He outlined the food festival and hunger drive idea later in the year. "Before that happens, though, there is an urgent need to feed the hungry today. Please donate generously over this Christmas season."

After wishing everyone in attendance a happy Christmas in English and Spanish, he told his audience there was a small Christmas display for the children. Opening his backpack, he proceeded to launch five white birds into the air.

Instead of the expected chickens, he was surprised to find five white doves with long multicolored paper streamers attached to each leg.

"I am told the birds represent the five wounds of Christ, our Lord," he said.

The birds flew slowly, circling the seated audience. They flew without sound or concern. It seemed, without panic or distress—those watching noticed that they appeared by some strange influence to grow as they flew.

Five times they slowly flew in formation above the seated worshipers. Each completed circuit saw them bigger than before. Many thought it to be a quality of light in the building, obviously flickering shadows as they moved, as there could be no other reason. Rational people understand that birds do not become bigger as they fly.

Yet, from an astonished silence, a chorus of exclamations and amazed comments were heard. Soon the excited commentary grew, as apparently did the birds.

After a few more minutes on the wing, the flock of five sailed slowly through the open door and rose into the night sky.

A few of the congregation seated at the rear, including the four Muslim visitors, quickly left their seats to gaze after the birds, which now appeared to be as big as swans, flying resolutely toward the east.

Father Evans, quite shaken by the experience, thanked the now-seated Pablo and moved forward with the mass.

Between the others seated, Maria and Simona stared open-mouthed at the altar. Before them, old Cousin Pablo—the master of all things ignorant, knowledgeable in nothing—had spoken before the assembly and was thanked by the priest and treated as an honored guest.

The world had indeed gone mad, but they were both secretly very proud of their old cousin Pablo the ignorant, now elevated to Pablo, the respected.

The talk quickly turned to the latest strange experience at Saint Mary's. Unlike the previous, now infamous appearance of a daemon, this vision had no demonic overtones.

White doves were the symbol of peace, the color of purity, and virtue. Everyone knew that everyone except the Chinese, who associate white with death and often wear it at funerals, but they are Chinese, and what do they know?

As the experience was discussed, so the five birds grew with each subsequent recounting. The knowledgeable ones who understand the habits and preferences of birds insisted such creatures would not fly in darkness. Everyone knew that—everyone except the birds, but they were only birds after all, and what did they know?

Chowdhury was furious. He understood now that the secret six were turncoats, with no respect for the will or guidance of either the prophet, Allah, or himself. A devil, a visible enemy of God and Islam, had made the infidel church home, and they would not, or could not accept that in the face of all the evidence.

More than that, the plotters were stupid and incompetent. How was it possible for grown men to lose a large truck filled with explosives? Chowdhury thought deeply on these matters, tugging at his beard. Eventually, he adjusted his turban and entered his car.

"I will have to complete this simple task myself," he muttered.

Driving to the church, he stopped beneath a freeway overpass to speak with an old vagrant stumbling along the path.

"You are assuredly a poor simple fellow, a tottering smelly old wretch." "But this night, fortune will smile upon you."

Removing a twenty-dollar bill from his wallet, he moved it slowly before the old man's eyes.

"These riches will be yours after completing a simple job for me," he promised.

Tucker Harris, artist, alcoholic, and railroad tramp, peered at the rotund figure before him.

Here was a foreigner with his accent and, indeed, not an average person as he had a laundry basket fastened to his head. It took several seconds for the swirling mist of alcoholic distortion to clear sufficiently so Harris could see the laundry basket was, in fact, a turban.

Harris, the drunk, the accomplished but unknown artist, had long considered himself a master of delicate business negotiation, although with no experience or formal training. And so, with a deeply furrowed brow, he weighed the proposal carefully before making any commitment. As he considered the unexpected proposition, he scratched his head, as was his custom.

Chowdhury smiled and pulled at his beard, as was his custom. After a minute or two of head-scratching and beard-pulling, Harris nodded. He replied slowly, as any professional negotiator would so that the fat foreigner standing before him may properly understand his position.

"Twenty bucks, eh? And at Christmas? Well, fuck you, camel jockey. Keep yer twenty and buy a hat instead of tying a cotton sack around yer ugly fat head. You might be happy working for shit, but not me. This is America, pal. Forty bucks, or stick the job in yer arse an find another sucker!"

Chowdhury stared open-mouthed at the rude, belligerent ignoramus. *Such an ungrateful old peasant.* Unfortunately, it was late in the night now and probably impossible to quickly find another idiot, so he reluctantly agreed to the demands.

Harris smiled serenely, secure in knowing that he was indeed a painter and the master of these sensitive negotiations.

"Very well, then. Here is the machine you must operate," Chowdhury said, producing a cigarette lighter from his pocket. "Upon my command, you will light a short fuse to ignite a small Christmas firework display at the church. I will wait in my car. As soon as the fireworks show begins, come to the car and collect the other twenty. So, I will give you twenty now and twenty when the job is done. Very easy work for the money."

"Okay then, no problem, camel face. When do I do this?"

"Come with me, peasant; I will drive you to the church now."
Fifteen minutes later, Chowdhury parked his car on Argyle, within sight of the church. Together they walked into the parking lot and to the graveside truck. Chowdhury pulled and untied the coiled fuse, then shortened it with his pocketknife.

"This will now take about eighty seconds after you light the fuse and before the show begins. I will go to the car. When you see my lights flash, light the fuse. Stand a few feet from the truck for safety. When I flash my lights again, come to the car, and I will give you the money and drive you back again."

"Got it, shithead. Gimme the lighter, and I'll wait for the first signal."

Chowdhury, smiling broadly, passed him the lighter. Nodding to the tramp, he turned and walked to the street, cursing silently at the thought of a vaporized twenty-dollar bill.

Father Evans stood at the door, shaking hands and thanking his flock as they departed. In many ways, this service was unique and unforgettable, a delightful departure from any he could recall. Perhaps he could incorporate a bird release with a small lesson as a permanent yearly feature for Christmas. All in all, it had been a good evening—a strange beginning with old Pablo's bird launch, but even that unexpected demonstration was received well by the worshipers and their children.

Abdul and the other four Muslim visitors thanked the priest profusely as they left. Walking through the parking lot, they saw an old man—probably homeless by his ragged paint-dappled clothes—standing at the rear of the graveside truck, looking toward Argyle Street.

A flash of light suddenly erupted, and the old man stepped away from the truck. Abdul ran a few feet to the truck and saw the burning fuse.

"What have you done?" he screamed at the bum.

"What's the problem, dickhead? I done what I were paid for. I lit the fuse for the fireworks show. Why does yer poor old mother dress you so funny?"

Abdul turned to the Muslims. "Run, get the women away, my brothers! The fuse is lit!"

He vaulted onto the back of the truck, as did Qasim. "I stay with you, brother Abdul. By the grace of Allah, we will remove this threat."

Henry, walking with Pablo, noticed Abdul and Qasim at the back of the truck.

"Brother Henry, run! Now! The old fool has lit the fuse!"

"Stand down, my brothers. Through the guidance and wisdom of Allah, I have set the detonators so they will not be able to light the charges. The prophet has seen to this, having heard our prayers for direction. Let the fuse burn until it is extinguished.

There will be no slaughter tonight. Then under his breath, *"You may, however, detect the unmistakable odor of fine German smoked sausage."*

Henry turned to the old man. "What is your name? We have met before, but you were using a different name in those days."

"Harris, me name is Tucker Harris now, sir. I just come here to do a job. Some towel-head give me a twenty, with another to come. I need the cash for paint and oil, perhaps a little whiskey" He pointed down the street to where Chowdhury's car was once parked. "That sonofabitch sand scratcher's gone. He's jacked me outta me paint money!"

"We will make it right for you," Henry said.

"That lying dogshit kaffir told me, 'just light the fuse for a small fireworks display. But this ain't no Christmas firework show is it?"

Henry shook his head. "It would have been a very serious explosion, Tucker." *And another small sacrifice.* The vampire handed Harris a twenty-dollar bill. "There is much more to come for you later, my friend." *I will soon redeem these wages,* he thought.

The old tramp nodded his thanks and slowly walked away. For some time, he was heard muttering to himself about motherfuckin lying towel heads and other invectives most unsuitable for Christmas time.

"Our thanks to you, brother Henry. The worst is over, I think. There is still much more to come, though."

"Yes, there certainly is, brother Fahim. A missing rental truck full of high explosives and the graveside truck to unload and make safe. Our meeting on the 28th and a long talk with Chowdhury. Pig shit be forever upon him."

CHAPTER 29

I woke late on Friday morning, deliciously lethargic, relaxed, and happy. I did not need to work today—the promise of a long weekend begging to be enjoyed in the company of my favorite vampire.

I suddenly remembered my promise to Henry. I would call him as soon as we had finished breakfast.

Henry sounded in good spirits when we spoke.

"How about tonight, then? You may postpone if you wish, but I will not forget this is your treat."

"Tonight is fine, my friend. Would you object to another guest joining us?"

"Of course not, Jack. It's been some time since I saw Anneliese. We will all have a good time."

I laughed out loud but was not surprised by his foresight. "A good time but not at my expense, I hope. The thought of two vampires at the same table is a little daunting."

"Good practice for you, my boy. You will need plenty of that with my Anneliese."

"Done deal, then, Henry. Between 8:00 and 8:30, okay for you?"

Anneliese was quite excited at the prospect of seeing her Uncle Henry again. She laughed at my misgivings about two vampires together at the same table.

"A few months ago, two vampires were at your table in the French café. You just refused to see me. Your little mother saw me, though."

"Obviously, I need practice seeing invisible people then. Perhaps Julie would give me lessons."

Anneliese smiled a slow humorless smile. "Perhaps, but it would be a very short lesson."

She growled the same deep, terrifying sound that I had heard Henry make and then laughed uproariously as I hurriedly stepped back.

How far we had come since our first meeting just a few weeks ago, and what a happy transformation from her initial toxic bitch persona at the bistro to this sweet, lovable woman. Perhaps despite everything, there might be hope for us.

Unfortunately for me, I found myself analyzing every facet of our relationship. Henry had suggested to "just let the world turn as it has always done and enjoy life." It was good advice for some, but it was my nature to disassemble and examine seemingly inconsequential bits and pieces and to put everything into a logical and well-reasoned order. I was paid to do just that at the institute.

Looming over any possible chance for a carefree relationship, any hope for a regular commitment between two people, was the specter of our age difference.

The fact that she was a vampire was in itself a daunting prospect, but more importantly, for me was her age—a thirty-nine-year-old man with a four-hundred-plus-year-old lady.

She was definitely the older woman. I have been with older and younger women before; ten or fifteen years was never a problem. Four or five hundred years was a little much.

The thought occurred to me that she would look as substantially gorgeous as she did now when I was long dead. It was an interesting and worrying possibility for me and a discussion that we would soon have to have. And we did so a few days later. I was afraid our years together would pass like dreams. I withered by age, Anneliese remaining as she was.

And, as I fancied hearing the crash and roar of autumn leaves falling all around me and many harsh winters waiting beyond the graveyard wall to shred me and bringing gifts of creaking bones and withered skin. The solemn words from an old folk song echoed from my childhood, returning now as a troubling memory and would do so for many weeks.

"It's not so much the dying; it's laying in the grave so long; I've been all around this world."

No matter what happened, I was determined not to be the weight of stone around her neck, pulling her down, or for me being cared for and nursed out of pity in my failing years. What a strange foreign world I shared with Anneliese. Nothing seemed real or familiar to me, and for Anneliese, a vampire perhaps but always a woman. Never was her humanity more evident than when we made love. She moved beneath me with little gasps and cries, and at those times, I felt only love, and my fears were washed away.

Henry and Anneliese, they both knew how time works and recognized the many layers of associated realities. They would have answers for me, and they would understand. So, with that reasoning, I felt hope and was somewhat comforted.

About 3:30 pm Christmas day, I called Henry. "So how about a Christmas update on the Saint Mary's situation? I can't find any news stories, so I assume everything is fixed. Oh, and Merry Christmas!" Henry laughed. "To you also, Jack. Saint Mary's stands in the same place that it always did. A close call, though. Shame you were not at the

mass. There was much to see. Tell you what. If you have the time, we could meet for coffee—say about 4:30? I think the Gutburger is open."

"The Gutburger is always open. See you at 4:30, then."

Sure enough, Henry was seated when I arrived, and we once again exchanged Christmas wishes. I listened in amazement as he proceeded with his account of the explosive placement, a lost truck, and the emergence of the unfortunate Harris. He recounted the details of Pablo's food speech and the release of five birds.

"Strange thing," he said. "This morning, I received a call from our brother Fahim. He told me that the large white birds were on the grounds of the mosque, contentedly walking in the grass and flowerbeds. Very strange, eh?"

"Not at all. These were your birds, so that anything can be expected. Perhaps I'll drive down to the mosque later and check them out. This Fahim—the same imam you inserted a carrot into?"

The vampire nodded. "The very same. He was an instigator in the plot but redeemed himself at the last minute. Like most of the others, when faced with the ultimate reality of many innocent lives being ruined or destroyed, he had a change of heart. The power of a carrot can never be underestimated."

"So it would seem. Perhaps vegetable insertion should be mandated for criminal activity. Felonies, perhaps."

"Never work," Henry said. "Too many would repeat the crime, deriving pleasure from the punishment."

"Have you a plan for stabilizing the explosives in the graveside truck? What about the roadside truck? If it was stolen, the bad guys could be in for a nasty surprise. They would certainly advertise their position."

"Yes, Jack, do check on the birds; interesting creatures they are. I have thought about the trucks. They are due for return by the 30th. This leaves a week. I think I will have Fahim call the police and report the one stolen. As for the graveside truck, a hospital visit to our bedridden expert for his advice. All these loose ends will soon be taken care of."

"What about Chowdhury," I asked. "He was the culprit, wasn't he?"
Henry shook his head and stared into space for several minutes before answering. "He will be dealt with appropriately and quickly. There is a plan in place to remove him. Plus, he owes me twenty bucks. "All were equally responsible, Jack, but in the end, he was the prime instigator. He is a classical sociopath with no compassion or concern for the welfare of his fellows. His professed religion is a cloak to shield his true face from his brothers. He is a present danger to the mosque and others."

We continued to discuss the salvation of the church and many innocent lives. The birds were also a fascinating subject for me.

Although I questioned Henry, he would give no details about the creatures except to say they had much more work to do. I nodded and grinned with no choice but to accept his reluctance to discuss them in detail.

He outlined his plan for a grand festival with the mosque and church contributing—ethnic food from both parties with proceeds to aid the impoverished. Tucker Harris would display his artwork and assist Pablo as required. A fine pair, Tucker and Pablo, don't you think?

"Okay, Henry, here is a little story for you about a fine pair. I had a worrying experience the other evening after dinner when I left for home." I described the walk along the deserted highway, and the replicated Broadway Hotel.

Rodger listened intently to my story. "You found your way back, so all is well. Be warned, though. There are many parallel universes and many adjacent realities that it is possible to experience. From your description, you were between two, not committed to either. How does this little adventure relate to a fine pair? You must have been thinking of Julie."

I laughed, thinking of the pair in question, but with no idea what else he was talking about. "Actually, Henry, I was thinking of an acquaintance of yours. A sweet young German girl named Anneliese."

Henry stared at me for many seconds. As usual, he betrayed no emotion. In retrospect, the only time I had witnessed a serious reaction to any comment was a flash of rage at my joking reference to Father Malloy.

"Well, young Jack, you are certainly spreading your wings and venturing into dangerous territory. Yes, I know Anneliese very well."

"And?" I prompted.

"And what? You asked no question, just stated that you knew the woman."

"Spoken like a true attorney practicing international law. Here is another story to consider, then." I told him of our first meeting when she sat at my table at the bistro and our subsequent Broadway Hotel adventure.

"Tell me, Jack, exactly what did you think when you woke in your bed, back in your apartment? I am most interested in your thought processes. As a researcher and scientist at the prestigious Aeron Glass Marine Institute, you display a curious lack of intent or direction. You seem to be stumbling around in a daze."

"You're right again," I replied, becoming increasingly annoyed by Henry's attitude. "Meeting you and witnessing some of the most extraordinary events you have been involved in or personally orchestrated has changed my life. Everything I was taught now appears irrelevant or incorrect. Suddenly I meet this breathtaking woman who seemingly disappears or materializes at will. So yes, I am confused."

"Dear Jack, please relax. You are becoming most defensive. I am not criticizing you; simply relaying my observations. As for showing glimpses into other realities, am I to be blamed for that? I did not invent these things. They simply exist. Consider yourself fortunate, perhaps. You have witnessed events and possibilities that few others have".

He held up his nearly full coffee cup.
"Look! Have you seen this trick before?" He flipped the cup upside down. I stared as he raised the cup until I could see coffee in the cup. Not a drop spilled. He righted the cup again, took a sip, and stirred it with a straw.

"Just a small distraction for you, Jack. Now don't be so testy. It is Christmas, after all."

He was right. I had no business being angry with Henry. He had spent days and nights saving the lives of many people. What had I done? Chased after a woman, bounced around like a fool, and little else.
"Yeah, you're right, Henry. Sorry. I think I'm angry with myself. While you were out saving a church and congregation, I was complaining about the weather. Anyway, that was a hell of a trick with the coffee."

He smiled. "Not as good as this one, though." Passing his hand flat over the cup, he raised his hand about two feet in the air. From the cup, the coffee followed his hand, retaining the shape of the cup like a frozen block, except I could see movement and a wisp of steam on the surface.

Not a drop was spilled when he returned the drink to the cup. I glanced around us quickly to see if anyone was watching these displays. Luckily there were only three of four customers in the restaurant, and none were looking our way, so there would be no awkward questions to dodge.

"Without a doubt, you are the master of coffee."

Henry grinned. "Just a little Christmas trickery for you, Jack. Please don't try this at home."

"A little more than that. You are suspending the law of physics with this 'little trickery' of yours."

"Not at all, young Jack. I am working with the laws. Nothing is changed."

"You will have to explain that one to me later, Henry. First though, another cup of coffee."

"All will be revealed, Jack, but later—over dinner at The Broadway. You see, I have not forgotten. Perhaps your mysterious lady will join us there?" I nodded with a grin. "Perhaps, but not likely. Anyway, the first week of the new year, I will call your office for a time and day."

Henry stood and extended his hand. "Don't worry, Jack. Just see the world move as it has always done. There is nothing for you to do except give thanks for the life you have. You could stop analyzing every nuance of your existence and enjoy yourself; everything will fit into place according to design."

I smiled and nodded, watching as he moved to the exit. I had heard his "by design" reasoning before and was not impressed.

Julie's parents were in town for another three days. They would spend Christmas Day together, and I would join them the next day. Although I had been invited to dinner at the house, I declined. Pete and Julie would have some meaningful time with their parents and grandparents. I had neither, so for me; there was no reason to intrude. I usually found myself alone during Christmas and was well satisfied with the arrangement.

It was 6:30, by my watch. I had no reason to hurry home, so I decided to stop at The Broadway and watch, as Rodger suggested, the world move as intended.

This was my first visit since my strange experience a week or so ago. I found no dirty yellow glow this time and no deserted highway either. The parking lot had few cars that evening. Not many patrons were out on this Christmas Day, apparently.

I went through the main doors and approached the now-familiar reception desk, seeing a face I recognized.

"Good evening, Sue. Merry Christmas" She stared at me, no flicker of recognition in her eyes. I was somewhat disappointed. "You don't recognize me then?"

She smiled and shook her head. "No. Sorry. Perhaps I was on a different shift when you came before."

"Yes, probably. Would you please call room 447 for me? Anneliese Reinecke. Tell her Jack Cordell is at the front desk."

"Hardly necessary, dear Jack. You certainly seem much better than when we last met."

I spun around to meet a pair of dancing brown eyes. Anneliese was in a dark red full-length dress, grinning at me. We were in each other's arms before I could say hello.

"Ah, this is much better," she whispered. "Are you hungry, Jack? It's about seven. A very good time to eat, yes?"

"The only thing I have an appetite for is you," I whispered. I pulled back slightly. "Wait, yes, let's eat. You have a lot of explaining to do."

The dining room was small. I remembered the white starched tablecloths and expensive silverware, but mostly my thoughts were on the brown-skinned woman in a red velvet dress.

I ordered wine. "Your recommendation for a Chardonnay. I will have the cheapest Merlot you can find." To his credit, the old waiter inclined his head and smiled without questioning or showing surprise at my choice. *The hallmark of a true professional*, I thought. After a quick discussion with Anneliese, they agreed on the Chardonnay.

I became focused on our conversation—unlike the last time in the bar when many words were expended, but nothing was retained.

"What happened the first time we met, darling? I woke in my bed at home with two holes in my arm. I tried to find you, but nobody at the hotel had heard of you, and the bar receipt was dated months ahead of the actual date."

"Yes, sometimes a problem Jack. We were out of sync with our time period. About a year ahead of where we should expect to be. So when you tried to find me that night, you became lost. I did wait in the lounge for you when I got your message."

"Of course, beautiful lady. That makes perfect sense, but not to me, though. I have no idea what you are talking about. I know only that I want to be with you, no matter what."

"Thank you, Jack, but before any more bold statements or declarations of love or lust, you really should know a little about me. A few details of my background and family."

"Good idea. Do tell."

"Oh, but first I want to eat, then drink, then go to bed. Do you remember the last time we did that?"

"No—I mean, yes, I remember drinking in the lounge and us getting into bed. Nothing else. My next memory was waking to some demented alarm clock

On Saturday morning, I think. I have to ask you this, Anneliese, did we?"

"Did we fuck?" She smiled. "No, unfortunately, you were sick—although you did try. You had the flu or some crud from the future that you were unprepared for. You will get it again in a few months. Most disappointing for me, but not as disappointing as you having to ask me about it. I was quite angry at the time. I bit your arm—you don't remember, do you? That was the only pleasure I took from the evening, apart from a couple of hours of your delightful company and bringing you home again. Oh well, everything moves according to the way it is supposed to do so."

"By design?" I asked.

"Ah, you have been chatting with my uncle. He is the design aficionado."

"You are a vampire, Anneliese?"

"Yes, and a damn good one too. My dearest Robert or Henry—whatever he calls himself now—is my uncle. I love him dearly. He is a great humanitarian. Many human characteristics are pure and enduring. Uncle possesses most of them."

"Yes, he does. He also has a rather inflexible view on crime and punishment."

Strangely I felt no surprise by her revelation. I think I knew she was a vampire from the day we met. Her direct confidence and the way she moved among strangers, like a seasoned politician or, more exactly, like her uncle. What was surprising to me was that I had no regret or concern.

If she'd told me she was Frankenstein, it would have made no difference. This woman was forever irresistible.

"I had coffee with him this morning. Although I will never tell him or anyone else except you, he is probably the most important person in my life."

"Are you in love with him?" she asked.

"No, I am in love with you, as you must have guessed by now. As I am sure you know, your uncle prefers men to women."

"He once told me that 'girls are okay, but you can't beat the real thing.' Is that your preference as well?"

"Oh, I am definitely a firm believer. Girls are fine, but you can't beat the real thing."

She laughed her happy melodic laugh, then took my hand from across the table.

"I want to be with you, Jack. I want the real thing. I know this will take some time. Please try to accept me for what I am. We are not so different. What I lack, you can teach me. My abilities can be learned. I will teach you. We can go through life and travel the world together without fear or regret."

The food was, as expected, to a degree of excellence.

Later the next morning, while I was recovering from the exertions and pleasures of the night before, I remembered my date with Julie.

"After this, we will have time," I said to Anneliese. "I will tell Julie and regretfully end our relationship. She will go back to Washington. I will stay with you. I do have to work, though. You, I suppose, are independently wealthy? On the other hand, I must continue a research project to pay the rent. Tell me about your family."

"Not much to tell, Jack. My mother was Brazilian, and my father was French. They moved to Germany, and I was raised in a strict authoritarian household.

Father was killed in the war. The family was very strict through four generations. You are correct: I do have money inherited from my family. I live a—how do you say?" She searched for the word. "A subdued lifestyle, but all my needs are provided for. Now with you, every need is satisfied."

"Long may it continue, Anneliese. This all makes sense, your beautiful Latin features, and the German name. Very exotic, my darling."

"Okay, dear Jack. Get dressed, get out, get going, and see your sweet Droolie. I will be waiting."

I felt a sudden shock, a sense of disappointment, and sadness. Instinctively I knew this was wrong. There was something very unpleasant behind her words.

More than just a jealous woman's anger, there was a bitterness that was entirely unnecessary and unexpected.

"Julie," I said. "Her name is Julie."

"Yes, darling, is that not what I said?"

"No, you called her Droolie, as well, you know. All very funny, but she is a good woman, really a decent person. The insults are not necessary. She has many fine qualities and is a hardworking mother supporting her son. Unlike you, she is not an independently wealthy girl."

"Ah, do please continue, Jack. Should I now expect a lecture about the nobility of poverty and the workers' struggle? There is nothing desirable to be found in an impoverished setting. I know her well, Jack. There is no need to explain or describe her to me so. Mulie, Joolie, or Droolie—it's all the same, no? We are with each other. You are now with me, not your impoverished little mother."

"Yes, Anneliese, but why the anger? She's done nothing to deserve these remarks, has she?"

"My, my, how very protective of you, Jack. Well, then, you really should be going. Have a wonderful time. You have my number. We all have choices to make, don't we? By the way, do you think I am angry now? How little we know each other."

I turned to the door, then paused. "Look, Anneliese," I said, turning back to an empty room. Her perfume lingered, but of her, there was no sign. Did I hear an implied threat with her words, "you think I am angry now?" She was right, though, when she said, *"how little we know each other."*

Was my opinion of her as a spoiled spiteful child correct? Based upon her few parting sentences, then yes. I could not help but remember the first time we met and her astonishing rudeness.

It was such a stupid argument to me. For the last twelve hours or so, we had been playing and loving, happy as two children. Anneliese had everything I wanted in a woman, and I realized how desperately I wanted her.

The image of her in that red velvet gown, walking like a queen in the hotel lobby, was one that I would never forget.

Perhaps this was a vampire thing. Come daylight, her mood and personality would change suddenly. I would talk to her about that because she had displayed the very attributes that would soon kill a romantic relationship, jealousy, and possessiveness.

The drive to my apartment seemed endless. I had a lot to consider.

Although I was prepared to accept her unconditionally, there was a malicious quality, a sudden sharpness to her words that worried me. The image of Henry with his elongated features and gleaming fangs was still very real to me.

Did I hear an implied threat with her words, "you think I am angry now?" She was right, though, when she said, *"how little we know each other."*

Was my opinion of her as a spoiled spiteful child correct? Based upon her few parting sentences, yes. I could not help but remember the first time we met and her astonishing rudeness.

A vampire sat on the short, damp grass of an ornamental garden at the Light of Hope Mosque. It was early morning in late December, with the first faint show of daylight pushing away the darkness.

It was just light enough to see the five white birds standing before him—small birds, no bigger than pigeons. To an onlooker, this would seem an almost comical sight. Five birds, standing in an orderly semicircle within arm's length of a seated male figure. He appeared to be talking to them, and they seemed to listen attentively to his instruction.

After some fifteen minutes, vampire Henry Smith stood. He followed a path to the street where his car was parked. The birds wandered away and were quickly lost from sight as they found shelter in the hedges and shrubs.

On Monday, December 28, the secret six gathered in the madrasa at the request of the manager Quasim.

"I think we all know why we are here. I hope during the last week, all of you have taken time to reflect on the seriousness of this situation." Quasim's voice rose in anger as he continued. "This madness that you and others have engaged in is unconscionable. You, as a group, decided to murder at least one hundred people, women, and children—not enemies of Islam but worshipers at a Christian church. Why? Because of a baseless rumor."

He looked at each of them, one by one. "Let us suppose this devil lived in the church. If that were true, then it would be removed by the authority of that church, not by a band of criminals and revolutionary terrorists. The evil is not at Saint Mary's Church but regrettably lives in the hearts of those participating in this outrage."

His audience sat like naughty children being scolded by an angry teacher, silent and with downcast eyes.

Quasim could barely contain his anger. "I am here as a representative of the managers and director. There are to be changes, effective immediately. No more meetings at the school without written consent.

No unauthorized use of the maintenance building. Every follower worshiping here will be notified in writing, and this information will also be posted on the notice board. As of now, the police have not been involved in this matter, and I hope their presence will not be required.

There are rental trucks to be returned. There is a towing and claimant fee to be satisfied with the city. The participants will meet any expense, nothing originating from our mosque. Explosive material will be neutralized based on advice from experts in the mining industry that I will select. This information will be made available to you within two days. A professional might be needed to oversee this work. Disposal costs will be met by those involved. If there are questions, the office number is available to you. I can be reached there."

He stood over them quietly for several moments.

"I pray Allah, in his mercy, will cleanse your hearts and minds. Our humble gratitude to our lord that through his wisdom, a great tragedy was avoided. May his light shine within us all. Peace be upon those assembled here."

Quasim returned to his office. The six chastened conspirators returned to their various occupations.

Sir Henry Smith was well pleased by the outcome of the meeting. He waited at the Gutburger for Chowdhury to join *Asr* in the afternoon prayer. The Pakistani would be met by five small birds, anxious to fulfill their duties and return home.

So it was that in the poor light of a cold winter's afternoon, Chowdhury walked slowly through the decorative gardens and approached the main entrance of the mosque.

He paused in astonishment as two small white birds flew down from the darkening sky and perched, one on each shoulder. Two more landed by his legs and climbed, sitting one on each slipper.

Others passing by chuckled at the strange sight and made many comments, saying this was indeed a sign of good fortune. Yet another landed on his *taqiyah* as he had removed his turban. Humorous as the situation was, Chowdhury was at a loss. He tried to raise an arm to dislodge the bird on his head. He tried to remove a bird sitting on his slipper by lifting a foot and kicking. His limbs betrayed him. Neither arms nor legs would move at his command.

He stood immobile on the path, overcome by great fear. People gathered around and stared at such a strange sight. He tried to call for assistance, but no sound escaped his lips. The birds felt much heavier now, an almost intolerable weight on his shoulders, head, and feet. The harder he struggled, the heavier the birds became.

I am being crushed by these tiny birds. How can this be possible?

Suddenly there was no weight at all. His ears were filled with a tremendous roaring sound, unnerving and distracting. A strong wind sprang up, pulling at his clothes and cutting hard into his face. He became aware of people yelling and shouting. Looking around, he saw, to his horror, that he was rising above the mosque.

Little pinpoints of light erupted all around him as he was twisted and turned like a child's toy thrown into the air. He forced his eyes closed and waited for death to release him.

There is an ancient and very beautiful mosque, an ornate edifice waiting patiently beneath the same skies as it has for nearly five hundred years. It waits calmly, securely, and confident in its construction's impeccable architecture and integrity. Now a venerated landmark and regal tourist attraction, it continues to fulfill the primary purpose of the design: a glorious temple dedicated to God and a great house wherein the faithful still gather to pray.

In the picturesque city of Lahore, where the Badshahi Mosque was built, the fundamental Muslim law of *sharia* lives in the hearts of the people. Although not yet strictly enforced by the government, most people there wish it to be so. The *sharia* way is the perfect totalitarian governance. All aspects of Muslim living and all human endeavors within the faith grow and flourish, illuminated by way of *sharia*.

It was on the paved entranceway in the great courtyard of Badshahi that Chowdhury alighted. He was seen by many of those who gathered to pray at the time of *Maghrib*.

They saw him descending majestically from the sky, a dumpling-like figure holding five white doves. Fortunately, the evening was warm and forgiving of his foolishly provocative dress.
At first glance, he could be mistaken for a fat woman in her underwear. Closer inspection revealed that the strange visitor was a portly male wearing women's undergarments. He sat for many minutes, bewildered by his surroundings. When he regained his feet, the birds abandoned him, flying in tight formation toward the west until lost from sight.

"What manner of devil are you? How is it you dress in the apparel of women? Who are the demons that brought you here?" The increasingly hostile crowd demanded answers quickly.
"I am Chowdhury, protector of the faith, a Pakistani prophet from the West. I was brought here against my will by five devils from a mosque in America."

For most bystanders, his reply was sufficient. He was a Western prophet from America, consorting with devils. His attire was undoubtedly sufficient. Covered in dirt, with a pile of bird droppings on each shoulder and one on his head, he wore a woman's brassiere and panties as well as red high-heeled shoes. The filthy Western prophet was immediately thrown to the ground and pummeled for such egregious blasphemy.

The arrival of security guards and city police saved him from further punishment by the outraged mob. Despite his noisy supplications to Allah, he was removed from the holy site and secured in a small jail cell. His clothes and shoes were quickly removed and burnt after photographic evidence was secured. Punishment then resumed.

After sufficient adjustment and corrective measures were applied, the battered Pakistani prophet Chowdhury was hosed clean of bird dung and dressed in an old blanket. From the holding cell, he was removed to the state mental institution in Lahore.

He was destined to appear once more with Khalid Al-Mihdhar. They would enter the United States within three years when their contributions to the mosque jihad had been forgotten, but before their involvement in the September 11th atrocities had begun.

The vampire heard from fellow worshipers at the Light of Hope Mosque about the strange heavenly ascension of the Pakistani Chowdhury. Many witnesses willingly attested to the bizarre occurrence. Everyone saw small white birds perch on him. Many agreed that he rose into the air for a short distance.

It was at that point that stories differed. Media attention was nonexistent, there being no sexual overtones or possibilities of priestly involvement with satanic practices. Some say that he simply faded from view. Others argued that he seemed to swell until he appeared as a great balloon rising into the clouds. All agreed that he ascended into the sky in one form or another. There was no public outcry or suggestions that Satan's work was in evidence. White birds were messengers of peace and purity, entirely appropriate on the holy grounds of a mosque.

Within a day or two, the matter was forgotten.

Driven by continuing pressure from the management and directors of the mosque, the secret six moved forward with plans to deactivate the explosive material and remove any lingering reference to the ill-fated jihad.

Henry Smith drove to the Baker Mining Company, bringing with him all remaining Tovex packs and Titadyn sticks from the suicide vest he recently dismantled. A representative from the company met with Fahim to inspect the explosive drums. Having determined that the material was safe to remove by road if the containers were adequately secured, they arranged delivery to Baker soon after the New Year.

Another general meeting at a time to be finalized early in the New Year was called by Qasim. During this gathering, there would be a review of progress from the secret six and consideration of a proposal that the mosque partner with Saint Mary's Church in a joint charitable effort to hold a" *food for the poor*" event.

All events and preparations at the mosque were moving toward a satisfactory conclusion—almost by design, it would appear.

I said a long goodbye to Julie and Peter by driving them to the Los Angeles airport and putting them on the flight to Washington.

It was a trial separation, I suppose, as Julie had not fully committed to living in DC. Pete was as excited as any teenager would be. We promised to stay in touch through email and phone calls.

Although I knew they would be terribly missed, the thought of the curvaceous Anneliese would soften the blow. Yet even then, I had serious misgivings. What or where was reality? How did I grow from a sheltered little boy and dedicated student to a serious researcher? How and why did I now enjoy the unlikely acquaintance of a vampire and his niece? Neither could be explained away, and there was no doubting the existence of either one.

As Rodger often said, "The world will move as it should by design. There is nothing you or I will do to change that."

Anneliese opened the door to 447 before I was able to knock. I was greeted by a huge smile and a long lingering kiss. "It is my solemn duty to treat you to a fine dinner downstairs. Afterward, a drink or two, then a fine treat upstairs." She held up her hand as I started to speak. "Not now, darling. During dinner, we will talk about all your concerns and grievances."

I nodded and sat on the edge of the bed while she finished her hair.

A strange way of speaking. That might be the key to our differences, I thought. Happily, there was no sign of anger or the sense of bitterness that I saw at our last meeting. I remembered the first time we met at the bistro, how she introduced herself and then proceeded to continue a conversation with astonishing levels of rudeness, arrogance, and sarcasm. Even then, a beautiful, intelligent woman shone through the bad behavior with a disarming charm and grace. I had the uncomfortable feeling that any reasonable person would have left the table without a second glance.

I was always a sucker for pretty women.

It was, as she promised, a fine dinner. We talked about our last truncated conversation before I left to meet with Julie.

"Why did you leave? Why not finish a sensible talk and discuss the situation?"

She stared at me. "Because I had no more to say. All that needed to be said was said. I told you I was angry with you and the Julie situation. What else would you like to hear? Do you wish to continue the stupid impoverished, yet noble peasant discussion? If you are looking for an apology, it will be a long time coming, my sweet."

I shook my head in amazement, trying to think of a possible response but finding none.

"Are you angry again?" I finally asked.
"Of course not, darling. You asked me a reasonable question, and I gave what I thought was a reasonable answer. Look, Jack, it is like I said last time: how little we know each other. Good things take time to mature, do they not? This is the perfect example here, yes?"
She held her glass of Chardonnay to me as an example.

"Look at me; I am another example." She laughed her girlish happy laugh.

I realized she was sincere. If we were to continue any sort of conversation, I should have no expectations of anything except an absolute direct response. She apparently had no sympathy for social niceties if not delivered with unnerving honesty.

"I think I know you a little better now. May I ask you a few personal questions?"
"Certainly. Answers at my discretion, though."
"Okay. Why were you so very confrontational and rude the day we met at the bistro? Surely you don't usually talk to people like that?"

"Of course not. You are a researcher, Jack. I provided an enigma for you to solve, the perfect bait. It worked very well, I think. You chased after me, and here we are together, my sweet."

"Yes, the perfect bait. You are a very clever lady. Are you the same entity as your uncle?"

"Yes, dearest one. Uncle involves himself in more situations with people, though. As a result, he changes shapes—vehicles, as he calls them—more often than I do. I don't know why he does that. Such aggravation. Think about it, Jack. Not only wearing the physical form but lifestyle as well. These folks usually have bank accounts, apartments or houses, existing debts, and sometimes horribly entangled relationships. As you can imagine, stepping into someone else's life is difficult. You never really know what you are getting. This is why uncle seeks out travelers and singles without too many roots. My preference is to retain my form for as long as practical."

"What a delightful form it is, Anneliese. Please don't change."

She laughed her happy little laugh.

"Getting old now, Jack. I have worn this coat since 1901. Still in good shape, though, don't you think?"

"About the best, I could ever wish for."

"We will put it to good use a little later, my love."

Another oddity in the way she spoke. I would have to come to terms with the way she referred to herself as if she were the owner of a car discussing her vehicle.

"Do you feel the same emotions as I do? Love and hate, anger, pain, happiness?"

"Yes, I do. All human emotions, but at a heightened level. The difference is that I am able to control responses to stimuli."

She laughed again.

"For example." Smiling, she took the dinner fork and drove it hard into her upturned wrist.

I jumped from the table and grabbed her arm. "What the hell are you doing? What in God's name did you do that for?"

She grinned, showing her wrist. Blood trickled from four raised wounds she had just inflicted upon herself. "Here, I chose to feel no pain. These marks are real, but I control my response to the damage. I am able to do the same for the emotions that you just listed. I will stop the blood-leaking soon; otherwise, the lovely white tablecloth will show the stains."

I sat again, shaken and very concerned for the crazy woman I had fallen for. "Obviously, this will be a serious learning curve for me."

"Well, my darling, while you are learning, I will make sure the lessons are interesting and enjoyable."

I nodded, reaching for her arm. Turning her wrist, I saw the bleeding had stopped. The angry reddened wounds, although visible, were much smaller and healing quickly.

"Tell me, during the course of our relationship, how much blood do you expect to take from me?"

"Please don't be afraid of me, Jack. I need very little human blood—actually, very little blood at all. I do need protein, though. Human blood is a great delicacy to savor a little at a time. We have been enjoying this world with you for thousands of years. In the early times, we were called angels. Some still know us by that name, although we seldom display our wings. We are known as vampires now and suffer from an undeservedly bad reputation. Blame it all on that old goat Bram Stoker. His Dracula was a good story, but only a story. Powerful enough though to affect readers worldwide and still do so after all these years."

She frowned, then waved her hand in a short, dismissive gesture.

"So, to answer your question, how much blood? Oh, gallons, darling. By the time I am finished, you will look like a sausage skin hanging from a nail: pale and thin, with nothing inside."

"Who in your family hangs sausage skins from nails?" I asked. "Are they new or used? In neat rows in the bedrooms or dangling on the front porch drying in the sun? A great visual, for sure."

I pointed at her hand. On her index finger, she wore a heavy silver ring. I had meant to ask her about it for some time. It was octagonal and deeply engraved with a Maltese cross, inscribed with letters or symbols around the band. It was the only adornment I had ever seen her wear.

"You're not a girl for jewelry or ornaments, are you? Do please tell me about the ring."

"Mother gave it to me. It was my father's. After the first siege, his body was badly burnt. One of his soldiers tried to help him, but he died. The page cut off his hand and saved it for my mum." She smiled. "Mother said my dad was very brave. I don't remember him, though."

"First siege? What war was this?"

"He died in the holy lands fighting the Saracens. A well-respected knight of the Saint John's order."

Yet another aspect of Anneliese that continually surprised me. She was a living historical record.

We finished our meal in good spirits, chatting and enjoying the evening. After dinner, we strolled along Broadway for about an hour.

The cold evening was offset by the warmth of our romance and the humor we shared as we walked.

Later in bed, as I ran my hands over her body, all thoughts of my previous concerns evaporated.

Father Philip Malloy was reaping the rewards that any popular television personality may reasonably expect. His "Father Philip Hour" had solidified ratings for the previous three months. The New Year ahead brought the promise of a renewed contract and conditional monetary gain.

Better yet, he avoided arrest and prosecution due in part to the innovative legal maneuverings and experience of his attorneys. He was well pleased with the results to date. Although somewhat expensive, the vaunted local law firm of Rubenstein, Weintraub, and Goldstein satisfied all his legal needs and always represented him with a degree of competence.

Flushed with new confidence and purpose, he returned his Mercedes to a factory-approved specialist, refinished entirely at enormous expense in a bright red metallic paint. No traces of the nasty door or hood insignia remained.

On the seventh day of the New Year at 4:30 pm, he parked his refurbished chariot in a prominent position at The Broadway Hotel. He was deliberately early for the meeting.

The arrival of four television production executives scheduled for 5:00 provided at least a thirty-minute cocktail opportunity. By 8:00, an elegant dinner and many more drinks were consumed. Their meeting eventually disbanded with much backslapping and hand-shaking. The air was filled with good humor and the expectation of great success in the near future.

Father Malloy had consumed many cognacs before and after dinner. A whole bottle of the delectable French *Leopold Gourmel* lay empty on the table. His dinner companions, who helped empty the bottle, left by taxi, offering to drive him home,

Malloy thanked them but did not believe there was any reason.

A ride home would mean the inconvenience of returning to retrieve his car the next day. He might be slightly drunk but was by no means impaired.

Although he staggered a little before he reached his car, he quickly dismissed any possibility of intoxication.

"I was," he muttered, *"raised on communion wine. A few brandies won't hurt. Not far to go anyway."*

He pulled out of the hotel, entering the Broadway traffic flow. He drove carefully along Broadway toward Main Street, approaching the

Main Street crosswalk. He was perhaps moving too slowly and most definitely weaving across two lanes.

The police car pulled away from the curb and slid into traffic three vehicles behind the priest.

"What do you think, George? That moron's set to hurt himself or someone else."

George nodded. "For sure. Drunk or asleep. Let's reel him in before there's a problem." George moved into the left lane, now in sight of the red SUV. He flipped on the sirens and flashing lights so there would be no doubt about their intent.

Their car closed the distance between them, and other vehicles dropped back, expecting both cars to pull to the curb.

Malloy jerked upright behind the wheel. The light and sirens seemed to fill his car with noise and confusion. The police must have been pursuing a vehicle and wished to pass him.

He noted a small knot of slow traffic ahead. He decided to overtake the cars before pulling into the right lane. The Mercedes shot forward.

Sean grabbed the radio and called ahead, informing dispatch that they were pursuing a fleeing vehicle driving erratically through traffic at high speeds.

A Salvadorian sailor, now a vampire and, most recently, an international lawyer, walked from his dingy apartment on Argyle Street and soon turned at the crossing onto Broadway. He walked unhurriedly, with the expectation of a fine meal at a good restaurant and pleasant company at his table—not an encounter with a large vehicle driven at high speed through the crosswalk.

He was a good vampire, a friendly Salvadorian Jewish vampire. Punctual and well-spoken. He exercised regularly, took fish oil and vitamin D supplements, habitually cleaned his formidable teeth, and flossed methodically. He was always clean and neat in appearance, with impeccable personal hygiene and regular bowel movements.

When walking, he engaged in deep breathing exercises to relieve any accumulated stress. He would also play his accordion. The soothing sound was a perfect therapeutic balm as the world occasionally closed around him.

The stoplights were in his favor, and the little flashing icon indicated he could cross safely. Everything was in its proper place and at the appropriate time. All pieces in the game were in play and moving inexorably forward as they should.

About halfway across the road, he looked suddenly into the blinding headlights of a speeding car, still smiling as the vehicle struck him.

Malloy felt the shock of impact, and his windshield shattered. He saw something move in front of his car, twisting in the air and then falling to the road.

Sir Henry Smith, a Dark Angel, lay like a broken doll, blood and fluids oozing and pooling around him. The red Mercedes skidded to a stop just beyond the crossing. Flashing lights filled the sky, moving in a jagged dance all around and reflected from store windows. The howl and wail of sirens cut through the evening, piercing and intrusive.

Police directed traffic in commanding voices and cordoned off the scene with yellow reflective tape leaving a few curious pedestrians. This was all routine for them; nothing here that they had not seen many times before. Two police officers knelt in the road, examining the broken body for any sign of life.

George returned to his car and removed a heavy shock blanket from the trunk. Sean continued to relay information over the radio.

Father Malloy was handcuffed and pushed into the back of a police car, mumbling angrily. He gazed at the action on the road with uncomprehending eyes. Nothing was real beyond the vehicle's windows in which he sat; nothing out there concerned him at all. He felt only the restraints chaffing at his wrists and restricting his movement. He would soon complain loudly about that sort of disgraceful treatment and make it known that he wanted another drink.

For George and Sean, there was nothing else they could do to help the victim. The body would remain as it lay until the arrival of the coroner. The blanket covered it, hiding the tragic sight from curious spectators.

George stood, leaning against his car, and stared at the lifeless form. He had witnessed images of death many times, always with a personal sense of sorrow. The spectacle of the dead or dying during a short tour of duty in Viet Nam continued to remind him of his own mortality.

Beneath the blanket, he saw something glow. Dimly at first, but unmistakably glowing yellowish-white light.

He shouted to Sean. "What the hell is that—that light, do you see it?"

Sean shook his head. "Shit, no idea. I see the light, but there's nothing alive under the sheet. Must be a flashlight." He walked to the lifeless form, George following closely behind him. Before they could lift the blanket, the light became so intense that brilliant incandescent daylight illuminated the surrounding area.

Both officers stepped back, George automatically reaching for his sidearm. They turned their heads, unable to look directly at the light.

As suddenly as it appeared, the light dimmed. Within a few seconds, there was only a corpse beneath a blanket.

George holstered his weapon again as Sean stepped forward and pulled the blanket from the lifeless form. Nothing had changed. No light, no signs of life, just a broken body lying in the blood and dirt.

It would be many months before Sean and his partner no longer discussed the strange occurrence, but it was something neither of them would ever forget. Others at the scene saw a light but assumed it was from police car headlights. No bystanders could corroborate the vision shared by Sean and George that night.

Paramedics arrived and quickly confirmed the obvious. The victim was most certainly dead. The coroner would arrive and, in time, after examining the scene, would allow the corpse to be moved to the morgue. Malloy's vehicle would again occupy space in a city holding area.

Within the hour, driver LeShawn loaded the SUV and swept broken glass carefully into the curb. Early the following day, city cleaners would remove the glass and hose any remaining blood into the storm drain.

And so, everything moved slowly, according to the way it should and as it had always done. Within one or two days, no trace of any accident would remain.

Anneliese and I waited at the dinner table, grumbling at first, then surprised and concerned.

At about 9:15, Anneliese stood. "Uncle Henry will not be joining us. Will you eat?"

Something about her voice, a strange dull intonation—almost a monotone and so unlike her typical vibrant pitch—made me curious and somewhat concerned.

"That's too bad; I been planning this dinner for a while. Always a pleasure to see him. I'll eat now if you will. Maybe tomorrow he'll join us if he can't make it tonight. We could meet here at the same time, perhaps. What do you think?"

There was something wrong with the way she stared at me, and suddenly a bad feeling darkened the evening.

"Did he call you?" I asked.

She shook her head. "No, he told me he wanted to say goodbye to us and wish us well." Then she clung to me, sobbing like a child. There was no trace of a vampire, just a small girl lost in pain.

I died a little when she told me of his demise.

The coroner ordered an autopsy and quickly determined the death was caused by multiple blunt force traumas, primarily to the skull and chest. An inquest held liable a speeding vehicle driven with reckless abandonment and disregard for public safety.

Father Malloy was subsequently charged with several violations, including driving under the influence. The most serious charge was vehicular manslaughter.

The local news media immediately pounced on the situation, regurgitating the old Saint Mary's Church daemon and child molestation stories. The television news outlet fielding the "Father Philip Hour" program soon canceled the show and tried to distance itself from further contact with the disgraced Malloy.

The trial judge, the Honorable Millicent Carlisle, refused bail, citing the prosecution's objections that the defendant was a genuine flight risk. Rubenstein, Weintraub, and Goldstein's law firm made very public their decision to no longer represent Philip Malloy. He had, after all, effectively murdered a brilliant young member of their staff.

The fortunes of the charming but self-absorbed priest continued to plummet.

I thought about the situation for a long time. My memories often returned me to the bistro dining room when Henry displayed his fangs in a show of rage. At the time, I believed his demonstration to be an overreaction to my levity and entirely unnecessary. Perhaps it was, although probably in hindsight, he saw a shadow of the events briefly yet to come.

I helped Anneliese with the inevitable red tape and seemingly endless details, all requiring attention. After she claimed the body, she told me that Henry had, about 200 years earlier, expressed distaste for any form of disposal other than cremation on a wood pyre. He had some concerns about deviant necrophiliacs rummaging around in his remains.

"Not that I have a problem with a person obtaining sexual pleasure from my cadaver, only that they are fair of face with firm bodies."

After much serious discussion, cremation was decided between us. A death certificate was issued, citing the cause of death as determined during the autopsy. Henry was to be cremated, although we realized this was forbidden or strongly discouraged under Islamic tradition. We reasoned that, as he was not a true believer in any organized religion, all would eventually be forgiven.

Together we searched his small apartment and removed his accordion and a small wooden box containing a rather elaborate Coptic cross fashioned from silver—also, an old worn copy of the Bardo-Thodol. His clothes were gathered in plastic bags and sealed.

Anneliese made clear that "under no circumstances were they to be sold or given to others."

"All personal items would be kept by family members or burnt. Any clothes must be burnt," she insisted, explaining that energy would remain in the various fabrics and cause harm to others if worn."

I did not understand any of her explanations and, therefore, did not believe them but thought it best to say nothing.

By the time the cremation was over, Anneliese had returned to her old feisty self. I think we were both in shock for a few days, wandering without direction.

Henry's ashes were sealed in a thick waterproof bag and held in an ornate stone urn. I collected the urn from the funeral parlor and stored it on a wardrobe shelf at my apartment.

I missed him terribly. It seemed as if a large part of my life had just disappeared without warning. I asked Anneliese about vampires and angels dying.

"Your kind are not indestructible then? Your uncle told me he would not live forever, but from some of his disappearing and reappearing displays, I assumed he was not affected by accidents as we mortals are."

"These things are possible for us by manipulating our life frequencies." She thought for some time before continuing.

"Simple projection, darling Jack; this is probably what you mean by *disappearing and reappearing displays*. Here is an example for you. Squeeze my hand."

I reached over and squeezed her hand. "Now, once more."

Again, I reached to squeeze her hand. She smiled and pursed her lips. There was nothing of substance beneath my fingers. I was squeezing the air, yet she stood before me, a perfect Anneliese. I ran my hands over her. The effect was the same: a perfect insubstantial replica.

"Try now."

I started as her voice came from behind me. Spinning around, I saw she stood before me, grinning. I turned again to face the replica, but it had vanished.

"It's the best way I can explain to you, simple-minded mortals." She laughed.

"Thanks very much. Do please excuse me for being a normal person." In fact, I was delighted that we had learned to joke about our differences without becoming angry or defensive.

"Please continue, my darling."

"In our daily lives, perception is a reality for us. You were squeezing the hand of a memory. I stood there while we talked, but I moved behind you quickly. I moved so fast that I left a ghost image of myself in your mind; you remembered me and where I had been standing. If necessary, I can *Think of* myself from one place to another."

"Aha, so the trick is speed, then?"

"Time and speed, of course. I am sure you are familiar with heat signature technology, yes?"

"Yes, warm-blooded living organisms emit an infrared outline of themselves. That image is invisible to the eye but can be read by instruments. Military night vision, for example."

"Correct, but not just living creatures. There is decomposing material, for instance—perhaps rotting vegetation. But we are discussing energy only in the infrared spectrum. Sit quietly in a chair for a minute or two, then get up and leave the room.

Your image remains visible to the instruments even though you have left the room. Now, remember, there are many invisible energy forms other than infrared."

"Okay, professor, but what happened to Uncle Henry, do you think? He said he had the ability to see into the future if he chose to do so. He told me these things were quite commonplace, so how did he not see his own death?

Anneliese nodded. "Of course, he was correct. Here is an easy explanation for you, Jack. Stand in an imaginary hole about seven feet deep by seven feet in diameter. Look around; tell me what you see."

"I see the walls of the hole. If I look up, I see the sky." She smiled and nodded.

"Good, now climb out of the hole and climb to the top of a nearby tree. Now let me know what you see. Are you with me so far?"

I laughed, "Sure, the higher view from the tree allows me to see things much further away,"

"Yes, exactly, darling Jack. I can see much further than you at any given time. I can see the imaginary hole you were looking from and the view from your imaginary treetop. The further objects I see are out in the future; the tree's ground level is the present. I know the distance, of course; now add the time component.

Although I can see events in the future, I am not able to see exactly when. At least, not with any certainty. Do you understand me so far"?

I shook my head, now with a perfect understanding of her lesson. At least her perspective analogy was clear to me; the *time component* comment was not. Something to re-visit at a later date, I thought.

"Brilliant explanation, sweetheart; just one thing, though. How did your uncle miss the accident?"

There was a long silence before she answered.

"To see, you have to look. Uncle was probably distracted; this is only my opinion. He would typically have sensed or foreseen a threat and easily avoided or contained the problem, but I suspect he was wandering along thinking about our dinner.

Stupid old man, it's hard to believe we may never see him again, Jack."

"*A Stupid old man wandering along*," she said, and with that cold reminder, I realized I might well have done the same thing. The disturbing memory of my recent experience walking to the Broadway from the bistro returned with a shock.

I had no excuse; I could not even claim old age, having recently turned thirty-nine years. Henry could have certainly cited old age as a factor, having more than six hundred and forty years to his credit. At that point, I resolved to exercise a little mental discipline when walking alone.

As I briefly considered our age differences, Anneliese held onto me again, tears streaming down her face. I pulled her to me, and with my face buried in her hair, I knew she could not see my tears.

I think it was then; that the cold reality hit me. I would never see him or listen to his voice again. Never again sit in the Gutberger with him and listen to him expound on so many subjects with authority. The uninvited painful memories came flooding back.

When I first met him in the early days, my disbelief trying to reconcile his claims and demonstrations of supernatural abilities with my scientific understanding and familiarity with a highly structured, logical environment. His sudden unnerving appearances and laughter at my reactions. My life was clearly divided into two parts—a life before Henry and my life after I met him.

And then there was the vile posturing criminal Malloy and his disgusting television show. Only *three times* over the legal limit, the police report said, so I suppose that was okay.

I remembered Henry's antisocial behavior, his sudden anger, and his compassion. I thought about our recent conversation when I asked for his advice on Annelise and our age differences. He smiled and put an arm around my shoulder, telling me he could easily tweak human DNA and extend human life. I argued the point knowing full well that DNA is not *easily tweaked or manipulated*. Anyway, having *'tweaked,'* then what? Was I soon to be returned to an embryonic state? I remembered all these things, and I remembered his laughter when he kissed me. There was so much unfinished business, so many more questions needed to be asked, and now I would never have the opportunity. I thought about these things, and as I did, I cried.

CHAPTER 28

Our personal lives continued with me spending every night and as many free days as possible with Anneliese. We decided to move to the Woodland Hills area. As I was the working one, the task of reviewing and pricing various properties fell to her. I think she was pleased with the project as it provided an ongoing distraction for her.

Another necessary task we would undertake together was disposing of the ashes. Anneliese suggested a small ceremony at Saint Mary's and the burial of the remains. Eventually, we decided upon a simple non-denominational service.

Henry had professed no particular religion yet was affiliated with many. We decided against Saint Mary's, choosing a plot at Forest Lawn in Glendale instead. The ceremony would take place within four weeks—enough time to make arrangements for burial and select a suitable plot. In fact, six weeks were needed as invitation cards had to be printed, then sent, and confirmations received.

The short ceremony was to be held on Monday, March 25, at 10:00 am, with those attending invited to join us for lunch at a local restaurant. We decided to wrap the urn in a white sheet and place it on a small oak pallet before lowering both into the grave.

Anneliese said she would jump into the grave with the urn. After placing it to her liking, she would then leap from the hole like a jack-in-a-box. I thought about that possibility for a while. Although it would provide an entertaining display for anyone watching, I decided it was defiantly not going to happen.

During a lull in the hectic arranging and planning, I read and replied to the apartment's emails and phone messages. Among the 316 mostly spam emails, I found five from Julie. I had left a note for her a few days after Henry died. She expressed deep sadness at Sir Henry's passing, a fine gentleman, in her opinion.

She chatted about her new apartment in the city and how Peter was progressing in school. From the tone of her messages, they were settling happily into their new life.

I wrote a long reply, apologizing for the late response, but with Henry's death and helping with burial arrangements, I hoped she would understand. I made a fleeting reference to Anneliese with no personal details, though.

I spoke with the priest Father Lewis Evans at Saint Mary's Church, who was a likable and very personable character. He had heard about the accident and expressed his sorrow, as anyone would.

He told me he remembered Henry as the charming friend of the old gardener Pablo. He certainly remembered the five large white birds flying around in his church. He said he would gladly find time to attend the memorial and say a few words appropriate to the occasion.

Anneliese spoke with a cleric or scribe, Fahim Ibn-Abidin, at the Light of Hope Mosque. She said the members there knew about the death and were devastated. Fahim told her a party from the mosque would undoubtedly attend the ceremony.

Replies to our invitations trickled in: four people from the law firm, six from the mosque, Pablo the gardener, and his two cousins Maria and Simona.

All in all, the preparations seemed well in hand for the burial. I arranged for a taxi to transport Tucker Harris to a cheap motel in Glendale, just a few minutes from the park.

Anneliese seemed in good spirits. She was moving forward with the typically detailed trivia that consumed much of her life since the death. Meanwhile, I found myself continually looking over my shoulder, expecting Henry to appear at any moment.

It was impossible for me to accept that he was gone.

The night before the ceremony, rain fell, clearing the morning for a bright sunny day. It was not by any means a dismal burial day.

We stayed in Glendale overnight, ensuring our timely arrival without the misery of a Monday morning commute. We were at the site before 9:00 to greet attendees.

Anneliese could not resist. Checking for watchers, she jumped into the grave and, as promised, sprang from the pit, an apparent effortless jack-in-the-box maneuver. I dismissed it as a vampire thing—another fascinating personality quirk for me to learn and love. I wish I had remembered to bring the camera.

"Am I still forbidden to lower the urn like this? she asked, grinning?" I glowered at her as seriously as possible but, in the end, had to laugh. I promised myself that I would defiantly practice my menacing angry animal growl.

Flowers arrived in a delivery van with many beautiful bouquets, including a large arrangement of white carnations from Julie and Peter.

By 10:00, all the visitors had arrived, including a closely shaved Tucker Harris, now resplendent in an old brown ankle-length overcoat. A large blue polka dot bow tie and a dark, very battered gray fedora hat completed his wardrobe. Despite his unique dress style, he seemed a perfect fit for everyone else in attendance and quite comfortable with his surroundings, nodding and chatting with many at the service. He even joined a conversation with the Muslims without using any foul language. I think Henry would have been proud of his protege and his transformation into a social butterfly.

The six representatives from the mosque were dressed in dark suits and wearing traditional Muslim head coverings. An earnest young man introduced himself as Qasim and thanked me for the opportunity to pay his last respects.

Father Evans likewise wore a dark suit, carrying neither a bible nor a prayer book. He smiled and shook hands with me.

I watched as he greeted the visitors from the mosque. They had met on a previous occasion, it seemed.

Anneliese strolled among the visitors, In her dark gray business suit, chatting and thanking them for their time. She was very self-assured and a perfect hostess in this setting.

Two partners from the law firm and the skinny receptionist gave their condolences, telling Anneliese that the firm was closed for the week—a small token in remembrance of the tragedy. Also, a large framed photograph with a plaque beneath it would be hung in a prominent position at the reception area entrance.

Not a bad turnout for an old vampire, I thought. But I wished he were here to see it for himself.

Anneliese stood at what would have been the head of the grave. She raised her hand, waiting for a few seconds before speaking. She introduced herself to the bystanders and then thanked everyone for coming.

"We are assembled here to recognize a sudden and most wasteful accident, a tragic and quite unnecessary death. This has been a terrible loss for me personally and a terrible loss for all who knew him as a friend or colleague. Now, my friends, this is an opportune moment for me to present to you Father Lewis Evans from Saint Mary's Church."

The priest stepped forward and stood beside Anneliese. He smiled and nodded to the small assembly.

"Good morning, everyone. Let me begin by saying that I am not here in any formal capacity, nor am I representing my church. I am here, as I am sure everyone is in attendance today, to pay my respects to a very good man.

I regret I never knew him well enough to list his fine qualities as a person or talk of the many achievements during his life but look around.

Because here, you will find Muslims, Catholics, Christians, Jews, and non-believers. These people are not here by chance but because of friendship and respect for the deceased.

We are not given to judge or concern ourselves with the reasons for any man's death.

CHAPTER 29

"We are all children of God and celebrate the life he has given to us." He paused for several seconds. "At this time, I would like to introduce brother Qasim from the Light of Hope Mosque."

As I listened to Father Evans, I realized that there was indeed a diversity of religious beliefs represented here. What about other groups, though?

Not a black face to be seen. No women's rights advocates or Americans with disabilities.

Animal protection leagues had no representation at all, nor did any gay and lesbian groups. It was an outrage that Child laborers' protective society and pregnant working mothers groups were underrepresented or ignored.

My musings were interrupted when I looked up to see Anneliese glaring at me. A glaring vampire is never a good thing; thankfully, her eyes were not yet red. I was introduced as an old and valued friend of the family. I walked over to stand beside Anneliese. As I was about to speak, it occurred to me that I had heard none of the words from the Muslim Qasim. No problem, I would employ an old imaginary *"no clothes trick"* my Mother taught me. My tiny audience became suddenly agitated.

They pointed to a small group of oak trees behind the grave with fingers waving and exclamations of astonishment. Six large white birds circled lazily above the visitors before perching on a low-hanging branch.

None appeared frightened or confused. These regal shining ornaments gazed solemnly over the watchers, unmoving.

Pablo, the gardener, became quite animated, babbling and waving his arms. For Father Evans and the six Muslims, these birds held a very special significance.

One of the birds, larger than the others, took flight again. After circling the area slowly, it alighted on another branch close to the others. It looked rather like a large white seagull with a cruel, curved beak and glittering golden eyes.

I watched, fascinated, realizing these must be the birds Henry had described to me. Anneliese squeezed my arm and took my hand.

"Look, Jack, I think he's here with us again."

I stared at the large bird, fancying that it shone with a brilliant golden light as the rays of the morning sun illuminated the feathers.

For many seconds everyone stood immobile.

Father Evans was the first to move. He walked carefully around the grave to stand within arm's reach of the bird. For some time, he stood, staring at the creature. Then, raising his arm, he spoke to it softly.

He continued speaking gently to the bird until Pablo joined him. They stood together for a few minutes, staring at the bird before walking slowly away. Many times they stopped, looking back at the tree and talking among themselves.

The priest seemed dazed, a man in shock shaking his head repeatedly.

Anneliese called for the two helpers to lower the urn. They lowered the pallet gently, pulling away two silk ropes when it was in position. At that point, the six birds took flight again, circling in a tight formation over the small group until lost from sight beyond the trees.

Nobody moved for some time, gazing after the astonishing flight. Anneliese walked among the group, thanking the attendees again for their time. "This is exactly how my uncle would have wanted to be remembered," she said. Everyone was given a buttonhole of two white carnations before they left. Harris pined his to the brim of his hat.

The visitors gradually dispersed, talking animatedly among themselves. After flowers were dropped into the grave and covered the urn, workers filled it and placed a small headstone, setting it as a marker.

All the visitors went their separate ways except Tucker Harris. We took him to dinner at a nice restaurant, pleasing him greatly. "What could be better?" he said, "good food and better company." And this, from a man I first met a few weeks ago living under a freeway overpass with a terrible attitude. All the questions he asked about the birds went conveniently unanswered."

The last few weeks had seemed like a lifetime to me, and I thought Anneliese felt the same. It was as though a great cloud had dispersed so the sun could shine through again.

We could now continue with our lives once more. I would resume my investigations and advance the project at the institute. Anneliese would continue searching for new accommodations and transitioning old Tucker Harris from the freeway embankment to a lovely little apartment Henry had arranged for him.

CHAPTER 30

Two days later, I mentioned the burial once again. "A perfect ceremony, don't you think? Respectful and fitting for your Uncle Henry. Even a flock of birds performing a small air show for the visitors."

"Yes, thank you so much for all the help, sweetie. It was almost perfect. If only my beautiful lover hadn't nodded off while Qasim was speaking."

"I was not asleep," I protested, "just thinking about true diversity at the ceremony."

"Yes, I know exactly what you were thinking. I was *reading* you." She laughed. "Oh, hope you don't mind, darling. I invited Father Evans to dinner tonight. He was so nice at the funeral, a genuinely helpful person with all the social protocol and arrangements. He seemed a little shaken by the bird's display, though. He will join us tonight. I hope that's okay with you."

"Yeah, of course, looking forward to it. He's a nice guy and seems almost normal for a priest."

Dinner was arranged at the hotel, and Father Evans was dressed casually, unfashionably preppy, and unfashionably punctual, arriving at 8:30.

"Good to see you again, father." I extended my hand.

"Please, not father, dear boy. No collar on tonight. Please call me Lewis."

I inclined my head—a likable fellow, a few years younger than me, with a freshly scrubbed, enthusiastic schoolboy look.

"Good to see you again, then, Lewis."

He nodded and took his place at the table.

"Anneliese will be down soon. I wanted to thank you for the help and your kind words at the ceremony. Those birds put on a fantastic display, don't you think?

"Oh, absolutely, they did. Not a problem. Always glad to help family, young Jack. Remind me to explain the birds to you—not this evening, though, too many distractions. Perhaps tomorrow for lunch at the Gutburger, *if* you can spare the time. You will see our birds again very soon. There is a large priest to package and deliver to Lahore. We have many more miles to travel and much work to do."

I had nothing to say. I just listened in shock, let the words flow around me, and tried to make sense of it all, or some of it, as that which was Lewis, now perhaps Henry Smith continued.

"To begin with, young Jack, there is a food drive for the poor. Actually, thinking about that, a *food drive and art exhibition* would be more appropriate and just as easily arranged, don't you think? Two diverse programs in one venue to attract sponsorship. Anyway, the stories of our lives, you and I, will continue, and we will travel on many roads together.

I am delighted you are buying dinner tonight, though. Better late than never, eh?" He smiled, inclining his head. "Lord Henry Lewis Smith at your service, and as always, dear boy."

> *"My Old Friend, Henry Smith, lay dead out in The Street.*
> *At the End of The Day, In A drunkards Way,*
> *Is Our Story Now Complete?"*

"Complete? No. Tales of vampires, angels, and men are never finished. Vampires and angels have the time to finish the work they began when the world was young. Men have no time at all to realize that bitter truth only when it is too late.

"Be in the world like a traveler or like
a passer on, and reckon yourself as of the dead."

Attributed to the prophet Muhammad.

www.ingramcontent.com/pod-product-compliance
Lightning Source LLC
LaVergne TN
LVHW041759060526
838201LV00046B/1056